GRAVE SILENCE

What Reviewers Say About BOLD STROKES Authors

ᴔ

KIM BALDWIN

"*A riveting novel of suspense* seems to be a very overworked phrase. However, it is extremely apt when discussing Kim Baldwin's [*Hunter's Pursuit*]. An exciting page turner [features] Katarzyna Demetrious, a bounty hunter…with a million dollar price on her head. Look for this excellent novel of suspense…" – **R. Lynne Watson**, *MegaScene*

ᴔ

ROSE BEECHAM

"…her characters seem fully capable of walking away from the particulars of whodunit and engaging the reader in other aspects of their lives." – *Lambda Book Report*

ᴔ

GUN BROOKE

"*Course of Action* is a romance…populated with a host of captivating and amiable characters. The glimpses into the lifestyles of the rich and beautiful people are rather like guilty pleasures.…[A] most satisfying and entertaining reading experience." – **Arlene Germain**, reviewer for the *Lambda Book Report* and the *Midwest Book Review*

ᴔ

JANE FLETCHER

"*The Walls of Westernfort* is not only a highly engaging and fast-paced adventure novel, it provides the reader with an interesting framework for examining the same questions of loyalty, faith, family and love that [the characters] must face." – **M. J. Lowe**, *Midwest Book Review*

ᴔ

RADCLYᶠFE

"…well-honed storytelling skills…solid prose and sure-handedness of the narrative…" – **Elizabeth Flynn**, *Lambda Book Report*

"…well-plotted…lovely romance...I couldn't turn the pages fast enough!" – **Ann Bannon**, author of *The Beebo Brinker Chronicles*

GRAVE SILENCE

by

ROSE BEECHAM

2005

GRAVE SILENCE

ISBN 1-933110-25-2

THIS TRADE PAPERBACK ORIGINAL IS PUBLISHED BY
BOLD STROKES BOOKS, INC.,
PENNSYLVANIA, USA

FIRST PRINTING: BOLD STROKES BOOKS 2005

CREDITS
EDITOR: STACIA SEAMAN
PRODUCTION DESIGN: STACIA SEAMAN
COVER DESIGN BY SHERI (GRAPHICARTIST2020@HOTMAIL.COM)

By the Author

MYSTERIES as Rose Beecham

<u>Amanda Valentine Series</u>

Introducing Amanda Valentine
Second Guess
Fair Play

<u>Jude Devine Series</u>

Grave Silence

ROMANCES as Jennifer Fulton

<u>Moon Island Series</u>

A Guarded Heart
Passion Bay
Saving Grace
The Sacred Shore

<u>Heartstoppers Series</u>

Dark Dreamer

<u>Others</u>

Greener Than Grass
True Love

Acknowledgments

I belong to that species of author for whom writing a novel is a lonely, antisocial affair. Family and friends are excluded, the phone is ignored, and the espresso machine works overtime. My dear ones, especially my partner, put up with all of this and still love me. Puzzling, but I cannot thank them enough.

As I worked on this novel, Shelley, Connie, and JD kept my feet to the fire—thank you. Radclyffe made the publisher/author relationship a rewarding and happy one, and Stacia Seaman took her usual care editing the end results.

I owe a debt of gratitude to several LDS friends—Carrie, John, and Rona, whose experiences and insights added much to my research for this novel. Writing this story would have been immeasurably more difficult without Jon Krakauer's superb account of Mormon fundamentalism in America, *Under the Banner of Heaven*, and without the courage of the women who've escaped these communities and who refuse to remain silent about the abuses committed within them.

Dedication

For my mother, Wyn
who defines family values for me

Author's Note

This is a work of fiction set in a reality that is stranger than fiction, that of the Mormon fundamentalist gulag on the Utah/Arizona Strip.

The Fundamentalist Church of Latter Day Saints (FLDS) mentioned in this story is a real organization, the largest of the Mormon polygamist cults. Many of the events I refer to are a matter of public record; however, the main story line is entirely fictional. Until quite recently, the FLDS was led by a man named Warren Jeffs, their self-proclaimed prophet. At the time this book was completed, Mr. Jeffs was a fugitive wanted by the FBI.

The FLDS cult and the mainstream Mormon church (the Church of Jesus Christ of Latter-day Saints), are not one and the same, although they spring from common roots. The mainstream LDS church banned polygamy as a practice in 1890 (it was never renounced as religious doctrine).

As I was finishing this book, I realized some people might see it as "anti-Mormon" and others as "anti-religion." I had neither agenda as I wrote it. The novel began the way many do—like most authors I know, I became intrigued and inspired by something I saw. I then proceeded to make up a story and characters so I could explain it to myself.

Hildale/Colorado City needs explaining. The existence, within the USA, of a Taliban-like, white-supremacist theocracy paid for by taxpayer dollars needs explaining. I didn't come up with any explanations, only more questions, and of course a mystery novel. I hope readers will enjoy *Grave Silence* for what it is—entertainment.

Lying is done with words and also with silence.

—Adrienne Rich

CHAPTER ONE

O n a still afternoon in early August, a couple of gas station robbers fished an old-style Samsonite suiter out of the Dolores River near Slick Rock. Bobby Lee Parker and Frank Horton had been dragging the murky waters under the Highway 141 bridge for the proceeds of a stickup they'd pulled two weeks earlier.

It was not their lucky day.

So far, they'd lost the final round of the watermelon seed–spitting competition at the Montezuma County Fair. Then Bobby Lee's mom showed up wanting to get high and helped herself to his last gram of weed. Now it seemed like the plastic garbage bag they'd stashed under some rocks had been washed away during the big storm that had startled locals earlier in the week.

Normally, this time of year, the Dolores between Slick Rock and Bedrock was a muddy trickle. The whitewater crowd abandoned the place by June, taking their kayaks and Discover cards back to Boulder. Soon after, the canyons were overrun with hikers busting their asses to see wildflowers and shit. A couple of these idiots normally got themselves mauled by mountain lions every summer. Then came the annual funeral procession of VWs packed with posers winding down their tinted windows and asking directions to Telluride. Bobby Lee had seen the worst movies of his life trying to get laid at that film festival.

He stared up at the bridge, where yet another dickhead had stopped his SUV so he could peer down at the river. The guy waved and yelled something about "boatable flow."

Ignoring him, Bobby Lee said, "Fucking perfect. They'll be down here with their fucking kayaks before we get done."

Frank let go of the suiter and stood upright, panting and wheezing. His light brown mullet was limp with perspiration, the combed-back sides drooping flaccidly onto his cheeks. "Damn, it's a heavy mother," he whined.

Reluctantly, Bobby Lee helped him hump the garment bag farther up the bank onto the flat. He figured maybe they'd lucked onto some other guy's heist. "Open it," he said and watched Frank plaster his DNA all over the striped canvas like the amateur he was. The zipper wouldn't budge.

Eventually Einstein remembered he had a knife and used it to slit the thing apart. "Oh, man!" he choked, lurching back. "That stinks worse 'n a dead skunk. We gotta get out of here."

Bobby Lee took a moment to digest the grisly sight of a decomposing corpse. He weighed his options. His midnight blue Chevy Silverado was parked at the Chuck Wagon Café a few yards from the bridge. The truck was well known in these parts on account of its Super Swampers and the custom-painted flames that licked across the rocker panels. A bunch of cars had gone by while he and Frank were searching the river, mostly tourists headed for the canyons. But tourists were nosey and took photos of every fucking blade of grass. Who knew how many of them had shot video that could later become Exhibit A in the kind of bogus trial Bobby Lee knew all about?

He stared around the riverbanks. They could haul the suiter under the bridge and bury it real quick while the earth was still moist, only he didn't have a shovel, so they'd be doing it with their bare hands and Bobby Lee had never cared much for manual labor. Or they could do what Frank wanted and shove it back in the river.

The bad news was dead bodies had a habit of showing up. In a few days' time, the Dolores would be a mud slick again and some dude would spot the lumpy Samsonite shroud. Murders were a big deal in the Four Corners, so the discovery would be plastered all over the front page of the *Durango Herald*. Someone would remember seeing Bobby Lee's wheels. Next thing, the cops would come knocking at his door. Who else around here owned a tricked-out show truck like the *Midnight Rambler*?

Placing his hand over his nose and mouth, he said, "We're gonna do the Christian thing. Whoever this dead chick is, there's a family needs closure."

Frank turned away and sucked in a breath. "You're gonna call the cops?" He removed his Terminator shades and shook them free of sweat. His pudgy face was incredulous. "They'll wanna know what we was doing down here. That cross your mind?"

Bobby Lee took a few paces along the bank to escape the stench. Frank was the kind who never saw the bigger picture. He had not graduated from high school. Bobby Lee, on the other hand, had finished two years of college before he had to suspend his education to serve time for an assault that was really self-defense. Unfortunately, the so-called victim was not just any retard who'd gotten antsy when his girlfriend flashed some leg at Bobby Lee, but the son of a Ute Tribal Council member. And seeing as the Ute owned the casino and employed half of Montezuma County, guess whose version of events the jury bought?

Patiently, Bobby Lee explained the psychology of law enforcement officers. "They'll be real surprised that we're reporting this, on account of our past histories. So they'll know we're not the guys who did it, otherwise we'd have been hightailing it out of here as per your proposal. Now they'd see that as suspicious behavior. Guilty conduct. Know what I'm saying?"

Frank mopped his face and flattened his hair back into place. "So when they ask us what we was doing down here in the first place, we tell them some bullshit about fishing?"

Bobby Lee shook his head. "Call of nature. We were relieving ourselves and that's when we saw it. You got curious because it looked to contain something large, so you cut it open with your knife."

Frank chewed this over for several seconds then asked, "Do I bury the knife?"

Bobby Lee did not call his buddy a dumbass, even when he acted like one. It was not Frank's fault his father was a no-good SOB who beat on his family. Bobby Lee was aware of several head injuries that had sent Frank to the hospital when they were kids, so he made allowances.

"No, Frank," he said like he took the question seriously. "Burying the knife is felon-thinking. If they ask for it, just give it to them. We got nothing to hide. Okay?"

"Aw, shit."

Interpreting this as approval, Bobby Lee flipped open his cell phone and dialed 911.

❖

Deputy Virgil Tulley hoped he would never get used to real depravity. There was only so long a decent man could stare into the chasm of horror before he got dizzy. On such occasions it was his habit to pick up his cell phone and call his ma in Ohio. Today was no exception.

Ma Tulley had important information to impart. "Your brother Billy lost his right testicle last week while they was dehorning."

"No kidding." Tulley crossed his legs.

"They sewed it back on, but Marybeth says that's just for cosmetic appearance' sake. He won't be a daddy again."

"They don't need any more kids, Ma."

"If I'd took that attitude you'd have never been born."

Tulley squinted up at the ceiling fan. One of the blades was loose. With each drunken gyration, it clicked like a cricket in the mating season. His skin prickled. Sweaty nausea had dried in a thin film all over his body. Lucky he kept a change of shirt at work.

"I got that Chinese sow," his ma said. "There's money in pet pigs nowadays. They walk 'em on a leash in L.A., you know. Get bored and it's always a good meal, I guess."

"Ma, people don't eat their pets." He glanced at the case file in front of him. "Most people, anyways."

"They got that Union County grand champion boar servicing gilts over Harper's place. We're next. Weighs seven hundred eighty pound."

"That's a shitload of bacon."

"Owner reckons he can do four sows in an hour."

"Who? The hog?"

A long-suffering sigh. "If you think you're gonna get a rise out of me with your trash talk, you're mistaken, boy."

"Yes, ma'am." Tulley snickered. He was a grown man. He didn't have to fear the pig paddle anymore.

"We're getting them snout coolers," his ma continued. "Had a farrowing decline last summer. Heat stress. That's what the vet says. What you got to do to prevent that is keep their noses cold."

"Like dogs," Tulley noted.

"What you call for, anyways? I got better things to do than listen to you bragging on that hound of yours again."

❖

A few feet away, Detective Jude Devine cracked open a can of ginger ale and rocked her chair back, legs crossed, feet on the corner of her desk. She surmised Tulley had been reading the Pohlman case file. Made it as far as the dog-burger bit, then called his ma. Nothing like a debriefing on hog husbandry to hustle a sensitive soul back to mundane reality.

Tulley was the youngest of eleven and had something to prove. The impressive trappings of a career in law enforcement were made to order for him. No one polished his badge like this kid. Not so long ago he'd applied to the sheriff's office for permission to have an exact replica cast in solid fourteen karat gold. Concerned about setting a precedent, they'd turned him down. Jude had to talk him out of taking the matter up in writing with Governor Owen. Gold scratches like hell anyway, she'd pointed out. Why not spend the two thousand bucks on something more practical?

Tulley had taken her advice. Within days he'd plunked his money down on a bloodhound described in the *Lawman's Best Friend* as "a true gallant descended from a line of champion cadaver hounds and felon trackers." The dog was surplus to requirements at Georgia State Penitentiary, where fancy new security was putting fine animals like him out of a job.

Jude had rustled up some not-exactly-kosher cigarette company sponsorship and persuaded her superiors to approve six weeks of handler training for Tulley at the Advanced Canine Academy. When he graduated, a posse of Marlboro executives hit town to stage-manage the occasion. They lured the Channel 9 people out of Denver to cover the story, and the front page of every local rag from Grand Junction to Cortez ran a picture of the suits benevolently awarding Smoke'm a monogrammed collar and five years' worth of Purina lamb and rice. In exchange for this largesse and the price of a K-9 vehicle, a Marlboro Man billboard—minus the brand logo—now dominated the vacant lot next to the Montrose & Montezuma County Sheriffs' outpost in Paradox Valley. The executives called this a "subtle artistic tribute" to their one-time icon, now banned across the land of the free.

Every time Jude looked at the twenty-foot cowboy's chiseled jaw, she reminded herself that this *homage* was a small price to pay for the full-service status deeply coveted by remote offices. No longer would she and Tulley wait in vain for the deputies of Cortez to mark their dance card. No longer would they be passed over in big-ticket cases because someone supposedly had to be on hand in the canyon area to investigate petty campsite thefts, hiker disputes, and cattle rustling. Jude was a sheriff's detective, even if she was only a woman, and her substation now operated one of just four K-9 units in the region. As far as the dispatchers were concerned, that meant Paradox could pursue and detain upon their own initiative.

So, when the 911 call came in about a suspicious discovery in a garment bag, Jude tapped Tulley on the shoulder and said, "Tell your ma good-bye and get that hound on a leash. We're not wallflowers anymore."

❖

By the time they reached the Slick Rock Bridge, an impressive lineup of silver and blue Ford Crowns were parked at the scene, lights flashing. Several state patrol troopers were directing the scant traffic and preventing guys with kayaks from heading down the riverbank. Another was taking statements from two males in their twenties. The shorter of this pair looked like the adult version of the fat kid everyone teased in school. Hands crammed into the pockets of his too-tight jeans, he stared at the ground as his cool-dude companion did the talking.

Jude parked her Dodge Dakota alongside Tulley's K-9 Durango, located her camera, and bailed out. Gesturing at the flashy Silverado parked in front of the local café, she asked her sidekick, "Recognize that truck?"

"Bobby Lee Parker." Tulley opened the back of the Durango so Smoke'm could dangle his dewlaps in the fresh air. "DUI. Served eighteen months for assault with a deadly weapon. Suspect in a couple of gas station robberies. Fond of the ladies, 'specially those in uniform."

Jude looked harder at the cowboy in question and it all came back. Parker had spent last New Year's Eve in jail after a brawl over someone's girlfriend. His mom, a local artist and president of the Concerned Citizens for Cannabis Law Reform, had bailed him out. A few days later he showed up at the sheriff's office in Cortez with a bunch of flowers and a poem for a female deputy. The young woman had actually dated him for a time, sparking a firestorm of gossip that even found its way to Paradox. He was, the deputy told her colleagues, "real suave for 'round here."

As she and Tulley approached, Parker snapped to and smoothed his frosted blond cowlick, presumably at the sight of a female, even one with shorter hair and more muscles than him. He was barking up the wrong tree, but Jude had no plans to advertise the fact. This was not Boulder, with its liberals and GLBT picnics. This was southwestern Colorado, a few miles from the Utah border, less than a day's drive from Matthew Shepard's Laramie.

After identifying herself and Tulley, she sought out the most senior of the troopers, a rangy fortysomething who introduced himself as Henson.

"What have we got?" she asked.

"DOA. Hundred yards thataways." He pointed down the riverbank.

"Smells real bad, ma'am." Parker flashed a grin that probably worked on females who had never been to the big city. Even standing still, the guy had a swagger. "Got a clean bandanna in my truck if you need to cover your mouth."

"What I need is for you to talk to Deputy Tulley, here." Jude returned her attention to Trooper Henson and invited, "Lead the way."

They followed a well-worn track through silver-green grasses and gnarled junipers to the banks of the Dolores. The once mighty River of Our Lady of Sorrows meandered north between walls of stratified sandstone, through the open spaces of Big Gypsum, into Slickrock Canyon and on to Paradox Valley. 160 million years of history were etched along its serpentine progress, from dinosaur tracks to the ruins of Anasazi Indian villages, to homesteader graves and the poisonous dust layer that was once Uravan, a uranium mining town bulldozed when its cancer epidemic made the news.

Jude had made it her business to get to know the area since moving out here, and spent most of her leisure time exploring on horseback. It was a world like none she'd ever known, a far cry from D.C. Lack of water kept rapacious developers away, which meant you could look out across a vast, natural landscape unsullied by human presence. Jude loved that. There was nothing like sitting on a horse high on a mesa, alone in this timeless splendor, feeling like a tiny speck on the ass of Mother Nature.

The track leveled out and she stopped and gazed toward the canyon mouth where a large cottonwood stood, impossibly alive and green in a barren sea of rock. From its branches, an owl stared at her, a rare sight in the garish brightness of day. *The harbinger of death.*

Jude shivered and continued along the riverbank, following the unmistakable hum of feasting insects. A few feet ahead, a squadron of flies hovered drunkenly around a vintage suiter split open to reveal what appeared to be female remains. The hair was long and the bloated facial features still vaguely identifiable. Jude pulled on some latex gloves and covered her nose and mouth with a handkerchief she'd pocketed for the occasion. The victim was young, maybe even a teen, fair haired and Caucasian, at least as far as she could tell.

Time since death was hard to guess. At a glance, Jude thought maybe a week, but submerged bodies decomposed more slowly than those left exposed, so it was more likely two or even three weeks. She did some math. The rains had struck six days earlier, so the body could not have been underwater any longer than that. Even with the August heat, the decomp rate seemed to be out of step with this time frame, which meant the killer must have hidden the body somewhere before he put it in the water. Poor planning, Jude thought.

Maybe it was a spur-of-the-moment killing and the perpetrator had to wait for an opportunity to travel to the dump site. He would probably have wanted to hide his victim some distance away from his home environment. Had he driven for a while, looking for a likely spot, or had he planned on the Dolores all along? He must have put the suiter into the river somewhere near Cahone, Jude calculated, for it to have drifted to its present location. There was no other direct access by road after that, until Slip Rock bridge.

She supposed it was equally possible that he'd dug a shallow grave right here in the muddy riverbed a week or so before the rains. The storm waters would have loosened the earth, and when the river started to flow again, the garment bag would have floated free. As a body dump strategy, it seemed like hard work and a high risk of disturbance, but maybe the killer had wanted this victim to be found. Either way, the body disposal seemed like the work of someone unpracticed.

Jude put a few paces between herself and the putrid discovery, and released the breath she was holding. Trooper Henson offered his Tic Tacs.

"Guess you'll be wanting that hound down here," he said.

"Not yet. We'll have to wait till the forensic team is through."

It was doubtful Smoke'm would have a role to play. Having been in the water, the bag wouldn't hold the killer's scent anymore. Still, it wouldn't hurt to see if the sniffer hound turned up anything of interest in the general vicinity, and Tulley was desperate for an opportunity to flaunt his K-9 handler skills.

"I better call in." Henson was clearly keen to go where the air smelled sweeter.

"Sure." Jude waved him away. "I'll finish up here."

She photographed the scene and wandered along the bank a few yards toward the cottonwood. The owl kept tabs on her, its demeanor one of vague affront. She was probably disturbing some rodent it was stalking. Her eyes drifted east toward Disappointment Valley and the adobe badlands skirting McKenna's Peak. The mountain rose silver and conical above the pomegranate landscape. Wild horses still roamed its slopes, the last survivors of human encroachment that had condemned their kind to near extinction.

The Old West no longer existed and its scars were plain to see. Yet, in the eerie majesty of this place, the untamed spirit of those times remained palpable. With an odd sense that prairie ghosts were watching, Jude returned to the body and lifted the canvas so she could see inside the suiter.

The dead girl was missing her legs below the knees. She was naked and heavily pregnant.

❖

Unfortunately for Bobby Lee and his faithful lackey, Frank, the Huntsbergers were so dirt poor they had to apply for assistance to bury Darlene. The only reward offered up was a mute nod from Mrs. Huntsberger when Jude fed her the standard bullshit about how her baby hadn't suffered and they would catch the scum who did it.

"They got the best tracker hound in the state," Clem Huntsberger said, as if there were a trail leading directly to the killer just waiting to be sniffed out.

Mrs. Huntsberger glanced nervously across the office at Smoke'm. The dog promptly plodded over and placed his big wrinkled head in her lap. As he gazed up at her, tears welled in the bloodshot perimeters of his eyes and rolled like crystalline pearls down his jowls. Overwhelmed by this show of solidarity from one of God's dumb creatures, Mrs. Huntsberger lifted her weathered hands to her face and began sobbing like she would never stop.

"I told you that hound was psychic," Tulley said as the bereft couple's pickup rattled off toward Highway 90 a half hour later.

"He's empathetic," Jude corrected. "That means he senses human emotions and reacts to them."

"Yes, ma'am. He does that too." Tulley reached down and caressed the hound's ears, an intimacy greeted with groans that vibrated up through the animal's throat folds.

"When you're done typing the parents' statements, keep on with those Samsonite dealers," Jude said briskly.

"Man." Tulley shook his head and peeled a fresh stick of gum, adding his last to the Wrigley's stalagmite growing from his ashtray. "That's another thousand phone calls. Shame her folks didn't notice anything before she disappeared."

"They're just plain decent people. Not the suspicious type." Jude wandered to the window and stared out at the Marlboro man. "Let's face it, no one 'round here expects this kind of thing."

Darlene had vanished two years earlier from the bus station at Cortez, aged sixteen. The Huntsbergers had reported her missing but the Cortez PD pegged her as a runaway. Her family had a run-down farm in Mancos, a two-bit settlement no young woman would elect to live in if she had a choice. There was only one witness statement worth a dime. A local drunk had seen a girl who fit Darlene's description getting into a white minivan. The police didn't set much store by his recollections and instead formed an opinion based on a girlfriend's statement that Darlene couldn't wait to graduate from high school and "get a life fifty thousand miles away from this shitheap."

It was the story of legions of girls like her. Darlene was not a troublemaker. She had average grades at school, helped her mom with the younger kids, and listened to Usher music. Her friends said she was shy and had never had a boyfriend. She made bead jewelry for a hobby and had a *Princess Diaries* poster on the wall of her tidy bedroom. Would she have gotten into a vehicle with a complete stranger? Everyone the police had questioned doubted it.

Jude was disturbed that they had treated the case like a routine missing person inquiry when the circumstances seemed so suspicious. She returned to her desk and sifted through her notes. How far would a killer drive to get rid of a body in these parts, given the price of gas? Her guess was Darlene Huntsberger had been murdered somewhere within a radius of a hundred miles, probably less. An accomplished killer who knew the area well might have tied concrete to her feet and dumped her in the McPhee Reservoir to get rid of the evidence. But this guy had zipped her into a garment bag to keep his trunk clean and had disposed of her body where it would probably be found. He had also had the courtesy to place her social security card inside the suiter's ID compartment.

A thoughtful but amateurish sociopath who trawled for a random victim in a remote part of the state? Jude seriously doubted it. More likely, the killer knew Darlene. Which meant there was a motive. In her experience a motive meant a boyfriend or husband. It looked like their victim had picked the wrong guy to dump. Had she left Cortez with a man she'd met somehow? She didn't have a computer, so it probably wasn't an Internet romance. How would she have met the guy? In a small-town world like this, how could she have hidden a boyfriend from everyone who knew her?

Jude contemplated the manner of her death. Darlene was eight months pregnant. Her tongue had been severed, but not at the time she was killed. The autopsy suggested four or five months earlier. Her entire body was pockmarked with wounds described in an additional forensic odontologist's report as "ovoid lacerations consisting of two facing symmetrical arches separated at their bases by open spaces. Along the periphery of the arches are a series of individual abrasions, contusions and lacerations reflecting the size, shape, arrangement, and distribution of the class characteristics of the contacting surfaces of human dentition." In other words, someone bit the hell out of her.

Many of the bites involved flesh loss but, thanks to her immersion in the river, no saliva evidence remained. As far as the pathologist could determine, the bites were inflicted around the time of death, so it seemed probable that biter and killer were the same individual—a guy whose folks had not prioritized expensive dental work when he was a kid.

According to Dr. Claudia Spelman, the odontologist, it was rare these days to see an "irregular mesiodistal width coupled with rare convex labial rotation in #7 causing it to overlap #8," otherwise known as the kind of teeth that made kissing anyone except your mom unlikely. Jude felt gloomy about that. If the killer had never had any dental work, there would be no record of the quirky fangs. Hopefully, this wasn't the only time he'd bitten someone. It would be nice if they could solve this case the clean and simple way, sitting on their butts in air-conditioned comfort, getting a hit on one of the databases. But she had a feeling they would need to come up with some other data to narrow the suspect pool. The obvious starting pace was the killer's M.O. Unusual, to say the least.

Darlene's sternum was fractured in two. This had been caused by a large object that had also perforated her heart—a metal spike of the kind logging protesters rammed into trees to prevent felling. Carelessly, the killer had left it embedded in her chest. But this was not the cause of death. Darlene had been silenced permanently when her throat was slashed ear to ear. The stake was a postmortem touch.

Jude wondered where it was from. The nearest logging protests were in the Dolores River canyon, one of the wilderness tracts now being opened up to drilling by gas and oil companies.

"With that fancy luggage and all, maybe he's white collar," Tulley piped up. "Bank manager by day, cannibal killer by night."

"We don't know if he ate the flesh he removed."

"Then why not just bite her?"

"Removing the flesh could be symbolic to him."

"The stake through the heart is symbolic." Tulley chomped hard on his gum. "The rest is just sick." His mouth stilled suddenly and his Madeira brown eyes flashed with inspiration. "Know what I think? This creep could be a Russian."

"What makes you say that?"

"They got themselves a big problem with cannibal killers over there. It's real common."

You couldn't rule out anything in a homicide investigation, so Jude gave the idea some room before she shot it down. "Experts think the cannibalism in Russian homicides is circumstantial, rather than fetishistic. The victim is already dead. The killer is hungry. There's a food shortage. So…"

"They're starving in Africa, too, but they're not eating their neighbors," Tulley said.

With notable exceptions like Idi Amin Dada and Jean-Bedel Bokassa, but Jude kept that thought to herself. "Yeah well, the Africans aren't drunk 24/7. Think about it. Russia has the highest alcoholism in the world. Alcohol loosens inhibitions. Societal mores that govern human conduct lose their power. The individual fails to suppress his most basic urges." She slowed down. This was not Quantico.

"I've been reading up on profiling, now that we're dealing with a psycho." Tulley indicated a pile of newly purchased volumes chosen from the FBI recommended reading list, also compliments of the tobacco industry. "Seems like the more you find out, the more you know you don't know, and you never will know. So you wonder what the point is. They'd never put a guy like me in charge of a big investigation, anyway."

Having met Ma Tulley on the occasion of the Smoke'm presentation, and having endured her dissertation on the hazards of book learning, Jude could understand Tulley's reservations. He had already amazed family and friends by overcoming the academic hurdles that stood between him and a sworn deputy's badge. There was no reason why he couldn't make it to detective. She suspected low self-esteem was what held him back.

"Anyone can fill their heads with facts and figures," she said. "But you can't learn gut instinct. The good news is, you were born with that."

Tulley's ears turned cranberry. Praise made him nervous. "Why'd you leave the FBI?" he blurted all of a sudden. In the twelve months they'd been working together, he had never asked that question directly.

"It's a long story," she said.

"Ain't none of my business, right?"

"Right."

"I heard some things, that's all."

"What things?"

"Just talk, same as always."

"Talk, huh?" What was new? A female FBI agent from Washington, D.C. is suddenly hired as a sheriff's detective in Colorado and stationed far from the action in a newly formed remote substation with one deputy and a part-time secretary. The entire staff of the MCSO and the Cortez PD was mystified.

Every now and then, Tulley reported a new theory to her—she'd been sleeping with her FBI boss and had to go when the affair ended; she'd messed up a terrorist investigation so bad she'd resigned and the FBI had to cover it up; the job was too hard on females and she'd only graduated from the Academy because her daddy was "somebody."

Jude let the gossip circulate unchallenged. Truth was stranger than fiction. For now, she was keeping the facts to herself.

CHAPTER TWO

No one at the Montezuma County Sheriff's Office or the Cortez PD enjoyed public humiliation. All too often when a big case landed in their laps, the media would sweep into town like a biblical plague and the accusations of incompetence would soon follow.

Who could forget the Fred Martinez murder? The Colorado public still thought the cops had dragged their feet making an arrest because the kid was gay and a Navajo. In fact, all they'd done was build a decent case without the resources available to big-city departments. They'd gotten a conviction, too. How come no one remembered that?

These days, Sheriff Orwell Pratt made a point of sharing the burden and with it the blame if anything went sour. Which was why he hadn't waited for Montrose to dump the Huntsberger case on his doorstep, with the accompanying bullshit about the resource burden of that goddamned film festival. Instead he'd offered to head up a three-county team as soon as the deceased was identified as a Montezuma girl. Since then, he'd held a press conference every morning. His strategy was simple: throw the TV people the same crap day after day and they'll lose interest. So far it wasn't working.

As Orwell glanced around the reporters gathering in the conference room, he was gripped by a fear that the case could become one of those that the public obsessed over. It bore the familiar hallmarks—a wholesome, pretty white girl, her unborn child, a respectable and outraged family, bizarre circumstances, the whiff of police incompetence. The media was always on the lookout for tabloid-type stories they could report over and over so they could avoid the real news, since that was a downer. That had to be why they were still camped out in Cortez, trying to turn this small tragedy into a big story. Orwell only prayed another bride would run away soon, or some cheerleader would vanish at a foreign resort, or there'd be a celebrity assassination at Telluride. Anything to take the heat off him.

This morning, the pathologist who'd performed Darlene Huntsberger's autopsy was in town to reinspect the body dump site. She had agreed to say a few words to the media, a fact for which Orwell, and the entire law enforcement fraternity of Montezuma, was pathetically grateful.

Dr. Mercy Westmoreland was a regular guest on *Court TV* and commanded respect, even awe, from knucklehead reporters. Orwell thought her aloof bearing and serene oval face gave her a quiet dignity that announced her as the serious professional she was. The honey blond hair scraped into a no nonsense bun at her nape sent a signal that she had better things to do than check herself out in mirrors. This was a woman who spent most of her time up to her rubber-gloved elbows in human fluids. What she had to look at on a daily basis would make most grown men puke. The sheriff admired anyone with the *cojones* to do her job.

He also admired the way the lovely doctor put media blabbermouths in their place without raising hackles. He wished he knew how to pull off that feat; he had his reelection to think about and could do with some tame reporters who would make him look good. But he had too much on his mind to watch his mouth, and his back, all the time.

As if by magnetic force, his eyes were drawn to the chief source of his daily indigestion, Detective Jude Devine. The woman had arrived in his bailiwick twelve months earlier, under cover of darkness, with a team of nameless operatives from Homeland Security. No one had bothered to ask if Orwell wanted a substation, least of all under the umbrella of a politically delicate arrangement with the Montrose County Sheriff, whereby they shared costs and responsibility for an unwanted outpost in Paradox, of all the godforsaken places. No, these asswipes just took over an abandoned schoolhouse and converted it into a sheriff's office, employed a valley woman to be the secretary, doing Lord knows what, then told him to base one of his deputies there. He'd picked Virgil Tulley, who had never quite fit in with the boys in Cortez for reasons Orwell preferred not to delve into.

Next thing, he was informed by the powers that be that Devine would be joining his department as a detective. Period. He was supposed to circulate the official story that she was ex-FBI and make up some bullshit to explain why she wasn't based in Cortez with the rest of his team. Knowing he would look like a real moron for opening an outpost where there wasn't enough crime to justify the budget, Orwell had confided in his staff that there was a big tourist development in the offing and the Japanese moneypeople needed to say there was law enforcement on site. He was heroically doing his bit to lure this foreign consortium into the area by establishing a remote office with Montrose, who could not fund it alone.

Ever since word leaked out, he'd been pestered constantly by most of Cortez, who were hanging out for the job bonanza. He only hoped no one would uncover the truth before his reelection, yet another reason media attention made his guts churn.

Devine met his eyes and produced one of her cool half-smiles. You couldn't warm to a woman like that, Orwell thought. Admittedly, it was not her fault she was too tall and too strongly built to appeal to most guys, not to mention a plain Jane. It was obvious she had not been blessed with the kind of mother who taught females how to make the most of themselves, like his wife did with their three daughters.

Devine's short dark brown hair was cut all wrong for her face, which was on the square side. And she had the kind of Roman nose that would have suited a guy better. But up close, you could see she had really beautiful gray-green eyes. They weren't big and pretty, instead they were heavy-lidded and sensual with eyelashes so dense and black Orwell's wife had commented on them. Most women would have made the most of this one attractive feature with cosmetics, regulations notwithstanding. Orwell had let it be known to his staff that he didn't consider eye shadow a disciplinary issue. The way he saw it, the fairer sex had a tough enough time retaining their femininity on the job. All he asked was that no one showed up for work looking like a hooker.

But despite the enlightened work environment, Devine didn't bother plucking her dark eyebrows, and didn't wear lipstick, let alone mascara. On top of it all, there was her surprising smoke-and-whiskey voice, all wrong for a woman in this line of work. Orwell wondered if she lowered her tone deliberately so she sounded more authoritative. He could only conclude she was one of those career types who thought she had to act like a man and would end up a lonely, frustrated spinster. Women's lib had a lot to answer for.

❖

Jude shifted her gaze away from Sheriff Pratt, who seemed to be fixating on her again. No doubt the media presence had him on edge, reminding him that he was the likely fall guy for some kind of federal government shenanigans. She knew he pictured his career in ruins every time he clapped eyes on her. That was one reason she'd pushed to head up the Huntsberger investigation. It was outside her real brief, but if she could help land a conviction that would bring kudos to the boss, maybe he'd chill.

Mercy Westmoreland had wrapped up the sound bites stage of her presentation and was now taking questions. Jude had one for her: *Doing anything tonight?*

She'd first met the alluring pathologist soon after starting her assignment in Paradox. They were both at a symposium on the recovery of human remains. Mercy had presented a guest seminar on air disaster victim identification issues. Afterward, she and Jude had exchanged a few words while they stood in line for burritos at the lunch buffet. The words themselves were not memorable, but Jude had had the strangest feeling Mercy was thinking about the two of them having sex the whole time they talked about the program, the bad coffee, and the long dry spell the Southwest was having. Jude herself had been happily distracted by that fantasy, picturing the cool, alarmingly well groomed Mercy in disarray. Hair down. Shirt unbuttoned. Lipstick smudged. She could almost feel that perfect skin smooth beneath her hands, that lissome body hot and damp against her own.

She had caught herself staring at Mercy's mouth as it shaped words, wondering how it would feel to kiss her. Even as they ate their Mexican food and compared notes with colleagues around their large table, Jude had covertly watched her. Their eyes had met several times and Jude had looked away first, determined not to announce her sexual frustration by acting like she had never seen an attractive woman before and wanted to jump her on the spot.

To her surprise, Mercy remembered their conference encounter when she'd arrived to examine the Huntsberger crime scene, and she'd greeted Jude like an old friend. A day later, Jude had attended Darlene's autopsy in Grand Junction, and Mercy had singled her out at the water fountain for a smile that seemed downright flirtatious. As the day progressed, this had evolved into the kind of eye contact that could be seriously misconstrued. Mercy had also prolonged their handshake during the farewell civilities at the end of the day.

Jude had since decided that reading anything into Mercy's manner was plain wishful thinking, the by-product of her reluctant celibacy. The Four Corners area was not exactly overflowing with eligible lesbians, let alone opportunities for discreet no-strings encounters. Jude would have to drive to Denver if she got really desperate. So far, she hadn't made the trip. Her life was complicated enough.

She permitted herself a long look at the golden girl of Southwestern forensic pathology. Mercy was your typical highly educated knockout, the kind Jude blew it with on dates. She was average height and neatly made with small high breasts and well-toned legs, at least that's how they looked beneath her beige linen pants. There was no wedding ring; her jewelry comprised a sensible wristwatch and small pearl studs. Jude was not standing close enough to catch her scent, but she could recall a beguiling musky fragrance from those few hours in the M.E.'s office. She could also recall the smattering of tiny cinnamon freckles across Mercy's nose and the faint scar below her left temple. Then there was her great ass and sexy walk, her slender hands and dancer's posture, the remarkable blue-jean eyes, and a seductive smile that hinted at a whole different woman beneath the cool reserve.

Yes, Dr. Westmoreland was the complete package. Looks, brains, minor celebrity status, and the X factor. Tons of it. Jude decided she was probably involved with a rocket scientist who grew orchids as a hobby, the kind of guy who didn't worry about being upstaged by his girlfriend. In a few years' time she would ask him to marry her and they would have two gifted children, then Mercy would go on Oprah to talk about combining family life with her glittering career. She was not a woman who would ever fade into anonymity, content with the mundane routines of domestic life. She was star material and everyone around her behaved accordingly.

A paunchy man waved his hand as a make-up artist powdered his face. "Gordon Reid. Fox News. Would you describe this as a ritual killing, doctor?"

"I can't speak for the killer's motives."

"There's talk this is the work of a Satanic cult." The Fox guy stuck to his game plan. "Is that a possibility?"

"I'm not here to indulge in speculation on faith-based violence. I can confirm that there was no attempt to remove the fetus and no evidence of goat's blood."

Another reporter fired off a question. "How was the stake driven through the victim's heart?"

Mercy rewarded this inquiry with a thoughtful expression. "In the Roman manner, I imagine."

Jude stifled laughter as the media bozos stared at one another in chagrined confusion, waiting for some intellectual giant to interpret this.

"So you're saying it was a mafia hit?"

"I'm saying the spike appears to have been hammered, a proclivity made famous by Pontius Pilate." This biblical reference only seemed to puzzle her audience even more. Without so much as a blink, Mercy translated, "People, she wasn't whacked by the local godfather."

A brief silence ensued. Several reporters then started speculating on the identity of said godfather, the Four Corners not being known for organized crime. Jude could see the ludicrous headlines tomorrow: *Mafia Link Denied in Vampire Killing.*

Mercy answered a few more questions with polite aplomb before pointing to an emaciated newswoman with a blinding platinum dye job. Suzette Kelly, the face of Channel 8, was wearing her signature look, a candy pink suit and a necklace of huge white pearls. Jude wondered what a big name like her was doing miles from Denver on a hick town news beat.

Like a barracuda parting a shoal of goldfish, Suzette carved her way to the front of the pack. "Doctor, would you care to comment on the rumors surrounding your personal relationship with Elspeth Harwood, the British actress."

Jude's small gasp was echoed throughout the room.

Mercy raised an eyebrow. "Suzette. You know I'd love to get into girl talk with you about celebrities. But alas," she flashed a coy smile, "I have an exhumation." Evading microphones, she stepped behind a couple of Montezuma's finest and vanished out the side door.

Staring after her, Jude found herself grinning like a fool. She wiped her expression clean of delight as Sheriff Pratt arrived at her elbow. He wasn't amused.

"Detective Devine, would you drive Dr. Westmoreland to the scene? Take a patrol vehicle. We can't expect her to ride in that truck of yours."

"I was planning on getting it washed, sir."

"You'll have to do that later. She's waiting out back." He hovered like there was something on his mind.

"Sir?"

"We don't want any trouble with Utah," he confided.

Mystified, Jude said, "Understood."

They shared a moment's stoic reflection.

"Alrighty then." Pratt tugged on his collar like it was too tight. "You better get going."

❖

"Guess you're headed back to Grand Junction this afternoon," Jude remarked after she and Mercy had made it through the mandatory pleasantries and had been driving in silence for a while.

Mercy stopped staring at the passing scenery and took stock of her. "Is that a roundabout way of asking me if I'm free for dinner?"

Jude had met some fast women in her time, but the question caught her napping. Could Mercy really be gay and not just a straight woman under time pressure? She tried not to sound startled. "Er...would you like to have dinner?"

"Business or pleasure?" Mercy said "pleasure" with a hot smile that took the straight-woman option off the table like it had never been there in the first place.

Unable to believe her luck, Jude asked, "What's your preference?"

"I'm kind of a sucker for pleasure."

Jude dragged her filthy mind off the word "sucker" and commented politely, "The social opportunities are fairly limited in these parts, aren't they?"

"No kidding. It's Denver or self-service." Mercy took a mint from her purse and popped it into her mouth. She offered the bag to Jude. "Want one?"

"Not for me, thanks."

"I'm trying to place your accent. Where are you from, originally?"

"Back east. D.C."

"Of course. I heard you were with the Bureau."

"Guilty as charged."

"A casualty of the partisan witch hunt?"

These days it didn't pay to comment openly about the stifling political atmosphere in the Bureau, so Jude made like she had no idea what Mercy was talking about. She'd requested an assignment out of D.C. anyway, so she said truthfully, "I was looking for a change of pace."

"Uh-huh." Mercy's enchanting blue eyes bored into her.

Jude told her what she wanted to hear. "Okay. So the environment was getting uncomfortable and I bailed."

"And you came *here*? Why, for God's sake?"

Jude tossed the question back. "Why are *you* here?"

"Because my father is dying and he needs me."

Jesus. "I'm sorry."

"Me too. He's all I have." As if the simple candor of the statement rocked her, too, Mercy added, "It sounds pathetic to say that. I mean, I have friends, of course. But my mother died a few years ago. She was an immigrant, so all her people are in Scandinavia. And my father's an only child."

"You don't have any siblings?"

"No. Just a few distant cousins in Atlanta."

Jude thought about her social-climbing older sister with the homophobe hubby and wanted to tell Mercy she wasn't missing out on a whole lot. But still, family was important, whether you liked them or not.

Her own parents had moved to Mexico recently, to enjoy a retirement where the dollar stretched further. They lived in Sayulita, a seaside fishing village near Puerto Vallarta. Selling their home in D.C. had given them enough cash to buy a luxury villa in the hills overlooking the Pacific Ocean, and have some left to add to their savings. Her dad's pension as a retired cop was barely enough to maintain a decent standard of living in the U.S., with the cost of health insurance going through the roof. Jude couldn't blame them for leaving. Money wasn't the only reason, but in Mexico their income bought a nice lifestyle with cheap medication and a maid service.

"So you're single?" Mercy cut to the chase.

"Yes. You?"

"Extremely."

What did that mean?

Before Jude could ask, Mercy said, "I suppose you're going to tell me you're shopping for the love of your life."

"Aren't we all? I mean, even if it's not conscious."

"I guess that's a yes."

"I'm trying to be honest."

"Never met Ms. Right?"

"Only in my dreams. Sometimes I get…entangled."

"What happens? You rent the U-Haul?"

"No, she does. And I get dumped for backing off."

"Ah, but you want to be dumped by then anyway, don't you?" Mercy smiled with the mournful contentment of a blackjack dealer listening to a tale of gambler's ruin.

How did she know? The pattern irritated the hell out of Jude. She knew she was a chicken when it came to relationships—anything to avoid confrontation. But she was making progress. Lately, she hadn't done anything really stupid. In fact, she hadn't done anything at all. No relationship meant no screwups.

"I'm not too successful in that department, either," Mercy informed her. "I got out of the worst relationship of my life three years ago. What's your story?"

"Ineptitude," Jude offered the bald truth. "I have trouble juggling work with a private life. It was a nightmare in both my quote unquote *serious* relationships. Since then, I've just focused on staying out of trouble. Guess you could call it the path of least resistance."

"Good, then I'd like to sleep with you," Mercy said, taking her breath away.

"It's completely mutual," Jude replied after stifling a choke. *In fact, what are we waiting for?* She got real. They had a crime to solve. She dragged her eyes away from Mercy's delicious body to the road ahead. Was this happening?

"Is tonight too soon?" Mercy inquired.

"No, tonight works." Jude's mouth was as dry as the dust their tires were kicking up. Unbelievable. They were negotiating a sexual encounter. There was a god after all.

"I know it seems rather forward. But we're adults, and there's some chemistry. Why waste time on the pretense of getting to know one another?"

"Agreed. Would you like to come back to my place or check into the Holiday Inn?" Jude wished there were better alternatives, but Cortez was no one's idea of a romantic getaway destination.

"Your place sounds good. Thank you." Mercy pondered the scenery anew, then shared, "I'm so horny I could fuck for hours. How about you?"

Jude almost drove off the road. "I haven't had any in a year."

"Excellent." Mercy shifted in her seat, laughing softly. "You've got me all wet just thinking about it."

Jude's palms slid on the wheel. They reached the Slick Rock Bridge and she swerved into the parking area and cut the motor. For a moment they sat in silence, then they unfastened their safety belts and faced one another.

Jude had a thought. "Who's Elspeth Harwood?"

"A former fling." Naked lust glittered in Mercy's eyes. Her mouth invited Jude's.

Unable to resist, she moved close enough for the kiss she'd been thinking about ever since they'd met. Mercy tasted of the mint she'd been chewing, her lips still sweetly coated. As far as kisses went, this one was right up there with the first Jude ever had with the first girl she'd ever loved. The gear stick and steering wheel cramped her style as she tried to find a more comfortable position. She reached across Mercy and located the seat lever. Instead of tilting back to a reasonable incline, the seat jerked flat, their combined weights overwhelming the mechanism.

"Oh fuck," Jude said.

"Exactly my thought." Mercy caught a handful of Jude's crotch and bumped hard.

Jude gasped. The backseat was looking pretty good right now.

"How far is your place?" Mercy asked.

"Not very." Jude could not believe she was seriously considering shirking duty so she could get laid. On the other hand, these were desperate times. "What about the crime scene?" she asked halfheartedly.

"It's not going anywhere." Mercy inserted the tip of her tongue beneath Jude's upper lip and slowly sucked. After a long hot moment, she broke off to confess, "And just so you know, the real reason I came down here was to see you."

❖

In the sack, Mercy was every bit as forthright as she had been in the car. "I'm in the mood for a little rough play. Nothing heavy."

All things being relative, Jude obligingly cuffed only one of the pathologist's delicate wrists to the headboard rail. "No marks, right?"

"Nothing visible."

She slid her hand between Mercy's supple thighs. Mercy resisted and twisted away.

"Oh, no. You're not going anywhere." Jude forced her onto her back. Softly, she said, "Be a good girl and it won't hurt."

"Fuck you." Mercy locked her knees together.

Jude yanked them apart. "If you're going to talk like a slut, I'll have to treat you like one."

"Perfect," Mercy murmured before slipping back into role. "You and whose army? How's it going to be when I notify your boss that his new detective forced me into her apartment and fucked me in the ass."

"And what will that Channel 8 reporter say when I tell her you loved it. You were on your knees, begging for it."

"Please don't," Mercy implored. "It would excite her *way* too much."

They started laughing. Helplessly, Jude cradled her forehead in her hand. The whole situation felt surreal.

"Hold me," Mercy said once they'd settled down. Her smile faded and there was a vulnerability in her face that hadn't been there before.

Sensing a change in her mood, Jude removed the cuff and gathered her into a firm embrace, kissing her cornsilk hair, wanting suddenly to know her better.

Mercy's voice was muffled against her chest. "Sometimes I'm so damned lonely I think I could die."

Jude's throat constricted and a rush of sadness made her feel ridiculously weepy. She pulled herself together before Mercy could notice. "We don't have to do this, you know."

"Oh, yes, we do." Mercy seemed unruffled once more, her vulnerable self tucked out of sight. She touched Jude's cheek. "Just this once. And then we have to be professional colleagues again."

Jude slid a caressing hand over her body. She was a babe. Lithe and silky smooth. Her flesh goose-bumped in reply to fingertips and tongue. They moved together softly, then hard. Mercy gave herself over to pleasure with thrilling abandon, frankly communicating her preferences. All the while, as Jude stroked and licked and fucked her into orgasm, Ms. Forensic Pathology bit and kissed, dug her nails in and talked really dirty.

Sprawled on her back some time later, she patted her chest and invited, "Sit here. I want you to come in my mouth."

Jude knelt over her and gripped the headboard. She had to hand it to Mercy. Her oral technique was impeccable.

CHAPTER THREE

Tulley was brooding. If he played with his gun anymore his palms would go numb, Jude thought. This had been going on for three days.

"What's eating you?" she asked.

He paused over the stack of hefty books he was slowly banging his head on. Dark amber eyes peered at her from beneath a coal-black cowlick. Even with his wavy hair cut shorter than usual, his deputy uniform, and the muscles he'd developed on the Bowflex that occupied their holding cell, he looked like an overgrown kid.

"Friday sure came 'round quick," he said dourly.

"Yep. It sure did." Jude figured he was stressing about the investigation.

So was she. They hadn't made a whole lot of progress and Smoke'm had failed to turn up the key evidence Tulley had fantasized about. He had, however, sniffed out a trash bag containing two thousand bucks in cash and checks belonging to a local gas station. No prizes for guessing what Bobby Lee Parker and Frank Horton had been looking for that day at Slick Rock.

"Tell me something," her gloomy subordinate said. "What would you give to a young lady?"

Jude blinked. Mercy's face loomed in her mind's eye, its pale perfection flushed. She could hear her gasping and groaning in the throes of orgasm. Instantly, wetly, she ached for another clandestine assignation. They hadn't spoken since that day. Jude tried not to conclude she had disappointed Mercy in some crucial way. Should she have kept her handcuffed, after all?

With an air of frustration, Tulley asked, "When you were younger, what kind of gift did you like getting? I read as how women don't like chocolates because they're worried about their figures. And flowers could bring on a hay fever attack."

"You're trying to choose a gift for a young lady?" Jude kept her face and tone free of astonishment. Tulley had a girlfriend? He'd never mentioned one, and he seemed so excruciatingly shy around women she'd assumed he was single.

"I already chose it. But I don't want to send the wrong signal."

"What signal would that be?"

Tulley reached into his desk drawer and produced a book called *The Rules of Dating for Clueless Christians*. A skirt of torn Post-it notes fluttered around the edges, marking pages for ready reference.

He opened the guide and read aloud, "'A well brought up young lady is easily spooked by expensive or overly personal gifts. She may think you are trying to buy her favors. Do you want the woman who could one day be your wife to feel cheap?'"

"I see the problem." Tulley was one of the faithful. Also new information.

"Is this what they're talking about?" He slid a small box across her desk.

Jude opened it and lifted a wad of perfumed pink tissue. "Nope. This is fine. A scarf is a thoughtful gift. Does she wear scarves?"

"All the time."

"Then she'll like this one. The design is very…feminine."

Tulley ran his forearm across his face. "I got some fancy wrapping but I can't get it looking right."

"Let's see." Jude made a little space on her desk and found a pair of scissors.

Between them they prettied up the box.

"That's nice." Tulley's shoulders sagged with relief. He stared at the wall clock. "She'll be here any minute."

"She's coming here?" Jude swung her eyes around the office.

Their secretary, Agatha, had taken vacation this week. The difference her presence made was one of aesthetics. Agatha kept the place tidy and under her sharp, schoolmarm stare, both Jude and Tulley diligently tossed wrappers in the trash, took bottles to the recyle bin, and refrained from piling crap all over their desks.

"She's real interested to see where I work," Tulley said.

"Great." Jude got busy straightening up her desk.

"I took out the trash."

"Oh, that was a big help. Get the vacuum cleaner and start over there." She pointed at Smoke'm's feeding area, a quagmire of ground kibble and rawhide fragments.

"I sure appreciate this," Tulley said.

"You owe me a beer."

After they'd finished cleaning the floor, stacking their books and files, and hiding their television and DVDs in the mock-cherry console that ran beneath the windows, Jude collapsed into her chair and popped open a can of ginger ale.

"How long have you been dating her?" she asked.

"We're not dating exactly. A while back she invited me to come to church with her and her folks, seeing as they live nearby and I've got no family here."

"That's nice. So this gift—you're planning on asking her out?"

Tulley looked miserable. Lowering his voice, he said, "Last few weeks, I got the feeling they were kind of expecting something. Then Mr. Critch gives me this." He indicated the dating guide.

"Yeah, that's definitely a hint." Jude studied the young deputy. "So, do you like this girl?"

Tulley's ears glowed like night-lights on either side of his lean face. "She's—"

A sharp little knock severed his reply and Jude found herself looking at a stocky, pink-cheeked professional virgin in her early twenties. Fluffy blond hair cut chin level, placid blue eyes, white frilly blouse, pink chiffon scarf, knee-length floral skirt, and unsexy sandals, she waited in the doorway, toying with the dainty crucifix at her neck.

Tulley leapt to his feet, sweating like a nervous wreck. "Hey, Alyssa. Come on in."

"Hey, Virgil." She swept into their office like she was doing them a favor. Her small nose wrinkled as she came to a halt opposite Jude's desk.

They'd forgotten to spray the room freshener. The place smelled of dog, desert, and donuts. Too late now, Jude thought, standing up to greet her.

Their visitor stuck out her hand. "You must be Detective Devine."

"Jude works fine."

The handshake was limp and ladylike. Jude could see why Tulley was losing sleep over the gift. Alyssa Critch looked like the kind of girl who could take offense.

"I've never been inside a police station." She gazed hopefully around. "Do you have actual prisoners here?"

"Uh. Not at this time." Tulley shot a mortified glance at the Bowflex.

"We're awaiting renovations." Jude made it sound like they would be incarcerating vicious felons as soon as some overdue carpentry had happened. "Until then we're not taking any chances. In the interests of the community."

Alyssa made a small wet noise like her mouth was watering. She'd be first in line at a stoning, Jude decided, noting the pro-life pin on her tightly buttoned collar. No contradiction there. The Alyssas of this world had scant compassion to spare for the post-fetal.

With a smug little smile, the girl said, "I know it's kind of early, but I hope you don't mind if Virgil leaves now. I made a picnic for us."

"Sounds great. Knock yourselves out." Jude glanced sideways at Tulley.

He was trying to hide the gift behind his back. She wanted to slip him a note that said: *She'll never give you any,* or perhaps something less subtle: *Run!*

He whistled for Smoke'm.

"You're planning on bringing that hound?" the damsel asked.

A new tide of red suffused Tulley's ears. "He won't be any trouble."

Saccharine sweet, Alyssa said, "Okay. So long as he rides in the trunk." Dogs ranked even lower on the charity chart than post-fetal life, it seemed.

But Tulley settled for the crummy option of going it alone with the possible future wife. "He can stay here," he said and met Jude's eyes. His disquiet was palpable.

"Good idea," Jude affirmed. "Wouldn't want him drooling on Alyssa's pretty skirt."

At that, Alyssa gave her a grateful smile, closely followed by a long assessing look. A pitying expression came over her features and Jude realized she had just been examined as potential competition and found sorely wanting. Naturally she was crushed.

"See you later." Tulley inched toward the door like a condemned man.

"Take your time," Jude said generously. "I won't need you until we interview that pervert at two."

Predictably, this excited a wide-eyed response from Alyssa. "I'll see to it he's back in plenty of time, Detective Devine. No decent woman should have to deal with deviants alone, even one as well qualified and capable looking as yourself."

"I'd sure appreciate that," Jude said. "I find Virgil completely indispensable when it comes to handling individuals who offend feminine dignity."

This lavish praise should have earned gratitude, but as Alyssa delicately pawed his bicep, Tulley cast a tormented look in Jude's direction. She wiggled her eyebrows suggestively. If he played his cards right, maybe he would get to first base. She'd certainly done her bit to improve his chances.

❖

After Tulley's truck disappeared, Jude changed out of her chinos and shirt into a uniform, took a spare cell phone from her satchel, and made a call.

"I'm in the clear for a couple of hours."

Her contact said, "Pay him a visit. Something routine."

"Apart from the homicide, we have several head of stolen cattle and someone took a dump in front of the Our Lady of Fatima monument. Take your pick."

"Jesus. It's a crime wave."

"Any idea where he's keeping the stuff?"

"Negative."

"It's fairly stable, right?"

"As far as military ordnance goes."

They signed off and Jude locked up the office and stuck a sign on the door that said: *Called to an emergency. Back at 2 p.m. Phone 911 if urgent assistance is required.*

She drove the twenty miles of dirt road to Black Dog Gulch with her mind lurching from Mercy's persistent tongue to the subject's lengthy profile. Harrison Hawke was your common garden white supremacist with a fenced-off compound in the middle of nowhere. His organization, the Christian Republic of Aryan Patriots, served up a smorgasbord of paranoid fantasies on its Web site and treated the mental midgets who subscribed to its newsletter to regular rants about Jews and African Americans. Nothing unusual. The FBI monitored countless domestic hate groups of this ilk.

Hawke's was small, especially after a falling out within the group over the Identity Church's position on abortion. In an attempt to claw back supporters lost to the National Alliance, Hawke had recently made boasts about having something big in the pipeline and the Bureau had connected him to several significant purchases of the plastic explosive RDX. They'd been following his movements since Jude arrived in the area, and it was time to start closing in.

His wasn't the only white supremacist cell operating out of the Four Corners. For some reason fringe organizations were buying up land on the Colorado side of the border with Utah. Jude had been sent into the area on a long-term undercover mission. Her general brief involved keeping tabs on the various players. More specifically, she was charged with gathering intelligence on several targets, including Harrison Hawke. Her masters imagined that by posing as a local law officer, she could gain access to this nutcase on the pretext of conducting routine inquiries. Then, as a woman, she was supposed to lower his guard.

Jude thought this was breathtakingly naïve but according to reliable sources, Hawke had a weakness for feisty women and was eager to recruit female supporters. He was the author of several short works on the role of females in his movement and presented himself as a kind of Klan knight in shining armor. He had publicly upbraided his male colleagues for their "backward attitudes toward our White women causing their political flight to the arms of lesbianism and race mixing." His Web site ruminations on the topic generally ended with the dire prediction: "Men that treat White women like they are mud will soon find it hard to get a date in the Aryan movement."

This in mind, Jude applied some lipstick and teased her hair up with mousse so it looked like a fashion cut instead of an advertisement for the lesbian lifestyle. She made a conscious effort to walk like a girl as she approached his house. The uniform was a nice touch, she thought. It fit snugly and even if she didn't have much of a waist, she had long legs and no flab. Besides, Hawke and his breed seemed to have some kind of uniform fetish. It was her guess that, despite his mistrust and loathing for law officers, he would find her look sexy. Hell, maybe he'd get off on her badge, too. Plenty of people had cop fantasies, herself included. She pictured Mercy in tight-fitting black LAPD regulation attire, a personal favorite, and almost whined.

Hawke lived in a dour concrete dwelling with ostentatious security and barred minimalist windows, the most prominent of which was discreetly stickered with an Othala rune, one of the many racist graphics Jude had encountered in her preparations for this assignment. No doubt these elaborate fortifications were supposed to provide protection come the day his place was under fire by puppets of the government looking to deprive him of his God-given constitutional right to own a rocket launcher.

She pressed the doorbell and a stern voice on an intercom said, "State your business, Deputy."

Jude held her ID up to the security camera above the steel door and said, "Sir, Sheriff's Detective Jude Devine. I'm conducting routine inquiries into the recent desecration of a local Christian monument. May I speak with you?"

"I have nothing to say."

"And that is your right." Hoping to strike a balance between authority and down-home Southwestern good manners, she continued, "Sir, I would sure appreciate it if you could contact the sheriff's office in Paradox if you hear anything at all about a group of radical extremist lesbians thought to be operating in this area."

From inside the house, chains rattled and bolts clunked. The door opened and a man with a shaved head stood in front of her, muscle running to fat, tattoos yawning over his flabby arms. Fish-blue eyes surveyed her with deep suspicion.

"Lesbians?"

"That's what we're hearing, sir."

"You think these deviants damaged the monument?"

"Can't really say. I'm just following up on any leads I can get."

"I didn't know there was a sheriff's office in Paradox Valley."

Yeah, right you didn't. "It's myself and one deputy, sir. Joint arrangement between Montrose and Montezuma. A requirement of the Japanese consortium."

"I heard about that." He muttered a racist epithet.

Jude forced her face to remain impassive. "Yep, seems like before long there's not going to be much of this country left for Americans." She manufactured a sigh and stepped back from the door. "Well, thanks for your time. You have a nice day, sir."

She had only made it three paces when Hawke took the bait, "You new to Colorado, Detective?"

Jude stopped walking and offered a polite smile. "You guessed that right. Originally from D.C."

"What brought you out West?"

He'd hear the official version sooner or later, if he hadn't already. May as well use it to her advantage. "I needed a change. I was working for the FBI but I, er…I wasn't comfortable with certain aspects of my work for personal reasons, so I quit. Figured local law enforcement might be a better place for me."

Her disenchanted fed act seemed to play pretty well with Hawke. Caution vied with curiosity in his expression. "Those aspects you're talking about wouldn't have anything to do with depriving Americans of their right to privacy, would they?"

"I really can't discuss that. All I can say is recent changes didn't sit well with my personal views and there comes a time when you have to stand up and be counted."

"Which is something I pride *myself* on," her subject promptly asserted. He ran a hand over his naked head, smoothing back imaginary hair.

Jude blurted, "My dad didn't fight for this country to have it taken over by—" She broke off in a display of professional prudence. "I need to be getting along now, sir."

Amazingly, Hawke went for it and actually took a step outside his fortress. Jude couldn't imagine he would be suckered so easily by a man. But it seemed like a combination of loneliness and sexism was working against him. The guy was obviously starved of female company, not to mention being so damned ugly even the most deluded sycophant in his movement probably wouldn't get naked with him. It had to get old, sitting out here all day examining your navel lint and trying to come up with astute new ways to sell theories about international Jewish financiers running America. Especially since nowadays anyone who bothered to read the newspapers knew the Chinese funded the deficit and big oil called the shots.

"Detective, listen," he was emboldened to declare, "you're not alone."

Jude greeted this gesture of solidarity with an innocent smile, like his meaning had gone right past her. Guys like Hawke knew their organizations were targeted by undercover agents and were paranoid by nature. She didn't want to appear too eager to bare her soul.

"I appreciate that, sir. If everyone in the community took such a supportive attitude it would make my job a whole lot easier. Bye now."

Their subject was full of surprises. He walked her to the Dakota and gallantly opened the door for her.

Acting like she was fighting off a girlish flutter, she touched her hair, checked the buttons at her collar, and said, "Well, thank you. Mr."—she consulted her notebook—"Mr. Hawke?"

"Correct. Harrison Hawke." He watched her face closely for a reaction.

Jude gave him a smile she hoped fell somewhere between coy and unaware and got into the truck. "It was a pleasure, Mr. Hawke." She started the motor.

He bared his teeth in an uneasy version of a smile. "Come by again if you're in the area, Officer."

She waved cheerfully and drove off, wondering if it could possibly be this easy. Bureau wisdom held that even the most cynical and unappealing males were easily convinced that a woman might find them irresistible. Hawke, it seemed, was no exception, her badge notwithstanding. But it was equally possible that he had made her as a fed the moment he set eyes on her, and was merely playing along to see what she was up to, keeping the enemy close. Jude smiled. She enjoyed chess, especially with an arrogant opponent. The win was so much more satisfying.

❖

When she got back to the station, Smoke'm was howling and Tulley was in tears. Her colleague had hauled out their small television and was watching a film in an apparent bid to distract himself from the source of his upset. Jude pretended not to notice the soggy Kleenex piled on his desk. Clearly, congratulations on a successful date were not in order.

She eyed the TV screen and groaned at the sight of subtitles. Still, it made a change from *Fargo*, his regular fix. "Foreign movie?" she asked, unbuttoning her shirt and stripping down to her white tee.

As a detective, she spent a fair amount of her time in civilian attire, but she wore a uniform when she wanted to make her presence felt. The canyon residents seemed to appreciate having visible law enforcement for a change.

"It's called *Osama*. It's about this girl in Afghanistan. She had to pretend to be a boy so she could work, otherwise she and her mom were going to starve." Tulley got all choked up. "Then the mullahs made her go to their weird religious school and chant the Quran and all. But they found out she was a girl because she got her period."

"Ugly, huh?"

"Now they've buried this foreign doctor up to her neck and they're going to stone her to death."

"Fucking barbarians."

"I can't watch it anymore." Tulley gathered the used tissues and consigned them to the trash.

Jude turned off the DVD and flipped through the latest stack of movies her sidekick had ordered off Netflix. "For Chrissakes, can't we get some normal films for a change?" she grumbled. "This stuff is so depressing."

"I want to learn about other places. Not everyone is like us."

"What about *Kill Bill Volume Two*? I bet that's a blast."

But Tulley was still hating the mullahs. "We did the right thing going in there. Those guys are evil."

"Yeah, well, we put them in power. Bin Laden and his asshole buddies got their start on our dime. This is called pigeons coming home to roost. Or, in his case, Stinger missiles."

Tulley absorbed this fact with the skepticism of a true patriot. "I think you're mistaken about that."

"I'm sure you do." Jude didn't want to get into it. Why disillusion the guy? She had to work with him. "So, how was the picnic?" It seemed safe to ask now that he'd regained control of his emotions.

"She liked the scarf."

That was a start. "You're back sooner than I expected."

Tulley looked uncomfortable. "She…Something happened."

Jude pictured an awkward grope and Tulley getting his face slapped. Personally, she wouldn't be sobbing over the likes of Alyssa Critch, but then she wasn't a born-again Christian male who thought he'd have to wait until his wedding night to get any. "Want to talk about it?"

"She was very…aggressive."

"What?"

"I didn't know what to do, her being smaller and a woman." He said this with a catch in his voice that emphasized something odd Jude had noticed in his speech pattern, a halting rhythm that seemed almost singsong at times. "If I'd pushed her, I might have hurt her."

"Are you saying she tried it on?" Jude felt stoned. *This* had him sobbing in his beer?

Mutely, he opened his collar and pointed to a dark purple mark. It was more than a hickey. The virgin had gnawed on him.

Jude managed not to laugh. "Guess you weren't expecting that."

"She handled me. You know—there." Unlike 99.9 percent of the straight male population, Tulley, it seemed, did not count crotch grabs by young females among his daily fantasies.

Jude reminded herself that unwanted sexual fondling was not a joke, even if the victim *was* a six foot male. "So how did you deal with these advances?"

"I told her it was too soon for hanky-panky."

Hanky-panky. The last time she'd heard that expression was from her grandmother, who made pronouncements about teen promiscuity and venereal disease throughout Jude's childhood.

"Maybe she was just trying to let you know she's not as uptight as her old man," she said, finding that hard to believe.

A more likely explanation was some form of entrapment, her suspicious mind suggested. Were there still people who believed a man had to marry a girl he'd "compromised"? In this backwater, anything was possible. Was it her place to warn Tulley? She felt like a big sister to him at times, but this was the kind of situation that called for a man-to-man conversation, a talk with a guy he could look up to. She was puzzled that he seemed to have no buddies. He had plenty of brothers, but none he was close to. From what Jude had observed, his family had issues with him leaving town and getting an education. She had the impression that instead of being proud of him, they felt betrayed on some level.

"So, how did you leave things with her in the end?" she asked, resigning herself to the role of mentor.

"She still wants me to come to church with them on Sunday."

"And how do you feel about that?"

"Okay, I guess." He didn't sound enthusiastic.

"Tell me something. Are you interested in this girl? As in, attracted."

"Well, she's decent and from a good family. She's—"

"I'm not asking about her qualifications as a prospective wife. I'm asking if you want to kiss her."

The ears changed color. "Not really."

"Well, I have to tell you, that probably means she's not the right girl for you."

"The book says look beyond the flesh."

"Okay. But it doesn't say ignore the flesh entirely, does it? Listen, think about other girls you've dated. How did you feel about kissing them?"

"It was okay. I've never had a steady girlfriend. Guess that would be different."

"You haven't? Not even in high school?"

"I was friends with some girls. But we weren't serious. Then I was at the police academy and then I moved out here." Tulley shook his head in sober resignation. "There's a woman shortage. Seems like all the nice girls already have boyfriends."

Listening to these feeble excuses, Jude tried not to leap to the obvious conclusion. Some people were late starters. Tulley's lack of interest in women and the odd lilting way he spoke did not have to mean he was gay. And since she wasn't about to pop that particular question, she said, "You could maybe let Alyssa know you'd like to be her friend but you're not looking for more than that right now."

"I don't think she'll take that real well."

"They never do."

Tulley's expression said he could buy that. "Why aren't you married? Never met the right guy?"

"Can't see that happening, I'm afraid."

"Ever get lonely?"

Jude contemplated the grinding hollowness she felt fairly often these days. "Sometimes. How about you?"

"It's been better since I got Smoke'm."

"Maybe you should think about spending social time with some of the guys. Isn't there a poker game Tuesday nights?"

He shifted restlessly. "Yeah, but they're not looking for anyone else."

Jude wondered what the deal was with Tulley and the other deputies. She'd heard a few remarks about him being a loner and sensed puzzled tolerance rather than hostility in their manner toward him. Come to think of it, they treated her much the same way. Maybe it had do with their unique status as a remote office. The Cortez crowd plainly envied them the perks of a cozy situation away from the sheriff's eye, not to mention their glamorous new profile, operating the only K-9 unit with a specialist cadaver hound. Some people got all the breaks.

Which was another reason she'd taken the Huntsberger case. She wanted to show the department that she and Tulley were willing to go the distance on a tough investigation. Which was exactly what this had been so far.

The Montezuma sheriff had assigned five deputies and two detectives to the case, under Jude's control, and six additional staff had been committed by the Cortez PD. Montrose and San Miguel preferred to be left out of the real work, since they had plenty to do getting ready for the Sweet Corn Festival on top of Telluride's annual shindig, and besides, Darlene was a Montezuma girl. Digging deep, they had helped put up *Information Wanted* posters.

Jude had the team sifting leads from the public and searching the databases going back twenty years for any other killings involving a biter or a stake through the heart. She and Tulley had been systematically interviewing every householder from Slip Rock to Muleshoe Bend and Big Gypsum. Now they were working their way south to Cahone. No one had seen any unusual activity near the river in the past several weeks.

She'd spent most of the previous day in Towaoc, discussing the facts of the case with several members of the Ute tribal council and cops from the Bureau of Indian Affairs. Helpfully, the council members had informed her that this was a white man's crime and no one on their reservation had the kind of snaggleteeth she was looking for. They had offered one significant fact. A young woman without a tongue had caught a ride with a local potter named Eddie House six years earlier, around the time of the Bear Dance. She was in a bad way and had stayed with him for several months. One day, while he was working in the pottery factory, she had hanged herself. Now her spirit was free to fly.

Jude had an appointment to speak with Mr. House in a couple of hours' time. Meanwhile, she wanted to look up the local pottery on the Internet so she could make a couple of educated remarks about his chosen art form.

"Did you get those posters up in Disappointment Valley?" she asked Tulley.

He nodded. "Mr. Huntsberger's coming in later to help with that some more."

"I think he's taken a shine to Smoke'm," Jude said. Clem Huntsberger usually showed up with a beef bone or a bag of liver treats he could ill afford.

The hound looked up at the sound of his name.

"That's one intelligent animal," Tulley said. "He knows that family's grieving. Every time he sees their truck, he makes a special noise like he's sorry for them. It's the only time he whines like that."

"You don't say." Jude gazed at a pottery bowl on her screen. A band of dull turquoise encompassed the base. Above it a precise geometric pattern was painted in black. The colors made a striking contrast against the fine pale ivory clay. It was actually beautiful.

"I believe one reason his breed makes such fine cadaver hounds is because of their emotional sensitivity," Tulley said.

"The olfactory receptors probably help too."

Tulley took her teasing in good humor. "Another great thing about him—animals never lie."

Jude contemplated that fact as she drove to Eddie House's place, a few miles out of Towaoc. Her own life had been punctuated by liars. Most notable in the recent past was the girlfriend who'd cheated on her and the close buddy on the job who'd spent a year not mentioning that he was the jerk she was cheating with. But top billing belonged to her father, decent in so many ways but unable to tell the truth in his personal life if it meant unpopularity. He wanted to be his children's hero, the man who promised them the world. When he reneged, he blamed their mother for the broken promises, a habit duly adopted by his offspring. Mary Devine was still held responsible by Jude's brother and sister for almost everything that went wrong in their lives.

Jude had weaned herself from that particular crutch in her twenties when she finally caught on that her mother's one big dream in life had also fallen prey to Patrick Devine's need to look good without having to deliver. Mary had yearned to set up her own business making gourmet chocolates, and as far back as Jude could remember, her father had promised each New Year's Eve that he would buy her the equipment to get started. Instead he would trade in the car, or the house would require new paint, or they would have a family vacation because he needed time out from the stress of his job, and his wife's dream would be deferred yet again. Their worst fights were over her wanting to get a job so she could pay for the chocolate project herself. Patrick Devine said he saw firsthand what happened to latchkey kids and he wasn't going to do that to his own. His wife was a stay-at-home mom. Period.

Not long before they moved to Mexico, he'd commented on the lean retirement they were facing and said what a pity it was that Mary had never done anything about her chocolate idea.

Occasionally, when Jude found herself telling women what they wanted to hear instead of being honest, she thought about her father and felt sick. She still had a way to go with that behavior pattern, which meant she needed to phone Mercy soon and ask to see her again. They had concluded their passionate episode on good terms, both agreeing that it would be better if they didn't sign up for a repeat performance. Neither could afford to be outed and the Four Corners area was way too small for them to conceal a liaison for long.

But Jude had lied through her teeth about being cool with that. It was not like she imagined love at first sight, or anything. But she thought Mercy was being overly paranoid. Why not arrange the occasional weekend out of town? They were smart enough to see one another every now and then without the locals finding out, weren't they?

She unclipped her cell phone and dialed Mercy's office number. No answer. She tried her cell and left a message. "Hey, Mercy, it's Jude. I'll be in Lands End one day next week following up on a few leads.

Maybe we could have a meal. Hope you're well. Phone me when you get a minute."

As she ended the call, she exhaled sharply and realized she had not drawn breath as she made it. She felt like a teenager who'd worked herself up to phoning a crush, only to feel a weird mix of relief and anticlimax that she'd had to talk to a machine instead.

She drove through Cortez and took U.S. 666 south. Soon after she'd arrived in Paradox, Jude had worked an attempted murder at a dude ranch out this way, interviewing Ute Indians and skinny cowboys with leather faces beneath a vast blue sky. She'd been stunned, then, by the contrast between life in these wide open spaces and the torrid city maze that was D.C. That awe, the sense of being remote from the world she had once known, was always present. Even more so on the lonely drive to Towaoc.

The Devil's Highway didn't earn its nickname for being pretty. A pothole-ridden band of gray asphalt cutting through a desolate landscape, the route to the casino could easily pass for the road to hell. On either side, broken glass and aluminum cans glinted in the merciless sun and a few sad sagebrush clung to life in the sulfurous yellow earth. No one had bothered to "adopt" this miserable stretch of road, unless you wanted to count Oliver Stone, who'd immortalized it in his movie *Natural Born Killers*.

The state transportation honchos had recently renumbered it to the less satanic 491 after extensive lobbying by the Ute casino board, the neighboring Navajo, and the state of New Mexico. Locals said the authorities weren't moved by the guys in suits or the lure of fancy lunches. They'd just gotten sick of replacing all the stolen highway signs.

The change hadn't caught on yet, or maybe it just wasn't that easy to transform the "number of the beast" to something innocuous. Even the small chapel run by the Trucking Troubadours for Christ failed to instill peace of mind among either tourists or locals. It was a known fact in these parts that the accident rate for the triple-six was twice the national average. Which said it all about who ruled in this wasteland, at least that was the inference.

Jude had laughed off the superstitions when she'd first arrived in the Four Corners, but every time she drove this route a strange unease crept over her. She wanted to dismiss the grim menace of the place as mere imagining, but as she stared out across the stark, khaki vista of volcanic cones and stunted mesas, she was overwhelmed with gloom.

It had been madness to move all the way out here, she decided. No matter how much distance she put between herself and the past, it would always come crawling after her. She could feel that ghost presence now, unsettling the orderly world she was trying to create for herself. *Leave me alone*, she thought. *I can't do this anymore.*

❖

Eddie House had a photograph of the girl he'd picked up that day after the Bear Dance. She was small and slender with long mousy hair and haunted gray eyes. He had also kept a few of the notes she'd written him. The hand was childish and the writer could not spell. Jude guessed she hadn't seen much schooling.

"Did she ever communicate about the loss of her tongue?" she asked.

House drew a slip of paper from the pile. It said: *I did not keep sweet.* He spoke slowly and softly, his eyes lowered. "There were things she wanted to forget. But she could not escape from them, even in her sleep."

"What exactly was the nature of your relationship with her?"

"I gave her a home."

Jude glanced around the living area. There had to be six dogs, and the large gray one at House's feet looked like a wolf. One of its hind legs was missing and its tawny eyes tracked Jude's every move. Eddie House also had a few injured wild birds in lofty enclosures along the front path to his home. He was a man with a weakness for strays, she gathered.

"So you and she weren't in...an intimate situation." Catching a look of affront, she added quickly, "I'm sorry. It's a routine question."

"She was a child," House said with dignity. "She needed a parent."

"Any idea about her family?"

"No."

"And she never wrote her name on a piece of paper for you? Not even her first name?"

"She was afraid."

"That's why you didn't talk to the police?"

"Yes."

Which explained why she was unidentified. After she'd killed herself, the police had tried to trace her so a death certificate could be issued. The case was left open. The girl had been buried by House, under the name Poppy Dolores. She liked the flower, he explained, and he had found her near Dolores, hence the last name. She was nineteen. At least that was what she had told House in one of her notes.

"What makes you think she was from Utah?" Jude asked.

House referred her to a note that read: *I come from Utah.* He added, "I knew it the first time I saw her."

"Why was that?"

"She was mistreated." Perhaps sensing he'd lost her on the math, he said. "An old prejudice, Detective. Utah holds bitter memories for my people."

"The forced march?" Jude referred to the shameful episode in 1881, when the Colorado Ute were evicted from their lands and marched 350 miles to a reservation in Utah. All who had weakened along the way were shot. Women. Children. Old people.

"There are many reasons. Did you know, a greater proportion of our people served in the Second World War than the white men of Utah, but still we couldn't vote?"

"I think I'd have a problem with that," Jude acknowledged.

Given the ugly history their races shared, she was amazed that any Native American could tolerate being in the same room as a white person. However, Eddie House had been welcoming and hospitable, if somewhat reserved in his manner. Since living in the Southwest, she'd found that the Native Americans she encountered had quite different body language from most other people she came in contact with, and they did not seem especially talkative.

It was hard to pick Eddie House's age. Around fifty, perhaps older. His hair was silver-white and dead straight, his face lined but not heavily wrinkled. He wore a thin leather thong around his head. From one of the ties hung several tiny beads of turquoise and coral, a piece of bone, and an unusual banded cream and brown feather.

"Is there anything at all she ever shared with you about her life?" Jude sifted through the other notes. Most were single lines. One stood out. *No one will help us.* She handed it to House. "Do you know what she meant by this?"

"She had bad dreams. One night, I made her a milk drink and she gave me that note. It was not long before she took her life."

"I'm very sorry."

He acknowledged her sympathy with a tranquil smile. "There is no death. Only a change of worlds."

"Chief Seattle?"

"Yes." For the first time in their discussion, his dark brown eyes rested on her squarely. After a lengthy scrutiny, he rose from his chair and said, "Walk with me."

He led her into an airy bedroom overlooking the ochre prairie toward the Mesa Verde, the three-legged wolf at his heel. From the top drawer of a simple pine cabinet, he took a neatly folded stack of garments and handed them to her. "She was wearing these the day I found her."

Jude unfolded what passed for high fashion in certain parts of the Southwest—white socks, black shoes, a long-sleeved, high-necked, ankle-length pastel gray dress with an over-sized white collar and matching sash. Women in this type of getup could sometimes be seen in Cortez, shopping with their husbands, Mormon fundamentalists from Utah who had recently started buying land in Montezuma County.

"May I take these?" she asked.

"She won't miss them."

"Will you?"

"I have this." He indicated the leather thong at his temple.

"She made that?"

"She was learning crafts for the market."

"It's lovely. What kind of feather is that?"

"Mexican spotted owl. I was healing one while Poppy was here. He comes back sometimes and leaves a dead rabbit at my door."

Jude smiled. "Like he's thanking you."

"We have an understanding. I divide the rabbit and cook my part. Then we eat together."

Jude floundered for something to say that didn't sound patronizing. "That's amazing. So he's quite tame?"

"No." He didn't expand on this pronouncement, instead returning to the subject. "I think she could have learned to make pottery. She had patient hands."

Jude refolded Poppy's clothes. "Let me tell you something, Mr. House. I believe Poppy may be connected in some way to the murder I'm investigating. Darlene Huntsberger? Do you know her?"

He shook his head.

"I'm going to catch the person who did it. I think he may have hurt Poppy too. And when I do, I promise you, he'll pay for his crimes."

A faraway look softened House's features and he extended a hand to stroke the wolf's mane. "I would find that satisfying."

CHAPTER FOUR

Naoma Epperson tucked her index finger beneath the chin of the girl standing before her. "Are you ready to be sweet?"

Bold dark eyes blinked at her from a fine-boned face. Naoma could almost swear she glimpsed defiance in their expression. Impatiently, she flicked a glance toward the junior wife standing a few feet away.

Summer was staring at the floor. One of her hands rested on her heavily pregnant belly and her face was as pasty pale as the bread dough rising on the kitchen counter.

"Did you speak with your sister?" Naoma demanded.

"Yes, ma'am."

Naoma dropped the silent girl's chin and shook her slightly by the shoulder. "Seems like she still doesn't understand the honor being given her."

Adeline Fleming was fourteen and thin for her age, barely a sign of breast or hips. It was beyond Naoma why her husband wished to elevate a girl so lacking in womanly attractions to spiritual wifehood. But it was not Nathaniel's place to question the prophet's commands, as absurd as some of them seemed. Neither was it hers.

"I won't marry Mr. Epperson," Adeline said. "He's old."

Naoma was so outraged by this ungrateful pronouncement, she cuffed the impudent girl across the face. "How dare you speak in that manner about a member of the priesthood. Do you forget you are under the master's roof?"

Summer rushed forward and took her sister's arm. "I'll deal with her, Sister."

"You are both trying my patience," Naoma warned. "Do you want to be cast out of this family?"

Summer shook her head emphatically. "No, Sister. I beg your forgiveness."

"Bake the bread and teach your sister to conduct herself in the appropriate manner. You have two days before the master returns from his business in Texas and she is to be sealed to him immediately."

Naoma left the room, aggravated. She'd had a feeling that girl was trouble ever since she'd walked in the door a week earlier. The new prophet had awarded her to Nathaniel, whose loyalty had also earned him the promise that he would soon be appointed first counselor. Adeline could consider herself fortunate that not only would she be married to one of the most powerful men in the High Priesthood, she would also be living with her older sister. Had she not been assigned to Nathaniel, her parents had planned to marry her to one of her uncles, a man of lower status in the church who had recently spoken out of turn. Two of his wives had been taken from him as a consequence and given to a cousin of the prophet. Adeline, like most young girls, had no idea how much worse her situation could be.

Naoma paused in the long corridor that led to her private sitting room, yelling at one of the laziest wives in their family. Yet again Fawn Dew's simple-minded son had fouled the hallway. The only reason Naoma put up with him was that he was a Downs. They were worth more money from the state.

"It's not his fault, you old bitch," Fawn Dew yelled back.

Naoma ached to beat the impertinence out of her, but she would have to bide her time. Fawn Dew was the prophet's daughter and Nathaniel's current favorite, and no one would cross her while she had more of his pillow than any other wife. The smart-mouthed little slut's day in the sun would pass, as they always did, and when that time came, Naoma would have her revenge. Anticipation of this pleasure helped her keep her temper.

Patience and self-discipline had served her well in her thirty years of marriage. At first, she'd been too stupid to do anything but accept her lot in silence, hurt and angry when her husband brought a second wife into their home just before Naoma gave birth to their first child. For ten miserable years she had suffered humiliation and insult from a procession of wives who thought they had replaced her in her husband's esteem as well as his bed. She had been little more than a slave, waiting on those glorified harlots and their revolting brats until the day came when the household was in so much chaos Nathaniel took her to task.

It was probably the only time she had ever been completely honest with her husband. She had told him it was not her fault that his wives thought they had him wrapped around their little fingers. He had made his own bed and could not hold her responsible. She pointed out that any man who allowed his junior wives to show no respect to the senior wife was disobeying God and the prophet, and that everyone outside of their home had noticed he was making a joke of himself. Other men, higher than him in the prophet's esteem, ran their homes according to Sarah's law. Hadn't he wondered why he was not promoted in the church?

She had offered him a deal. She would manage a well-ordered compound with wives and children who behaved themselves. In exchange, he would meet certain conditions. Alternatively, he could continue to live in a zoo and Naoma would no longer compensate for the lazy harlots he kept adding to the household. They could fight over the chores among themselves. It was his choice.

Nathaniel responded by asking what she wanted him to do, and in that moment, Naoma had understood exactly how to survive the hellish life God had condemned her to lead. If she could give her husband what he needed and wanted—relative tranquility and unlimited access to young women—she would have as much power as any woman living the Principle could hope for.

That evening, Nathaniel had lined up his wives and children and instructed them that his home would now be run according to Sarah's law. That meant they would obey Naoma in all things because she was his blessed wife, the mother of his firstborn. She would determine who was sent to his bed, and any wife who did not keep herself sweet would be deprived of this honor. If anyone failed to show Naoma the respect to which she was entitled, that wife or child would be severely punished.

Naoma had duly delivered on her promise. Wives who misunderstood their situation soon found themselves carrying out the filthiest chores, wearing the oldest garments, and begging her for mercy. Children who cried and made demands discovered their behavior had painful consequences.

Unlike some first wives, Naoma was thrilled that her husband had ceased sharing her bed. Sometimes she thought she must have reached a spiritual plane where she no longer needed the physical attentions of a man. But the truth was, that side of marriage had always repelled her and child-bearing was an affliction she was happy to forgo. Her sole concern was to ensure that Nathaniel would never elevate any other wife above her. To secure her position, she allowed him his favorites for a time, but when it seemed he could be developing a special respect for one of them, she would ensure her conniving sister-wife did something to disgrace him.

Nathaniel seldom pushed his luck. They both knew their accord made it easy for him to have exactly what he wanted: a place in the prophet's inner circle, community prestige, the toadying obedience of his family, a steady diet of sex with docile young girls. And, of course, freedom from the financial burden of caring for his ever-expanding family. Naoma saw to it that the government shouldered that load, just as the prophet instructed.

❖

"You can't speak to Sister Naoma that way," Summer hissed as she marched her sister toward the henhouse.

Adeline had always been difficult. Even when they were small children, she was the first to get in trouble and the last to run from a fight. Finally, the problem became so serious, their mother couldn't manage her—not with fourteen other children to take care of. So Adeline had been sent to their aunt's home in Salt Lake City, supposedly so Aunt Chastity, who was not blessed with children, could teach her how to behave. A terrible thing had occurred some time during the three years she'd spent there. Aunt Chastity had fallen under the influence of Satan and had allowed Adeline to watch television and attend the public school. Out among the heathen of Babylon, she had acquired wrongful thinking. And her clothes!

Their parents had discovered the disaster after Summer's oldest brother called on Aunt Chastity and found Adeline dancing to devilish music and wearing shameless attire. Naturally, when they heard the news, they rushed to the city to save her from corruption. Aunt Chastity had been shunned ever since and the family no longer spoke of her as a relative. She was Mrs. Young, even if her husband had divorced her for her wicked conduct.

A week ago, the Flemings had arrived at the Gathering for Zion Ranch with the good news that Adeline had been chosen to be the master's fifteenth wife. They'd made Summer's duty clear. It was her job to make sure that her sister forgot the evil ways she had learned among the apostates and kept herself sweet. So far, Summer wasn't having much success.

"He's an old ugly man," Adeline said. "I am not marrying him, and no one can make me."

"They can too." Summer clasped her belly as the baby kicked. Surely it would be a boy, wriggling about so much. The thought dulled her excitement about her first child. In the Epperson family, girls were more highly prized, and mothers had to let go of their sons sooner.

"I'll be out of here before they get a chance," Adeline said. "I'm going back to Aunt Chastity. She wants me to go to college."

"College is a dangerous place for decent women," Summer said.

"That's bullshit. If I go to college I can get a good job and live in Salt Lake. All my friends are there. They'll be going to BYU."

"What's BYU?"

Adeline rolled her eyes. "Duh! Brigham Young University. It's a good school. I want to be a veterinarian. That's a doctor for animals."

Summer had never heard of such a ridiculous thing. "Don't speak of these ideas to anyone," she warned. "You'll get us both in terrible trouble."

"If that old man comes near me, it won't be me that's in trouble. It'll be him, because I'll go to the police. He'll end up in jail, just like the man that kidnapped Elizabeth Smart."

Fear made Summer's skin damp and cold. She grabbed Adeline's arm. "Please don't say such things. Wives who go to the police are brought back. The master is very angry if that happens."

"What do you mean, they're brought back?"

"It is forbidden to speak of this." Summer picked up one of the shovels propped against the side of the small barn and unfastened the latch. "Bring the wheelbarrow, Addy."

The pungent odor of chicken manure made her gag as they stepped into the barn. Summer trampled a path through deep hay on the floor and began shoveling litter from beneath the perches. She moved awkwardly. Tasks like this made her back ache.

Adeline took the shovel from her. "I'll do that. You shouldn't be doing heavy work."

"I must keep strong so I can have a healthy baby." She massaged her lower back. Sister Naoma wanted her to pray for a Downs, like Fawn Dew's son, and Summer felt guilty that she hadn't. But one of the other sister-wives had given birth to a dwarf not long ago. Surely Naoma could be content with that.

Adeline continued to talk nonsense as she dumped shovel-loads into the wheelbarrow, finally declaring, "Aunt Chastity says women shouldn't have babies until they are in their twenties."

"Mrs. Young is apostate," Summer stated the obvious. "You should not heed anything she says. She is influenced by the devil."

Adeline leaned on her shovel and stared incredulously at Summer. "Boy, are you ever brainwashed."

"No. It is you who has been corrupted," Summer cried. "You must pass through the refiner's fire so you are worthy of the celestial kingdom. Please, Addy. Humble yourself. Remember, it is the husband who introduces a woman to Christ. You have to marry or you will not find salvation. This is the path God has chosen for you and—"

"That's such crap!" Adeline tossed her shovel aside. "I seriously doubt that God thinks any of this is a good idea. I'm leaving this place before old man Epperson gets back here, and you're not stopping me."

Summer had barely formed a reply, when a voice boomed from the doorway.

"But I am." Sister Naoma advanced into the barn carrying the thick belt-strap she kept handy for discipline.

"Just try it, you fat cow." Adeline quickly stooped and reached for the shovel.

Terrified, Summer did what she knew she had to do. She stamped down hard on her sister's hand, making her drop the tool. Naoma grabbed Adeline by her hair and dragged her a few feet.

"Leave us, Summer," the head wife said.

For a moment Summer considered falling on her knees, begging for mercy for her sister, but she knew the look on Naoma's face. All that would happen if she made such a plea was that she would be beaten also, and she was too frightened for her baby to take that risk.

She lowered her head and said, "Yes, Sister Naoma. Thank you."

As she hurried away from the barn, she could hear Adeline's screams. Her sister was a fighter but she was no match for the head wife. Naoma easily weighed two hundred and fifty pounds, and she knew exactly how to inflict punishment with her boots and her belt. Summer had only had to suffer one of those beatings and she had kept herself sweet ever since. Only a foolish wife defied Naoma. It was best Adeline learned that now.

❖

Jude poured herself a glass of Glenmorangie and added a splash of water. The setting sun flooded her living room with ruby light, making her blown-glass bowls and vases pulsate color as if lit from within. She sank back into her favorite burgundy leather chair at the window and contemplated the fierce beauty of her environment. The jagged violet of the Uncompahgre Plateau stretched along the horizon beneath an artist's sky awash with crimson, pink, and flaming orange. She never got used to this view. It changed every day, and each season revealed it differently.

Dragging her gaze away, she opened the file on her knee and reflected on the contents of Darlene Huntsberger's stomach. The M.E.'s report listed "mucus material without particulate matter"—not exactly a bonanza of useful data. However, the proximal portion of her small intestine had contained shreds of paper and a key. Mercy said these would have been swallowed about six hours before Darlene died. She was supposed to be getting back to Jude if they managed to reconstruct the paper shreds.

Darlene's death had not come easy. From the autopsy, Jude had been able to reconstruct a scenario for her colleagues at the briefing earlier that day. Darlene had been the subject of repeated physical abuse over a period of two years, presumably at the hands of the individual or individuals who'd abducted her. Multiple, differently aged posterior rib and scapular fractures, broken teeth, and patterned burns were textbook indicators of domestic battery.

Some five or six months prior to her death, she had lost her tongue in a criminal assault almost certainly conducted by the same persons responsible for her long-term battery, and in all likelihood her murder.

The killing itself could be classified as a ritual killing involving sexual sadism. Jude had brought in a criminal psychologist Mercy recommended, Stamer Knutson. His profile of the man they were seeking had even made Pratt sit up. She leafed through the transcript of his presentation, marveling again at the way competent profilers analyzed the psychological fingerprints left by a killer.

Knutson believed that the long-term abuse made it unlikely that the killer was a stranger. Darlene, he stated, was an atypical victim of intimate partner abuse. Find the partner and they would find their killer. Yet there was one problem with that theory. He was convinced that the biter was not the same man who'd been abusing Darlene since her abduction and probably not the killer. There was no evidence of old bites inflicted before the date of her death, and given the depth and intensity of the dentition, there would have been scarring.

Knutson found that the bites were consistent with "a disorganized individual carrying out a frenzied attack on the victim. Whereas elements of control and planning were present in the single, deep throat wound, the spike through the heart, and the method of body disposal. This could indicate partners in the killing." They were looking for "an older white male who exercises dominance over a younger, more overtly unbalanced companion." And, Knutson asserted, "The sacrificial aspect to the case indicates that one or both may be extremely religious."

His profile had been submitted to VICAP, and if the analysts at the FBI's academy in Quantico found any similarities with other homicides in their databases, Jude would be notified.

She thought about Poppy Dolores, missing her tongue and suffering profound psychological problems. The clothing she'd been wearing when House picked her up was like nothing Jude had ever seen before moving out here, home sewn and designed to cover the wearer from head to foot. Long sleeves, a large boat collar that seemed more appropriate for a toddler's outfit than a grown woman's dress, white knee-high socks…who wore anything like this in twenty-first-century America? Only members of a few religious sects.

Had Poppy Dolores been a victim of Darlene's kidnapper? Jude wondered how many others like her there were, and where they were now. Was Poppy the only one who had ever escaped?

A familiar, crushing helplessness stifled her breathing and trapped a mouthful of Scotch in her throat. Coughing, Jude dropped the file onto the coffee table and reached for the pitcher of water. No matter what she did, where she went, how far away she got, and how much time passed, she realized she would never escape this despair. Bleakly, she removed her boots, reclined the chair, and forced herself to relax into the deep cushioning.

She knew she couldn't allow herself to think that way. If ever there was a place where she could make a fresh start, it was this. All she had to do was give herself permission.

❖

"Is it nighttime?" Adeline mumbled the question. It hurt to speak. One of the head wife's blows had cut her bottom lip badly.

"Almost," Summer whispered. "I'm not supposed to be here."

"You have to let me out." Adeline pointed at the bolt that secured the cage she'd been thrown into. It was shielded by a sheet of tin and she couldn't reach it through the heavy steel mesh.

"I can't. She'd know it was me. You have no idea what it's like."

"I get beat half to death and now I'm locked in a dog cage. You think I don't know what it's like!"

"You should be thankful it's not worse," Summer retorted.

"What about him? What did he do to end up in here?" Adeline gestured toward a second cage a few yards away. In it a young boy was hunched in one corner. She'd been trying to talk to him, but he wouldn't speak.

"He is expelled but he keeps trying to come back. We have to keep him here until the master comes home."

"Why?"

"He might fraternize."

"What do you mean?"

"With our daughters. That's why he was cast out. We are not allowed to speak to him." Summer kept her back to the other cage, not once turning to see the child it housed. In a panicked voice, she begged, "Please don't listen to the devil's voice inside of you, Addy. Fight temptation!"

"There's no devil's voice inside me," Adeline scoffed, amazed that her sister still believed everything she was told.

Summer had always been a goody two-shoes, desperate to please their daddy, like he even remembered their names. She was always the one who read an extra hour of scripture and rushed to tell their parents if any of the other kids were disobedient.

"Hush! Listen to me. If you don't humble yourself, I don't know what will happen." Summer clutched the mesh. She was crying. "They will wait for me to have my baby, then I know I'll be punished. I don't want to lose my baby."

"What are you saying? You think they'll hurt your baby?"

"They could take him from me and give him to someone else. Unfit mothers are punished."

"Then come with me," Adeline urged. "Tonight. Let's get out of here and never come back."

"Where would we go?"

"I don't know. We'd hide."

A small voice piped up. "They'll find you. Runaway wives never get out."

Adeline squinted at the bony boy in the cage a few yards away. "Oh yeah?"

Summer shook her arm. "Don't speak to him. It's forbidden."

"Who says? That cretin you call a prophet? Guess what, Summer— he's a big phony. They all are."

The boy rattled his cage door. "If you let me out I can take you to a place."

"What kind of place?" Adeline asked.

"We can hide there for a few days. It's up Seeds of Cain mountain. No one knows about it."

"If it's such a great place, how come you're back here living in a dog cage?"

"I came to see my mom. I thought she would help me."

"Your mother is one of the wives?"

Adeline felt sick knowing that this kid's own mother had allowed him to be locked up in a cage with nothing but a few crusts of bread and a dog bowl filled with water. If that could happen, anything could happen. Was everyone in this place totally insane? She hadn't believed some of the things Aunt Chastity said about the prophet and his followers, but she knew better now.

The boy said, "She's the eighth wife. Heavensent."

Summer's expression shifted from fearful to completely frantic at the sound of her name. To Adeline, she babbled, "She's a poofer and it's his fault, and if they catch me talking to you I'll be a poofer too." She cried some more.

"Shush," Adeline said. "If you keep bawling like that someone *will* hear you and you will be a poofer, whatever that is."

"It's when someone vanishes. She was here, then she was gone. As in, *poof!*"

"Dead?" Adeline could hear how squeaky her own voice was.

"I don't know. Sister Naoma says they sent her to Canada to another husband."

"My mother's gone?" The boys' question was more like a strangled wail.

Even Summer turned around. "Yes," she hissed. "So there's no point you keeping on coming back. You're in mighty big trouble, all for nothing."

"Please, Summer, let us go," Adeline begged. " I'll take him with me and we'll never come back, I promise."

Summer hesitated, rocking back and forth on her heels, one hand clutching the small of her back. In the deep shadows of the barn her face was hard to read, but Adeline could sense she was weakening. She reached for the bolt then wavered and fell back.

"I can't," she said. "The devil is speaking through you. I cannot be tempted."

"No, it's not the devil, it's me!" Adeline fell onto her knees. "Please. It's me. Your sister."

But something hardened in Summer's face, and Adeline knew in that moment that her big sister was lost to her.

CHAPTER FIVE

When Jude got into work the next morning, Bobby Lee Parker was slouched against his fancy truck in the parking area. He wore black jeans, red shirt, and a black Santa Fe hat. This was angled down like he was sleeping standing up.

She pulled up alongside, wondering what could possibly have prompted this visit. Convicted felons did not usually pay social calls on law enforcement. She glanced past him into his lovingly waxed Silverado. The driver's door was open and Bobby Lee had company. A small fair-haired figure sat hunched in the passenger seat. Twelve years old, maybe. He was asleep.

Jarred by the sight, Jude had to shake herself. Like all slight, fair-haired twelve-year-old boys, this one made her skip a breath or two. Refocusing, she gathered up her satchel and food supplies, climbed out of the Dakota, and locked the doors, aware all the while of Bobby Lee's gaze sliding over her.

"Mornin', ma'am." He sidled around his truck and tipped his hat with ostentatious gallantry. "Allow me to help you with those."

"There's no need." Jude tried not to move too sharply as she unhooked the station key ring from her belt. All she needed now was to drop the lot, proving herself a girl. "What can I do for you, Mr. Parker?"

"That's a question I could answer a whole different way in different circumstances." Bobby Lee grinned like this was a toothpaste commercial.

Jude said, "Get to the point."

Only slightly crestfallen, he pointed to his passenger. "I knew you'd want to see this kid, Detective Devine." He said it like *Dee-Vine*. "Picked him up hitching out of Dove Creek. He's got some information for you."

"About?"

Bobby Lee extracted a folded sheet of paper from his shirt pocket. It was one of the Information Wanted posters the MCSO had plastered up everywhere, seeking leads in the Huntsberger case.

With patent satisfaction, Bobby Lee announced, "He had contact with the girl."

"So did half of Cortez."

"Yeah, but not recently." He paused for effect. "The kid saw her a couple of months ago."

Jude peered at him over her sunglasses.

"It's the God's honest truth. Least that's what he says. Figured you'd want to talk to him."

"I do." Jude headed for the station. "Bring him in."

She unlocked the front door and the internal security door, and dumped her stuff on her desk. Through the window she could see Bobby Lee trying to drag the kid toward the station. After a minute or so, she went back outdoors.

"What seems to be the problem, Mr. Parker?"

"He's real nervous of the police, ma'am. Minute he saw the sheriff badge on your sign, he made a run for it."

"A feeling I am sure you can relate to," Jude said dryly.

"If you're referring to my past, that's all over now." Bobby Lee's tone suggested he was hurt by the implication.

"Son, what's your name?" Jude asked the boy.

Silence.

"He goes by Zach." Bobby Lee shook the kid's shoulder. "Hey. Wake up, pal. There's a burger and fries when you're done telling the detective what you told me."

Jude could almost see the boy drool. He looked starved, bony arms and ankles protruding from filthy overalls a few sizes too small. The flies couldn't get enough of him either. She could hardly wait to have him cooped up indoors exuding the stench of unwashed body and cat piss.

"Zach, nothing bad is going to happen to you," she said. "And if you're hungry, I can rustle up some breakfast in the station."

Huge, limpid blue eyes stared up at her from a gaunt face. "Please don't make me go back."

"Back where?"

He lowered his head and mumbled something.

Bobby Lee removed his hat and swished it to disperse the flies. "He's afraid of being sent back to his hometown on account of people there who beat on him."

Jude was cautious about making promises to a runaway. She would have to take this kid to child services once she'd interviewed him. If family back home were looking for him, he would be returned unless there was proof of abuse and neglect. And it would not be up to Colorado Social Services to make that decision. The first thing they would do is hand his case over to Utah.

"While you're here with me, no one will hurt you," she said. "Now come on indoors."

The fight seemed to go out of him then, and he sagged against Bobby Lee, who uttered a startled yelp and recoiled in dismay, propping him at arm's length. "Shit," he told Jude, "he's fucking unconscious."

They carried him into the station and put him on the bunk bed in the holding cell. He weighed almost nothing. Maybe eighty pounds.

Jude got a glass of water and gently slapped the boy's cheeks a couple of times. "Drink this," she said as he came around.

"Oh, man. Disgusting." Bobby Lee was sniffing his own hands. "That smell…it transferred itself."

"You can go," Jude told him. "Thanks for bringing him in."

"At your service, ma'am." The Romeo of Cortez produced a slip of paper from his jeans and handed it to her. "That's my number if you need me for anything else."

"Appreciate that." Jude kept her attention on the task of reviving her smelly visitor. "How about you leave the door open on your way out. We could use some fresh air."

"Your wish is my command." The booted feet stayed where they were.

Jude looked up. She could swear he batted his eyelashes. "Was there something else, Mr. Parker?"

A shit-eating grin. "Anyone ever tell you, you have beautiful eyes, ma'am? I just wanted to look into them one more time."

Jude gave him a long, hard stare. "Get out of here before I arrest you for that gas station heist."

Bobby Lee held her gaze without flinching. "Don't suppose you'd care to discuss that over a fine meal?"

"If you have something to say to me, we can talk about it after I've read you your rights," she replied.

"Hard to get. I like that in a woman." He looked her brazenly up and down. "Give me a call when you need some satisfaction. Doesn't look like you're getting a whole lot of that."

Fresh out of smart replies, Jude could only stare in mild shock as her would-be date sauntered away. Men never hit on her, a state of affairs that made her thankful. There was enough shit to deal with on the job without colleagues trying to get into her pants. She figured most guys she met were too intimidated to indulge themselves in fantasies about winning her over with their manly charms. It seemed as if they sensed she was not available, even if they couldn't be sure why.

Hearing a groan, she returned her attention to the boy on the cot, and asked, "Feeling better?"

"Yes, ma'am." He eyed the cell door, his expression haunted.

Sensing an imminent bolt, she took one of his clammy hands. "Let's go sit in the other room and I'll fix you some breakfast."

He couldn't get out of the cell fast enough. Jude sat him at Tulley's desk, automatically checking the wall clock. The deputy wouldn't be in for another half hour. She took a can of soda from the fridge, pulled the tab, and set it in front of the boy. A shot of glucose seemed like a good move.

He gulped some down and said, "Much obliged, ma'am."

Jude pulled a couple of frozen entrees from the freezer, stuck the first of these in the microwave, and set up her tape recorder. "What's your full name, Zach?"

He looked cagey, a film of perspiration shining on his upper lip and brow. After a beat, he seemed to conclude that neither life nor liberty were in immediate danger and replied, "Zachariah Nephi Carter."

"And how old are you?"

"Eighteen."

Jude froze. Eighty pounds. Barely five and a half feet. The voice and development of a twelve-year-old. Eighteen could not be possible. She wondered if he was lying for fear of being returned to his family. Careful not to show any sign of disbelief, she asked, "What's your address?"

He fidgeted. "I don't have a place right now. Last few months I've been doing odd jobs in exchange for meals."

Apparently not enough of them to put any flesh on his bones. The microwave bleeped and Jude hauled out the dinner and ripped off the plastic. She set it in front of him with some utensils. "We can talk while you eat."

He hesitated. "You're not giving me your own breakfast, are you, ma'am?"

"No, it's a spare. And since you've troubled yourself to come help with our inquiries, it's all yours."

He fell on it like he hadn't eaten in weeks, the fork quivering in his hands. With a mixture of anger and sorrow, Jude watched him devour the small serving. Zach Carter was plainly malnourished and he hadn't got this way overnight. If he was a runaway, maybe he had good reason.

"Where are you from originally?" she asked him.

"Utah."

Eddie House's words repeated in her mind. He could tell Poppy was from Utah because she had been mistreated. "You're not living with your family?"

"I was unworthy."

Unworthy. It wasn't just teen-speak. His face wore naked despair. She put the next meal in the microwave, figuring the first wouldn't make a dent. Setting his unworthiness aside for a later discussion, she said, "So, Bobby Lee was telling me you knew Darlene."

He paused between mouthfuls. "I didn't know that was her name. She said it was Diantha."

"What makes you think Diantha was Darlene?"

"I saw the picture. It's her, for sure."

"How did you come to know her?"

"She lived near my family."

"Where is that?"

He hesitated. "Rapture."

"You were friends with her?"

An incredulous stare. "No."

"Then how did you know her?"

"She was kind to me after I was cast out. For a while, I hid in places. She found me and she didn't tell anyone where I was."

"Where was that?"

"In a barn on the Gathering for Zion Ranch. She was one of Mr. Epperson's celestial wives."

"Come again?"

He stared at her uncertainly. "A man must have three wives to enter the celestial kingdom, but because the government is in league with Satan, he can only be legally married to one woman in this country. So the marriages are celestial."

"Okay. Now I get it." It amazed Jude how well he could articulate the dogma of his sect. "How many wives does Mr. Epperson have?"

"I'm not sure. Lots. He's an important man."

Lots of wives. Jude could hear Pratt losing it. This was the kind of lead detectives prayed would drop into their laps, information that could save months of investigative labor. But for Pratt, it would mean only one thing—trouble with Utah. Yet again, Jude would be associated with a pain in the butt.

Resigning herself to the inevitable, she asked, "What's Mr. Epperson's first name?"

"Nathaniel." Zach cringed as if he fully expected to be struck by lightening.

"When did you last see Diantha?" She took the next meal from the microwave and handed it over.

"Maybe four months ago. It was after the winter."

"When did you leave your family?"

He shoveled food into his mouth. "The prophet excommunicated me last year, but I didn't leave town till the dog day."

"The dog day?"

"The prophet said we couldn't have dogs anymore. So the Sons of Helaman rounded them up at the drywash and shot them all."

Stunned, Jude said, "Do you mean stray dogs?"

"No. All dogs. They even had my dog Sam. I tried to get him, but they beat on me with their guns and ran me out of town again."

"You're saying they killed every dog in town? Even people's pets?"

"Yes, ma'am. The prophet says there are no dogs in the celestial kingdom, so we need have no care for them, or any other animal, during our earthly life."

What kind of outfit was this—Stepford on crack? "Didn't anyone try to stop the killing?"

He shook his head. "They couldn't. They would be excommunicated."

"What exactly does that mean?"

"You won't be lifted up to heaven. You are banished...cast forth to dwell in Babylon. No one can speak to you." He burst into tears. "Diantha spoke to me, and she brought food. That's why she had to atone and be purified. God commanded that she live henceforth in silence."

"This is why her tongue was cut out?"

He blinked. "How do you know about that? It's a secret."

"Not anymore. We noticed when we examined her body."

He set down his fork and cradled his head in his hands. "It was my fault. I led her into temptation."

"No, Zach. You didn't do anything wrong and neither did she. What happened to Darlene was a crime." She repressed the urge to tell him she was going to hunt down the people who did it and make them pay. It wouldn't take much to spook him. If he thought the Eppersons could end up in jail, he could stop talking for fear of retribution. She redirected the questioning slightly. "What about your mom? Couldn't you go to her for help after you were excommunicated?"

Zach looked at her in amazement. "My mother would never disobey the master of holy principles."

"The master...you mean God?"

"No. My daddy."

Where was a stiff drink when you needed one? Jude had heard plenty about the Utah polygamists since moving to Montezuma county. It had been all over the local newspapers recently that a bigshot in the FLDS had bought a ranch a few miles out of Mancos. According to the reports, polygamist leaders were selling up holdings in Arizona and Utah now that state prosecutors were finally investigating them for child sexual abuse, welfare fraud, and tax evasion. It seemed like these guys were little more than a gang of criminals hiding behind the mask of religious belief. The strategy had panned out pretty well for them. They'd been molesting young girls and bilking the system with complete impunity for decades.

"What about your friends—kids your own age?" Jude could not imagine a teenager without buddies willing to defy authority figures. "Didn't they try to help you?"

He paused over a bite. "I didn't want to make any trouble for them, so I stayed away. It is forbidden for the righteous to associate with me."

"That's mighty Christian of them."

He blinked and focused on her as if seeing her clearly for the first time. His expression was an odd mix of fascination and disapproval.

"Something wrong, Zach?"

"I haven't seen too many women wearing men's clothing, is all. Being as it's harlot's attire."

Jude bit back an automatic response. Here was a kid who had probably never seen a television and had been brainwashed since infancy inside a cult. Was it any wonder he had no sense of the real world, his thinking twisted by Taliban-like beliefs. She shuddered to think of him trying to find his way, a stranger in his own country. He would have a hard time fitting in with regular people.

"Most people in this country don't believe that to be the case," she said. "They don't live the way people in your community live."

"Yes, I understand. That's why the gentiles will not be admitted to the three degrees of glory."

Jude was intrigued. Zach's ability to think for himself seemed to have been erased, yet he could express quite complex ideas. She was reminded of an expression bandied about by the technical support staff at the Bureau to explain the limitations of her computer—dumb terminal: seems smart, but cannot function as an independent entity.

Ignoring the last dumb-terminal response, she asked, "The town of Rapture. Where is that?"

"Near Hildale and Colorado City."

Huge surprise. The twin towns were only the biggest hotbed of polygamy outside of Saudi Arabia. "You're a long way from home," she said.

"I got a ride with a truck driver." Pensively, he added, "At first I was afraid to be among the gentiles and the seeds of Cain, but folks have been real kind." He indicated his empty meal trays. "Thank you for the breakfast. I think that was about the best meal I ever tasted."

Jude pointed at the trash bin. "You can throw the meal containers in there and rinse the utensils in the sink. If you need the restroom, it's down the hall to your right."

Lesson one. Don't wait for women to clean up after you. Zach seemed to catch on easily enough. He tidied his trash away and even asked if there was anything he could fetch for her. Jude could sense an eagerness in him that verged on desperation. Survival was his primary consideration. If that meant doing "women's work," she had a feeling he'd get with the program.

"I need to ask you some more questions now that you've eaten," she said when he returned from the restroom. "First up, do you know who murdered Diantha?"

"No, ma'am."

"Do you know anybody who didn't like her? Who was maybe angry with her over something? Apart from her talking to you, I mean. Did she ever mention anything like that to you?"

"Can't say she did."

"Tell me about the Eppersons."

He considered this for a beat, then revealed nervously, "Mr. Epperson is a real important man. He's a high priest and counselor to the prophet." He vacillated. "We're not supposed to talk about the priesthood to gentiles."

"I understand. I promise no one will ever know you spoke to me about the way your church is organized. Okay?"

Her mind flashed to the press conference a week earlier. Mercy Westmoreland had publicly dismissed the idea of a ritual killing, but it had come up in the subsequent briefing. Stamer Knutson believed that hunting the local Satanists would be a waste of time. The type of brutality inflicted on Darlene was almost entirely the province of the obsessive husband, the lone psychopath, or of foot soldiers for the world's most virulent strains of religious fundamentalism. Historically, the black-magic crowd had produced a few wackos, but they were rank amateurs compared with their God-fearing counterparts.

"Tell me, Zach, does a high priest like Mr. Epperson follow the prophet's orders all the time, like everyone else does?"

Apparently, this was a silly question. Eyeing her quizzically, Zach explained, "The prophet is God's mouthpiece on earth. He is the one man who has the keys of sealing. He must be obeyed or death."

"Gotcha."

A decent single malt, she decided. Talisker, or maybe something sweeter like the Caol Ila she kept for special occasions. These happened so seldom she was in danger of turning her twelve-year-old bottle into an eighteen, and thus taming its smoky Islay character. She checked the wall clock again and accepted harsh reality. It would be at least eight hours before she could kick back and think about something other than the bottom feeders of this world. Meantime, she felt like she was interviewing an extraterrestrial. Trying to decode its language so she could make sense of the life being described.

Adding to her sense of the surreal, was a growing awareness that Zach had much more to offer than a useful clue or two. She could not believe her luck. Something the *Law & Order*–viewing public didn't realize was that cases could be solved by happy coincidences almost as much as by sheer investigative slog. Posters on mailboxes really worked, triggering memories and shaking clues from a community. This kid had obviously seen one in his travels. He might never have said anything, only the Fates had been kind. What were the odds of the gregarious Bobby Lee being on the spot and giving this bedraggled youngster a ride?

Eventually they would probably have come up with the information about "Diantha" given the direction the investigation was headed, but Jude decided she was owed a break after all the cases she'd ground her teeth over. Zach was a gift from above and she could only be thankful.

"So…" She pulled the interview back onto the domestic track. "How many in your own family?"

"I have fourteen sisters and ten brothers still living. My father has eight spiritual wives."

"Your father and Mr. Epperson must be wealthy men to provide for so many people."

"God blesses the elect."

"I see." Which meant the wives and kids were all collecting welfare and food stamps. This was fast becoming an issue in Cortez, with the recent FLDS arrivals. "Tell me about Darlene's silencing."

His face returned to its former waxy pallor. "She had to be purified and her demons cast out. The pain was greatest for the servants of righteousness."

"Are you saying other people had organs hacked off, too? Or did the er…righteous suffer different agonies?"

Some disconcerted blinks. "It was pain of the spirit. God's work tests the will."

"Do you think God ordered that Darlene's tongue had to go?"

"God speaks through the prophet. He is the one who holds the keys."

"Yes, I got that." She wondered whose words he was parroting. "So the prophet ordered someone to cut Darlene's tongue out?"

He shrugged stiffly. "The rules are known to all."

"And Darlene disobeyed..."

He nodded. "Women must live in perfect obedience and modesty. They must be pure and delightsome."

"Clear something up for me, Zach. Who are women supposed to obey?"

"The Heavenly Father. The prophet and the priesthood. Their father and their husband. Their uncles and brothers..."

"Okay, I get the picture."

"And they must obey the head wife."

Jude could imagine how that particular tyranny would function. Guys like Epperson ran their own private harems. Women competing for favor and resources would have to take their resentment and anger out on someone. Children and junior wives were the obvious targets.

"So who actually carried out the prophet's command—who cut out Darlene's tongue? Can you tell me that?"

He fell silent, his hands gripping the edge of the table so hard his knuckles glowed white.

"Don't be afraid," Jude said. "You're safe here. I won't let anyone hurt you."

"I will be struck down."

"Zach, who do you think is more powerful? God or the prophet?"

Tough question. Eventually, he replied, "The prophet is the one mighty and strong. He has the power on earth, and the Heavenly Father has the power in the celestial kingdom."

"What's the prophet's name?" At first, she'd assumed he must be talking about Joseph Smith, the guy who founded Mormonism, then she remembered reading references to a present-day "prophet" in newspaper reports about the new compound being built in Mancos.

With hushed awe, Zach said, "It was Warren Jeffs, but now... I'm not sure. He's gone and they're saying Mr. Rockwell is the true prophet."

"Do you know Mr. Rockwell's first name?"

"Elias." He drew a ragged breath and confided, "Even Uncle Warren's Sons of Helaman have gone across to him."

"When did Mr. Rockwell take over?"

"I don't think he's accepted the keys yet. There are others who say they are the one."

Which meant this Jeffs individual was still in charge when Darlene was silenced. Jude entered his details into the computer. The narrow, pasty face that popped up on her screen belonged to a guy who could have been labeled a nerd, only he didn't look smart enough. A high forehead, long nose, and weak chin made his round, startled brown eyes seem too close together. This cartoon-character effect was topped off with a wet rodent mouth and an Adam's apple too big for the scrawny throat it bobbed beneath. In addition to the good-looks deficit, Warren Jeffs had made the criminal big time; he was on the FBI's Most Wanted list.

Jude read through the description and cautionary notes and smiled. Life had suddenly gotten a whole lot easier. Arizona had issued a state arrest warrant, because—Newsflash!—Jeffs was wanted for sexual assault on a minor. If she crossed paths with him, she could grab him up on the existing indictment and Colorado could put their case together afterward. There had to be a conspiracy charge in there somewhere. It sounded like no one in the twin towns drew breath without the prophet's say-so.

"Do you have any idea where Mr. Jeffs is?" she asked, covering the obvious base.

Zach reacted to this casual inquiry with a vehement plea, "I don't want to talk anymore."

His wet blue eyes begged for understanding, and Jude could sympathize. The kid genuinely believed the gates of heaven had just swung shut in his face. He was also afraid of the thugs who'd already assaulted him. But she sensed something else at work. Even his rank, unwashed odor could not disguise the smell of terror that oozed from him.

"Zach, what are you so afraid of?" she asked gently. "Please tell me."

"Those who betray the secrets of the priesthood must atone in blood. Obey the prophet and we are blessed. Disobey, and it's death." He broke into exhausted sobs. "You don't know what they're like. They'll find me and give me to the demon."

Jude got up and found a box of tissues. She took these over to him and put an arm around his frail shoulders. "Calm down, and blow your nose. There's no such thing as demons."

He mopped his tears with odd, frantic motions, apologizing and assuring her he would stop crying immediately. Watching him, Jude felt a wave of grief rise from her chest to her throat. She wanted to kill someone—for Zach and all the children like him, the ones who didn't know the meaning of childhood. She wanted ten minutes alone in a room with Epperson or Jeffs.

Intellectually, she knew that the murderous rage she glimpsed in herself at times like this was very old and could never be given an outlet. But there was a part of her that clung to it, reveling in it, dreaming of the day when she would come face-to-face with the man she'd been hunting for almost twenty years. No way would she exercise judgment and restraint. No way would she deny the primal thirst for revenge and dress it up in modern clothing. Justice was a nice ideal, but her quarry did not deserve the civilized ritual of a trial, the fair-minded deliberations of a jury.

Jude was not going to arrest him, she was going to kill him with her bare hands. She would help him discover the limits of his pain threshold. Something touched her arm and she looked down to find Zach staring at her with an odd yearning expression. She realized her fingers were digging into his bony shoulders, and released him.

"You don't know what it's like," he said.

"No, I don't." Jude propped herself against the edge of the desk. "But here's something to think about. The prophet threw *you* out. I'd say that means you don't have to obey his rules anymore. You can't be bound by the rules of an organization that excommunicated you. *They* made that decision, not you. Do you understand?"

His face became strangely immobile, as if a spanner had just landed in the works of his brainwashed thought process.

"What will I do?" he murmured eventually. It wasn't really a question, more a stark expression of his disorientation.

Zach Carter had never learned how to think for himself. Without rules to follow, and lacking critical reasoning skills, he was in a limbo, displaced and vulnerable. Jude wondered if there was a help agency that could work a case like this. If he really was eighteen, he was too old to be a ward of the state, so Social Services would not be able to do a thing. Yet he was clearly unequipped to assimilate into the real world.

He would need education, therapy, and a safe environment. Protective custody seemed like a reach. But if she could get a statement naming someone in the assault on Darlene, if not the murder, that would make Zach a key witness. She could easily persuade Pratt that any of the nutjobs implicated would pose a threat.

A plan took shape in her mind. "What say you stay here at the station for a while? You could sleep in there." She indicated the holding cell. "You'd get all your meals. No one is going to come looking for you at the sheriff's office, are they?"

He looked astonished. "Can I stay tonight?"

"Absolutely. And for the next week or so while we think about what you're going to do with your life." She made the offer irresistible. "We do have a few rules you'll need to follow."

He nodded eagerly. Rules were something this kid knew all about.

"There's yard work and this building wants a coat of paint. So you'll be working in exchange for your food and shelter."

"Yes, ma'am."

"We'll arrange some schooling for you." Agatha was a retired teacher. If they let her loose on this kid, she would be off their backs over sloppy office habits, a win/win for all concerned.

"I liked school," he said wistfully. "But I had to work on the ranch so I quit in the seventh grade."

"Well, you have some catching up to do." Jude invented a couple more rules, since they seemed to comfort him. "You must eat all the food you are given. And you must always wash your hands after using the bathroom."

"Do I use the soap? I saw it there, but I wasn't sure. Back home soap was only for my sister-mothers."

Whatever happened to cleanliness being next to godliness? "In this station everyone uses soap," Jude said.

"I can get cleaned off right away, if you show me where the hose is." Zach jumped to his feet.

"You won't be needing the hose. Did you see the shower stall in the bathroom?"

"Yes, ma'am."

"You'll wash in there with warm water. I'll show you how it works."

Jude took a slow breath, controlling the anger rising from her gut. She supposed, with thirty or so kids, daily hot showers were not practical for polygamist families. Clearly, Zach had spent his life getting clean by hosing himself down outdoors. She was relieved that he seemed eager to wash. His disgusting body odor had given her a headache.

"After we're done talking, you can take your first shower," she told him. "Then I'm going to drive you into town and get you some new clothes. We'll swing by the doctor, too. I want him to take a look at you."

Zach's face was instantly pinched with alarm. "I don't need any doctor. If I deserve to be healed, God will heal me."

"Yeah, I had a feeling about that." Jude glanced toward the window, expecting Tulley's truck at any moment. She wondered if he would have better luck getting Zach to talk about Darlene's "silencing." The kid was fading fast, the aftermath of a square meal hitting bottom. He rested his head on one hand, eyelids drooping.

"You look sleepy," Jude said. "Want to rest up some before we head out?"

He regarded her gravely and she realized that giving him options only made him nervous. "You can lie down for a while after your shower," she instructed. "I'll wake you when it's time to leave."

He hovered for a moment. "Thank you for being kind to me, ma'am."

"Isn't being kind to others what God wants us to do?"

Again his face stilled in concentration, eyes slightly narrowed. Jude saw something new mingle with his fear and weariness. He looked older suddenly.

"I saw it," he said. "They made me watch."

Jude listened. This time he didn't look away.

"It was Mrs. Epperson. The head wife."

"She had the knife?"

He nodded. "Mr. Epperson had a revelation. He said she was chosen to be God's instrument."

How convenient. "So Mr. Epperson told her what to do?"

"Everyone had to read the scriptures and pray. Then he told us what the Heavenly Father revealed." He lowered his head and cradled his face with both hands. "Diantha tried to run away—" He broke into hoarse sobs. "And I didn't help her."

Chapter Six

"S hit." Sheriff Pratt closed his office door and sagged into his chair, groaning like he had heartburn.

Accustomed to this reaction from her superior, Jude sat down on one of the padded beige vinyl chairs opposite his desk. "So I figured I'd take Tulley with me," she said. "He could use the experience."

A small bead of perspiration ran down the side of the sheriff's nose. He flicked it away with a finger. "I'm not so sure about this. Can't we work up another approach?"

What did he have in mind, other than dropping the investigation? Trying not to sound impatient, Jude said, "We'll keep a low profile."

Pratt plainly wanted to wring his big, tanned hands. Instead he tortured an empty cigarette packet. "Can't see how that's possible, given you two are going to stick out like sheep at a rodeo."

"Obviously we'll go see the sheriff first, since we'll need to be sworn in to his jurisdiction. I don't know how this is going to play out, exactly. We'll have arrest powers from Arizona, but most of Rapture is on the Utah side of the border."

"Well, I'm guessing a warrant might be hard to come by. Don't waste your time asking the judge—three wives and twenty-something kids."

"I thought Utah was cleaning up its act. Didn't they sack the last police chief and half the force?"

"Roundy and his crowd...yep. Decertified. Clear case of the fox guarding the henhouse. One of them served a year...unlawful sex with a minor."

"So maybe this new sheriff will be looking to make a good impression. He has to have a working relationship with Utah, and their attorney general seems to be ratcheting up the pressure on these polygamists."

Pratt grunted. "I'll believe that when I see it. Listen, we're not looking for trouble. You know what I'm saying."

"No, sir. Not really."

Pratt sucked his top lip in and chewed briefly on his mustache. He seemed to be considering his words very carefully. "You have to understand something, Devine. You're not in D.C. anymore. Out here, we don't have big-city manpower. We cover a large area and we're right on the border. All of the above means we need to keep a harmonious relationship happening with the different agencies."

"I'm hearing you."

"I'll spell it out. Utah...they've got money. A lot more than the rest of us. And they don't like bad publicity. They have their own ways of dealing with internal situations like this."

"It's not an internal situation. Darlene was a Colorado girl."

"I'm talking about their religion."

"But these polygamist sects aren't mainstream Mormons. The church disassociated itself from them a long time ago."

"Yeah, well. They sure don't like the public looking into that particular relationship, and you can see their point. Those crazies in Colorado City are a big embarrassment."

"Because they're a snapshot of what the Mormon church used to be before they reinvented themselves?"

"In a nutshell, yes. I gotta tell you, there's not a whole lot of separation between church and state in Utah."

"The Iran of the Southwest, huh?"

"Some parts more than others, but you got the general idea."

"Point taken. So, I guess that means they won't just hand Epperson over if we ask nicely, so we're stuck with having to make this happen our own way."

Pratt muttered something. Jude guessed he could see the hole he'd dug for himself. She waited for him to come up with some delay tactics. Instead he grumbled, "What are we supposed to tell those idiots camped out in front of the town hall? The last thing we need is a pack of embedded reporters tagging along for the ride."

"We don't have to tell them anything."

Last she'd heard, they were more interested in the rumors about Mercy and the British actress than the hunt for Darlene's killer. Half of them had left Cortez and were now sniffing around the medical examiner's office in Grand Junction.

"I want you back here in three days," Pratt said.

"So, I have your approval to make an arrest if the evidence is there, sir?"

"Let's not pretend you need my approval for anything you do, Devine." Pratt lowered his voice to a harried murmur. "Any idea when you'll be out of here? I mean, in regards to your real...mission?"

"I wish I could discuss that. I truly do."

"If it's a nuclear situation, I don't want to be the last to know. Is that too much to ask?"

Jude guessed he'd tried to make that sound like dry humor, but fell short of the mark. "I promise you, sir. If I ever think there's a reason to evacuate this area, I'll tell you. Protocol or not."

At this reassurance, he went pale. "So you're saying there *is* something going down?"

Damned if you do and damned if you don't. Jude sighed. "Not that I'm aware of at this time."

"Nothing would surprise me. We got ourselves some major nutcases out here."

"We surely do. And on that subject, what can you tell me about those Utah folks who bought the ranch outside of Mancos?"

"Lot of money and a lot of womenfolk. You know my position—if they don't ask for trouble, they won't get any."

"They weren't too cooperative when we called around there last week." They'd interviewed all the Huntsbergers' neighbors, in fact, most of Mancos, asking if anyone remembered seeing a white minivan hanging around before Darlene disappeared. The new residents hadn't been living there at the time but had reacted to the routine questions with extreme paranoia.

"Yeah, I heard," Pratt said. "The boys thought they must have stumbled onto a methamphetamine lab."

"Is there anything we can hold over them so they'll quit with the sons of perdition crap and answer some questions?"

Pratt took time out from mangling his cigarette pack. "They've applied for a building permit. Paid the urgent processing fee."

"I wonder if they made all the necessary disclosures."

"Insufficient information…yeah, that's a problem." Pratt ran with the ball. "Can't get approval if you're not telling the whole truth. They wouldn't let the assessor into any of the existing buildings, so what's the guy supposed to think?"

"You can bet they're exceeding occupancy levels," Jude said. "Maybe approval has to be delayed while additional evidence of purpose is gathered."

"I'm guessing they won't be holding a parade once they hear the news. Better free up a couple of deputies to accompany the building inspector, just in case."

"Wise idea. That's the kind of situation that can get heated."

"You bet. So, what do you want from them?"

"Everything they can tell us about Nathaniel Epperson and this power struggle that seems to be going on in the FLDS."

"Which stands for what?"

"Fundamentalist Church of the Latter Day Saints. That's the biggest of the polygamist factions that broke away from the Mormon church."

"Beats me how they manage," Pratt marveled. "It's all I can do to make one wife happy."

"I seriously doubt any of these men give a crap about their wives' happiness," Jude said. "This is just white slavery by another name."

Pratt seemed lost in thought. "Darned if I know what we can do about that kid you brought in," he said eventually. "We get them drifting through here, panhandling and sniffing substances. Stealing goddamn cars from the Ute, who, by the way, get called Lammanites by our friends in Utah. Whatever that means. Anyway, half of them don't have birth certificates or social security numbers. No one knows what to do with them."

"Well, Zach's a key witness."

"Not to the murder."

"If we get this to trial, he'll testify to the mutilation."

"What are you proposing?"

"Protective custody without the paperwork."

"Keep talking."

"I don't want his family to know we have him. Tulley has volunteered to accommodate him for a while, and I'm going to see about getting his education started again."

"I thought you were taking Deputy Tulley to Utah with you."

"Agatha will keep an eye on Zach while we're away."

"You don't think he'll get skittish?"

"I think he'll stay where the food is." Jude took a few sheets of paper from her satchel and slid them across the desk to Pratt. "This is his medical report. Not for the faint-hearted."

Pratt skimmed the top couple of pages then slid his chair back to peer through the Venetian blinds to the outer office, where Zach was devouring a pizza. "God damn. Is this for real?"

"Which part? The tapeworm? The old fractures...the starvation... the scars on his back? The semi-castration..."

He faced her again and this time the pained resignation was gone and a grim anger had replaced it. "These people are vermin and we're going to put some of them behind bars. I don't know how the heck we're going to get them extradited, but we'll cross that bridge when we come to it."

Jude shared his pessimism. While Zach was sleeping that morning, she'd done some homework and learned that, with a few high-profile exceptions like Tom Green, polygamists were seldom brought to trial in Utah. The state seemed to be run by a small number of genealogically connected men who publicly distanced themselves from the fundamentalists but allowed them to operate unchallenged. In recent times, the new attorney general had signaled an end to Utah's indifference and had frozen the assets of the FLDS sect. But there hadn't been the flood of arrests antipolygamy activists were hoping for. If justice was to be done, Epperson and his wife would have to be convicted in Colorado.

"All we need to prove is that they kidnapped Darlene and took her across state lines. Then we can involve the feds," she said.

"Any idea where she was murdered?"

"We don't have a crime scene, as yet. If we can get the Eppersons in for questioning based on Zach's statement about the assault, maybe one of them will make a slipup."

Pratt made a sound halfway between a laugh and an asthma attack. "You think the Rapture sheriff is going to let you run that interview in his office?"

"I guess I'll just have to persuade him. They want to keep the polygamy stuff out of the newspapers. That's a lever we can use."

"Good luck with that." Pratt glanced down at the medical report again. "Utah's not going to like this. Not one little bit."

"I'm up for it. Are you?"

Pratt sighed. "We already let that family down once. We're not doing it a second time." He pushed his chair back and stood up. "When I look Clem Huntsberger in the eye I want to be able to tell him we did everything we could."

Jude got to her feet, mildly surprised by his determination. She hadn't been sure if Pratt would have the balls to ride shotgun on this case. He'd been distinctly uneasy when she first briefed him on Zach a few days earlier, insisting that they didn't have a smoking gun and just because it sounded like Diantha was Darlene, they had no proof. Jude had half expected she would have to sidestep him and take what she had straight to the FBI field office in Denver. It was good to discover he had a spine, after all.

"I'll keep you posted," she said. "Thank you, sir."

He shot her a warning look. "Be careful. People like them think they're above the laws of man. They think they've got God on hold. That's according to my wife."

"Well, God isn't going to help them this time."

If some bunch of child-abusing, dog-massacring wackjobs thought they could hide behind religion to justify their crimes, Jude had news for them.

CHAPTER SEVEN

The morning began with a dream, the kind that hovers just out of memory's reach. The moment Jude awoke, she knew it was about Ben, and almost as soon as she'd acknowledged that, the shutters of her mind closed, leaving her straining to recall what she had glimpsed.

Sometimes, in the days after these dreams, tiny fragments would flutter across her thoughts. She was always quick to trap these in the net of her consciousness, adding them to the disjointed mosaic that never quite became a clear picture. In her idle moments, she would arrange and rearrange every piece of the puzzle, searching for a secret code that would unlock their meaning. She had done the same with the facts of the case a thousand times over.

Ben had vanished three weeks after he turned twelve. Her memories of him were filed as neatly as entries in a Webster's dictionary, a consequence of her frequent recourse to them. Their reliable sequence comforted her. The memory of wheeling him in his stroller when she could not reach the handles, of climbing into his cot with him. They had been natural allies, separated from their older siblings by five years—an eternity, it seemed back then.

Ben was born in 1970, the year Nixon sent troops into Vietnam and National Guardsmen fired into a crowd of protestors at Kent State. According to the Fifth Dimension it was the dawning of the Age of Aquarius. Jude's dad always said they were "crazy times" and talked about "damn hippies." Her mom sounded wistful when she mentioned those days, which was seldom. She couldn't talk about Ben for more than a minute or two before taking refuge in chatter about something she just saw on the television.

Jude remembered his hair, fine white fluff that smelled of baby soap. She remembered being told off for biting his toes. She remembered taking him to school on his first day, teaching him to ride a bike, going to his Boy Scout events. Together, they had built the tree house they escaped to when their parents were fighting. They had not had time to become enemies. She had never had to put up with a pain-in-the-butt younger brother who humiliated her in front of cool friends. Ben always seemed a little younger than his age, as boys often did before the testosterone kicked in. He was gone before his Adam's apple appeared.

Jude got out of bed, telling herself not to go there. What was the point in shuffling the same hand of cards over and over? She could change nothing. The facts were the facts. He had vanished. The case was still open. Her single-minded quest to solve it had led her to law enforcement, a degree in criminology, the FBI. She often wondered if she would have made those choices had things been different.

Before Ben disappeared, they had talked about going to school together one day, training to be pilots, having their own plane so any time they wanted they could fly away to some glamorous destination. The pyramids. The Amazon. The Australian outback. Jude still had the dress-up pilot uniforms their mother had made for them. She had never worn hers again after the day that changed everything. It was folded away, along with her childhood. From that moment on, her compass had been fixed on a different pole. On each anniversary of his disappearance, she told her mother the same thing—that she would find him if it was the last thing she ever did. Lately, the promise sounded hollow.

Jude hung over the basin in her bathroom and scrubbed her teeth. There had been times when she'd thought she was close to a breakthrough. But nothing had ever panned out. Ben's trail was stone cold. She knew she should find some way to let go. That was part of the reason she had left the Crimes Against Children unit and moved into intelligence work, part of the reason she had relocated. She was thirty-six. It was time she came to terms with what had happened and moved on with her life like a rational person. Her older sister and brother had done so long ago. Even her parents seemed to have let go now. Selling the house had been a big step for them.

Jude had thought about buying it, if only for the tree house, but her mom had kicked up a fuss and in the end, Jude had accepted they all needed to let the place go. Her parents had held on to it for almost twenty years, frightened to leave in case Ben came home one day and they weren't there. Jude supposed they'd finally accepted that the day they'd prayed for was never going to happen—that Ben was dead. She should accept it too, and she'd tried, but hope had a complex root system. No matter how determinedly she hacked away at it, it refused to die. Without a grave to visit, she could not say good-bye and believe it.

She showered, dried, and wandered across the oak floorboards, her damp feet making satiny prints on the polished surface. She stared out the bedroom window for a few minutes, numbly seeking consolation in the view. The FBI had found a house for her a few miles out of Montrose. It was originally someone's rustic mountain retreat, built before the area was infested with trend-hounds buying up accommodations in what realtors loved to call "the Switzerland of America." Because of its age, it lacked the pretensions of many newer homes in the area. No hot tub, no marble bathrooms, no cobblestone fireplaces or theater room, or multilevel lofts.

Jude enjoyed its woody simplicity and the inescapable views of the Uncompahgre Plateau, and after ten years in an apartment building in Adams Morgan, she loved the privacy. The house was set back from the road on a few acres of sparse forest. Jude still couldn't get used to living in a place where you checked for bears and mountain lions before working in the yard.

She moved away from the window and took some underwear from the top drawer of her Welsh chest, making a point of ignoring the picture she kept there—an artist's rendition of how Ben might look as an adult. There was no need to refresh her memory. She automatically compared every male face she saw, searching for a match.

After she'd dressed, she made coffee and stared at her phone. Mercy had finally returned her last call. Jude replayed the message.

"It's Mercy." The voice was tight. "Next week is kind of difficult. My father is having a rough time. But dinner some time sounds like a good idea. I'll call you."

Discreet? Lukewarm? *I'll call you.* Did that mean: *don't call me?* Jude wanted to be a human being and phone back to say she was sorry about her father, and offer help, as people did. Mercy had no one; that's what she'd said. Yet the tone of her voice seemed discouraging. Jude listened one more time, trying to picture the facial expression that would have accompanied the words. She didn't know Mercy well enough to guess. The only boxes she could tick with any certainty were: professional, flirtatious, and orgasmic.

Still, only a self-centered jerk would not call a woman she'd slept with whose father was dying. Preparing herself for a frosty reception, she dialed Mercy's cell phone. To her astonishment, a woman answered in a British accent.

"Hello. Dr Westmoreland's phone." The voice was husky from sleep, or who knew what else.

Jude checked her wristwatch and collected her wits. A sexy-sounding foreign stranger was answering Mercy's phone at 6:30 a.m. It had to be the actress.

She rolled out her serious cop voice. "This is Detective Devine, Montezuma County Sheriff's Office. Is Dr. Westmoreland available?"

"I'm sorry, she can't take your call right now. Would you care to leave a message?"

Jude vacillated, wondering if she should make up some work related bullshit, or say something more meaningful. "I work with the doctor and I heard about her father," she said, hoping to hit a note of polite but impersonal sympathy. "I was calling to let her know she's in all of our thoughts at this difficult time."

Mercy was smart enough to interpret that.

"Thank you, Detective. Let me make a note of your name. Devine, was it?"

Jude refrained from replying: *Elspeth Harwood, was it?* Coolly, she replied, "Yes, that's right."

"Thank you for calling. I know Mercy will appreciate it."

Jude wasn't so sure about that. She said good-bye and hung up. Ex-flings didn't fly into town from England when your father was dying. Mercy wouldn't risk her cover being blown by the tenacious media if this woman was not important to her. Whatever was going on between Mercy and the Brit, it was not past history. She sipped her coffee and tried to figure out if she was angry, disappointed, or jealous. Mercy wasn't the first woman to lie about being single so she could score, if lying was what she had done. Maybe she and Elspeth had an open relationship, or one of those on-again-off-again situations.

Jude decided it was none of her business. It wasn't like Mercy had suggested their encounter would be repeated, quite the opposite. Neither did Jude nurture any romantic illusions about the two of them. Far from it. Sure, she'd have sex with Mercy again in a minute. But that's all it was. Sex. These days, that's all it ever was, and probably a good thing too. She wasn't looking for love. Who needed the drama?

Aggravated with herself for letting the phone call get under her skin, she focused her mind on work. In a few hours' time, she and Tulley would fly into Las Vegas, then drive up to Colorado City and Hildale, the twin border towns otherwise known as Polygamy Central, USA. A few miles east lay Rapture, a satellite town where some of the FLDS elite had ranches, Nathaniel Epperson and his tongue-slasher wife among them.

Jude threw some clothes into an overnight case and phoned Tulley. "You ready?"

"Yes, ma'am."

"How's Zach?"

"Pigging out."

Jude could swear the kid had put on ten pounds in the days since he'd arrived. "Is he okay about the arrangements?"

"I told him he has to mind Smoke'm. He's keen. He had a dog back home that died."

"Yes." Jude hadn't mentioned the dog massacre to Tulley. They didn't have time for him to get on the phone to his ma right now.

"I was thinking, he should stay at my place," Tulley said. "He reckons he'll be okay by himself, and Agatha says she don't mind picking him up on the way to work and bringing him home later."

"Fine by me. He'll probably feel safer up there too."

"Yeah, he's petrified these Sons of Whatever are going to come after him. The same ones that beat on him and ran him out of town. He says they've killed kids before."

"He's witnessed actual killings?"

"Not exactly. It's just stuff he's heard."

"Go on."

"He says it's mostly kids like him that aren't welcome in the town after they get excommunicated. If they keep hanging around, they end up dead. He says they make it look like an accident and say the kid got run over by a car. Or sometimes they just take kids out into the desert and shoot them and bury them out there."

"Ask him for names. We can see if the sheriff knows anything about it, once we get out there. It's weird," she mused. "They're so sexist, you'd think they'd value boys more than girls."

"Here's what I think." Tulley's voice had a rare gravelly intensity, like this was something that kept him awake in the small hours. "The old guys who run this outfit want a whole bunch of wives, but there's only so many women to go round. So they get rid of the extra males out of their church and make them leave town. It's like the cuckoo bird. You know...throwing the others out of its nest."

"Eliminating younger, better-looking competition," Jude completed the train of thought. "Yes, that makes sense."

She called to mind Warren Jeffs' yokel face. Fiftysomething with prominent front teeth and a bug-eyed stare, he sure looked like he'd washed up at the shallow end of the gene pool. Out in the real world, he'd be lucky to get a date, let alone convince seventy women to join his personal harem.

Tulley was on the same page. "That Jeffs dude—if he wasn't running that cult, he'd be flipping burgers and taking shit from waitresses."

"Instead he gets to hole up in the religious version of the Playboy mansion," Jude added. All that and tax-free status because his little empire was a "church." Clearly, she was in the wrong business.

"Are we going after him?" her sidekick asked.

Jeffs was on the radar but not as part of the initial plan. Yet Jude could almost feel her trigger finger itching. The thought made her smile. Being out West had rubbed off. She could hear Tulley breathing and sense his hopeful anticipation.

"Much as I'd like to nail his scrawny ass to the wall, Epperson is our priority," she answered. "If we can get him, I have a feeling we'll get all of them."

Adeline spat cotton fibers from her mouth and worked a hole in the arm edge of her bra until she could push the underwire through. For once, she was thankful that Aunt Chastity had insisted on buying her old-fashioned bras with cups instead of the sports type she saw at the department store. She hadn't complained, she was so grateful not to have to wear scratchy full length undergarments anymore.

Of course, her parents had put an end to that devil's work as soon as they'd gotten her home. Out came the stupid ugly chemise and knee-length underpants, and all they could talk about was how she would no longer feel the burning in her bosom if she didn't wear modest attire and how she had to remember every man was a snake and she must not allow one near her. Like that would be a problem.

She pulled the underwire from the bra and bent the sturdy half moon of metal to form a hook. Then she removed the long ribbon threaded through her hair and tied it to the hook.

"You have to watch and tell me if I'm close to the hole in that bolt," she called to Daniel.

Weakly, he lifted his head and pushed some matted brown hair out of his eyes. "Okay, go." He shuffled around in his cage to get the best view.

Adeline slid her arm out of the cage, stretched as far as she could and probed around with the tip of her wire hook. "We're getting out of here," she said loudly and positively, trying to bolster Daniel's confidence, and her own.

"I don't think I can walk," he said.

"You can too. We're going to Salt Lake City. My Aunt Chastity is a good woman. She'll take care of us."

"Up just a bit more and thataways." Daniel pointed.

Grunting and sweating, Adeline pushed up until she felt the hook connect with something solid.

"Down some." Daniel was excited suddenly, both hands gesticulating.

Adeline lowered her arm a fraction and felt the tip of the wire slide into a hole. She strained to feed the hook in, grazing her arm against the cage.

"It's through!" Daniel's voice shook.

Adeline fed her ribbon up, praying it wouldn't catch on anything, jiggling a little so the weight of the hook would carry it down. When the pink painted tip came into view below the tin strip she almost screamed. Fingers trembling, she grabbed it and tied the other end of the ribbon to it, making a pull cord.

"Please God, don't let this break," she begged and dragged down with both hands.

The bolt put up surprisingly little resistance. Adeline thought her heart was going to burst from her chest as she gave a final tug and the cage door swung ajar. Telling herself not to do anything dumb, she called to mind the plan she'd spent all last night thinking about. Leave the pull cord, so that bitch Naoma can see Summer didn't let them out. Get water. Wait until the Sunday morning gong sounds and when everyone is in prayer and scripture reading, get out and walk fast. They planned to take a route no one would expect, away from the road and northeast into the desert.

Daniel's hiding place was about six miles away on the slopes of Seeds of Cain Mountain. They could stay there until the searchers gave up, then they could walk in the mornings and at nights until they made it to a road. If they could get far enough away from Rapture and the twin towns, they would see cars with people wearing normal clothes. They could flag one down and hitch a ride to Salt Lake City.

Adeline was so excited she could hardly breathe. Shivering, she used the wire to etch an inscription into the earth in front of her cage. It was a saying Aunt Chastity had on the wall of her parlor. *Ubi dibium ibi libertas.*

"What's that?" Daniel asked as she unbolted his cage and helped him out.

"It's Latin. That was the language the Romans used to speak when Jesus was on earth."

"Before he came to America?"

"Jesus never came to America. That's a Mog fairy tale." Adeline giggled just hearing herself say that. It felt really good to call Mormon "Mog" here, of all places.

Daniel was staring at her like she'd just asked Satan to take her to the prom. He said, "Shh," and looked down at the inscription. "What does it mean?"

"Where there is doubt, there is freedom," Adeline quoted.

He looked puzzled, but they didn't have time for her to explain the concept of using your common sense instead of being hooked into Mog-think. She pulled off her long knit underpants and thrust them at him, too serious to laugh at the expression of horror on his face.

"You're going to get eggs while I get water. Tie them up in this. Not too tight or they'll break."

Juggling the pants like they were hot from the fires of hell, Daniel hobbled to the barn door with her and they peered through the cracks to the back entrance of the henhouse where a bucket and several large plastic bottles stood beneath an outdoor faucet. On Sundays, no one usually gathered eggs until after prayers.

"I'm scared," Daniel said.

Adeline gave his hand a brief, hard squeeze then pushed the door open just enough to get through. "Let's go," she said, and they hurried across the dusty earth.

While he was in the henhouse, Adeline filled the big bottles, terrified that someone would hear the soft hiss of the hose and the wet rattle of water against plastic. Just as she screwed a cap on the third, Daniel emerged with the pants full of eggs. He was wearing the first smile Adeline had seen on his face in the two days she'd been locked in the cage. They scuttled back to the barn and closed the door once more, both breathing loudly. While they waited for the prayer gong to sound, they rigged up a carry bag for the water bottles, tying together the edges of an old towel they found among the rags Daniel had been sleeping on.

Daniel hoisted the pack over one shoulder and said, "I'm awful hungry."

"We can't do anything about that now." Adeline's mind ran ahead. "Soon as we get clear of this place, we'll have ourselves an egg." She had no idea how they were going to cook it, but she figured they could suck it down raw if they had to. She'd seen *Fear Factor* on Aunt Chastity's television—or, as her parents called it, that tool of Lucifer.

At the dull clang of the gong, Daniel gripped her arm. She could feel him shaking. For some reason his fear made her feel stronger and braver.

"We're going to count to a hundred," she told him. "Then you're heading for that place you told me about, and I'll catch up with you."

He turned fearful eyes on her. "Where are you going?"

"To the laundry." She handed the eggs to him.

As he began to ask questions, she hushed him and started counting. She had everything planned. All they needed now was a miracle.

CHAPTER EIGHT

"Wouldn't want a breakdown out here," Tulley said as they drove out of a one-horse town called Fredonia.

"Understatement," Jude agreed from the passenger seat.

The landscape was a desiccated deep vermilion, its extreme isolation unnerving. Living in canyon country for a year should have prepared her for a place like this, Jude thought, but the Uinkaret Plateau was in a league of its own. A parched strip of badlands straddling the Arizona/Utah border, it was barely inhabitable. You could drive off the road out here and die of exposure before anyone but the local buzzards noticed your overturned vehicle. They'd passed a solitary truck as they left the town and had had the two lane highway to themselves ever since.

"We're about thirty miles from Hurricane," she said, refolding the map.

Tulley glanced at the clock on the dash, doubtless calculating how much longer they would be navigating terrain where human life did not belong. "Guess we'll start running into some traffic soon," he predicted hopefully.

Jude had her doubts. This was the only highway to the promised land. If there was any traffic in and out of Colorado City and Hildale, they were looking at it. She said, "We'll be there before you know it."

Tulley seemed to make a conscious effort not to dwell on their blighted surroundings. "My ma says folks should mind their own business about people that don't believe the same as them."

"I can see where she's coming from."

"In this country anyone has the right to be a heathen, that's what she says."

"Your dad still around?" Jude asked.

"No, ma'am. He was killed by a drunk driver when I was a kid. I don't remember him real well."

"I'm sorry."

"How 'bout your folks?"

"They live in Mexico now."

"You got brothers and sisters?"

"One of each." Jude tripped slightly over the half-truth. She usually avoided mentioning Ben, but it seemed wrong to deny him to Tulley. "I had another brother, but we lost him quite a few years back."

"I'm sorry to hear that. Were you close?"

"Yes."

They lapsed into silence. A golden eagle swooped into view, plummeting toward the harsh earth at breathtaking speed. Tulley braked and pulled over to the side of the road, and they watched as the beautiful predator spread its huge wings and extended its feet. It barely struck the ground before rising again with a snake squirming in its talons.

"Raptors are bird royalty," Tulley murmured breathlessly.

His solemn awe made Jude smile. She could almost hear Ben. He had been eternally fascinated by wildlife. "I have a soft spot for owls," she said.

"Yes, ma'am. That's a heck of a bird." Tulley steered their rental Toyota back onto the highway. "Very mysterious."

"Explains why I find them interesting." It was the same with women. She only got stuck on the ones she would never figure out. No wonder she couldn't make a relationship work. Her mind leapt to Mercy but she immediately redirected her thoughts into less complicated territory, asking Tulley, "By the way, how's it going with Alyssa?"

"She says I should talk to her dad."

"About?"

"The future."

"I see."

"She's a nice girl."

Jude had said exactly the same thing to herself more than once in the course of her own blighted love life, like somehow you weren't allowed to take a pass on a nice girl in case you never found another one. She had ended up in two really lousy relationships with nice girls because she'd felt so guilty about hurting their feelings that she didn't back out when she should have. They'd ended up hurt anyway, and one of them had cheated on her because of it. Jude had concluded long ago that she was better off with women who were, to put it bluntly, not so nice. They knew how to take care of themselves.

Wondering how she could give Tulley good advice without referring to her own experiences with women, she asked, "Are you looking for a girl to settle down with right now?"

"I don't think I'm ready for that." He lowered his window and spat his gum. Hot air rushed into the car.

"Then you need to find someone who feels the same way. It would be wrong if you let Alyssa think you're ready for commitment when that's not true."

"I tried to tell her. But she says males are slow in that department and everything changes when you have kids."

"Yeah, no kidding. The divorce statistics make that point loud and clear."

"I never thought about it like that." He seemed heartened. "Two of my brothers got divorced when they had little kids. Ma was real mad."

"The kindest thing you can do is let Alyssa know there's no chance you're going to get married any time soon. That way she's free to find another guy who wants the same thing she wants. Otherwise you're leading her on."

"I see what you mean. That would be wrong."

"Very wrong."

Jude continued to puzzle over Tulley's attitude. Most twenty-five-year-old males were not choosy about how they got laid and with whom. Weren't his hormones talking to him at all? She studied him covertly. By any standards the deputy was handsome, even more so since he'd been working on his muscles. In a town like Cortez, he could probably date anyone. Jude had seen the way cops' wives looked him up and down. Maybe that explained the cool attitude of his colleagues.

A pair of dark amber eyes met hers and registered faint surprise. Tulley's long eyelashes descended, and for a moment he could have passed for a disconcerted girl. Jude groaned inwardly. He had completely misinterpreted her stare.

To address any faulty assumptions right off the bat, she said, "I was just wondering what type of woman you're attracted to, Tulley."

His unease was transparent. "I don't rightly know."

"Are you attracted to me?"

"I…well, I like you." The driving got erratic as he tried to let her down gently. "I can see that you're a very intelligent person and I respect you as a fellow peace officer and all. You're the kind of detective—"

"That's a no, then?"

"Yes, ma'am." He wiped his palms on his pants one at a time. "Zero attraction."

"Good," Jude said cheerfully. "I'm not attracted to you, either. You're not my type."

Tulley was visibly relieved. "I knew it. A woman like you would never want to date me."

"What makes you say that?" Had Tulley finally figured out she batted for the other team? "The age difference?"

He laughed. "Heck no. The brain difference. You'd get pretty impatient being with someone who only had an average-type mental capacity."

"Oh, please."

"Just telling it like I see it."

"So, if I stumble on a rocket scientist, I'd better watch out?"

"Not much chance of that in the Four Corners."

"Between you and me, I can live without the excitement." Jude toyed with the radio, trying to find a channel that wasn't a sea of static. Tulley was dead right, of course. The women who made her heart beat faster were those brainy, tastefully slutty types who should carry a surgeon general's warning: *Will likely cause damage to your heart and won't give a crap about it.*

"I'm going to take your advice," Tulley announced as they lucked onto a Johnny Cash song. "Soon as we get back, I'll tell her."

"Good plan," Jude said, and they both sang glumly along to the corroded baritone of the Man in Black.

"Think if we solve this case there might be a promotion in it?" Tulley asked when the music changed.

Apparently this was Suicide Radio—Leonard Cohen was next up. Jude turned down the dolorous emoting. "Nothing to stop you applying for one even if we don't make a case."

"There's guys with more seniority. But a conviction on this one would look real good."

"We don't have a whole lot to go on. I wish there was a goddamned crime scene."

"I wish we could tie that suiter to the guy."

"No kidding." Jude resumed surfing the airwaves for something other than Bible-thumping talk show hosts and wrist-slashing hits of yesteryear. Were they that far from civilization?

Tulley mused, "It's weird about the social security card."

Not for the first time it struck Jude that there was something distinctly domestic about that particular act. It seemed like the kind of thing a woman might do. Maybe it wasn't the killer who was Mr. Neat and Tidy. Maybe he had a female accomplice. Or maybe she wasn't an accomplice, but was actually the killer. Zipping the body into a bag and tucking the victim's social security card into the ID pocket seemed somehow more plausible as the actions of a woman.

According to Zach, Mrs. Epperson had cut Darlene's tongue out about five months ago. Had she also murdered her and disposed of the body? Would she have killed one of her husband's other wives, acting on her own account? Could it be a crime of passion, one wife jealous of another? Jude had her doubts. It seemed pretty obvious from her research that these polygamist women didn't do a whole lot of thinking for themselves. She could not imagine one of them committing a murder without her husband's say so. More likely she'd followed orders. That was the way things worked in polygamy-land. Al Qaeda didn't have the worldwide monopoly on pumping out brainwashed devotees.

She thought about the Lafferty case, one of those she'd studied before setting off for Utah. Two polygamists had brutally murdered the wife and baby daughter of their youngest brother. Her crime had been to help one of their wives leave her battering husband. Naturally the culprits evaded personal responsibility for their actions by claiming God had commanded them to carry out the crime. Did they truly believe that?

Having worked in child protection, Jude had no illusions about self-deceit. Molesters usually espoused self-serving beliefs that enabled them to get about their lives free of guilt. They blamed their victims and clung to psycho-babble theories about children as sexual beings.

They denied the reality of their victims' pain because it contradicted the belief system that supported their behavior.

It struck Jude that in many ways religious extremists had a similar mindset. They, too, seemed strangely narcissistic and determinedly blind to any fact that could undermine their beliefs. They, too, avoided taking responsibility for their behavior by assigning it to forces over which they had no control.

Was it any wonder that child sexual abuse was widespread in the FLDS community? Their lifestyle created the ideal environment for it. Children were brainwashed from birth to obey adults without question, and women were subservient baby-making machines who were not even supposed to laugh. From what Jude had read, they never saw a television or read a newspaper and most had virtually no education. Added to the mix was a fundamentalist version of Mormonism that held that all men were gods in the making and their prophet's declarations, however banal and self-serving, came direct from the Almighty.

A cult like the FLDS would be a magnet not just for men who wanted multiple wives, but also for would-be child molesters. Talk about hog heaven. Just thinking about it got her so aggravated her skin felt scratchy. What kind of idiot system allowed a bunch of men to get away with crimes any ordinary person would be serving jail time for, all because they called themselves a church and blamed their conduct on God? What was the difference between them and some creep who said "voices" made him do it? Worse still, these fundamentalists received millions of dollars in handouts from the government they despised. It was just plain crazy.

Burning to arrest someone, Jude stared out the window at a tobacco tinted cloud haze looming ahead. A highway sign announced Colorado City & Hildale. The indistinguishable twin towns were sandwiched in a valley between the vast chasm of the Grand Canyon to the south and the towering cliffs of Utah to the north. A barren plateau stretched out on either side, etched starkly against a lapis sky. It was a remarkable backdrop for one of the ugliest towns Jude had ever seen.

Colorado City was a scab on the raw majesty of its surroundings. The place reeked of cow shit, decay, and the acrid smell of chemical smoke. Roaming cattle wandered between abandoned cars and piles of junk, trash blew along unpaved streets, and a grim, heavily polluted stream drifted torpidly through the center. The town had originally been named after this sorry tributary—Short Creek—and it had a sordid history.

For more than a century, the Arizona Strip had sheltered hard-line polygamists, whose numbers swelled when the mainstream Mormon church buckled to government pressure and disavowed plural wives in 1890, claiming God had revealed celestial marriage could no longer be practiced on earth. Although this about-face ensured statehood for the besieged territory of Utah, it contradicted previous doctrine that enshrined polygamy as a "Sacred Principle." The fundamentalists weren't buying the new revelation, which they saw as convenient flip-flop and an attempt to mainstream the church. They also wanted the right to keep on marrying their wives' twelve-year-old sisters. So, they abandoned Salt Lake City and retreated by the hundreds to the boonies where they thought they would be left alone.

For a time they were. Then, in the 1950s, Arizona got fed up with the welfare burden of the isolated community, and cattlemen weren't happy that their grazing fees were being used to pay for polygamist schools. Expecting to receive public acclamation for taking a stand against child brides and welfare scams, the then governor of Arizona, Howard Pyle, ordered a massive police raid. This appeared in the state budget under "grasshopper control."

The outcome was a public relations disaster. Howls of outrage greeted front-page pictures of weeping children torn from their mothers' arms, and the Arizona authorities found themselves accused of religious persecution. Eventually all the arrested polygamists were reunited with their families and thanks to the backlash, the state turned a blind eye to the community for the next fifty years. There were now some forty thousand of them, twelve thousand living in Colorado City and Hildale.

"I was thinking about those bite marks," Tulley said as he slowed the car to a crawl.

Jude had to think twice before she made the mental leap back to the Huntsberger autopsy. "Did you pack that model?"

"Yes, ma'am." He stopped the car, reached behind her seat, and produced a plastic bag containing a set of mock teeth the forensic dentist had worked up for them. "You wouldn't forget if you saw teeth like these when someone smiled."

"That's what I'm hoping."

Zach had assured them old man Epperson wasn't the proud owner of the exotic fangs. The kid had never seen teeth like them, in fact. Jude couldn't imagine a woman inflicting those bites, so even if Mrs. Epperson had murdered Darlene someone else had to be involved, someone who needed serious dental work. If it wasn't her husband, it had to be a relative. Women in her situation didn't come into contact with the public, so it wasn't like she could rustle up some lowlife to help her out.

There was also the matter of the body dump. Would a woman be capable of lifting a heavily pregnant woman in and out of a vehicle alone? Highly unlikely, Jude decided. If Mrs. Epperson had managed to slit Darlene's throat, she had not disposed of the body without help.

"We going direct to Rapture?" Tulley asked.

"Yep. Sounds like the new Mohave County transplants are the only cops 'round here that missed joining the prophet's fan club."

She stared out the window at a mountain of junk piled on an empty lot and got irritated thinking about the contents of Darlene's stomach again. So far, not a word from Mercy, and Jude had been procrastinating over the follow-up call she needed to make. How long did it take some lab technician to glue a few bits of paper together and look at them under a microscope? Jude located her cell phone and dialed the medical examiner's office while Tulley studied a map of Colorado City. A secretary answered the phone and put Jude through to Mercy, who sounded surprised to hear from her.

Jude said, "Dr. Westmoreland. Thanks for taking my call."

Mercy replied, "Are you in Utah already?"

"Yes, that's why I'm calling."

"Ah…the paper shreds from your legless victim. Didn't one of my staff speak to you about that?"

Mercy had left the chore of phoning her to an underling. Terrific.

"No," Jude said coldly.

"Would you hold a minute, Detective." Paper rustled and Jude heard muffled voices. Then Mercy said, "Yes, we have something for you."

"Bring it on."

Unexpectedly, Mercy laughed and her tone oozed desire all of a sudden. "I wish."

Jude figured whoever had been there with her must have left the room, and apparently Mercy thought it was okay to flirt even though her Brit pal was keeping her bed warm at home. Bothered by the images that leapt to mind, Jude said, "And?"

"We sent the materials to the QDU and they came back to us with a ten-digit number. Got a pen?"

Jude jotted down the number Mercy read, at the same time feeling embarrassed that she'd expected a level of amateurism from the small M.E.'s office. Mercy had sent the paper scraps to the FBI crime lab and the experts in the Questioned Documents Unit had come up with the goods.

"It could be a phone number," Mercy said.

"I guess she ate it to prevent it being found."

"Or someone tore it up and forced it down her throat. Can't have been easy swallowing little shreds of paper without a tongue."

"And you're absolutely sure the tongue was cut out, not torn in an accident or something?"

"Yes. Did you turn up anything in the hospital records?"

"Not so far. We're on it." Jude transferred the digits into her laptop.

Mercy's tone switched from crisp to sultry. "How long will you be away?"

"Two days."

"Maybe we could get together when you come back."

Jude wanted to sound chilly on that idea, but her breathing betrayed her and her voice came out husky. "Don't you have company?"

"Ah. Elspeth said you'd called."

"Yes."

"Thanks for that, by the way. It was decent of you." She said it like maybe that was out of character.

Bugged, and conscious of Tulley right next to her, Jude said, "What's the deal?"

"About?" All innocence.

Jude was silent, signaling she was not at liberty to speak openly.

"Elspeth?" Mercy asked after a beat.

"Yes."

"You can't talk right now?"

"That's correct," Jude said.

"So, do you want to see me?"

As one of two sexual partners—was that what Mercy was asking? Jude supposed she could get all righteous and indignant, but who was she to tell Mercy how to live her life?

"Yes," she said finally and was certain she detected a small sigh of relief.

"Good. I think we need to talk."

"Probably."

"And in case you were wondering, I do want to sleep with you again."

"Okay." Sharing was better than nothing, Jude told herself.

Mercy laughed. "Don't sound so excited."

"You've been very helpful," Jude said stiffly. Tulley had the car in gear and was easing them out onto the potholed dustbowl that passed for the main street of Colorado City. "I need to go."

"I know what you need," Mercy said sweetly.

"I have no doubt."

"If you're good, maybe I'll let you fist me."

Jude dropped the phone. The very thought of Mercy gloved around her hand made her light-headed. She groped under her seat and retrieved the device. Mercy was still there.

Perspiring, Jude said, "Thanks for mentioning that, Doctor."

"My pleasure."

"I'll be in touch."

"Don't make me wait too long."

Jude consciously elevated her mind and managed a casual farewell while she could still keep her voice even.

"Rapture?" Tulley asked, pointing at a highway sign.

Jude stifled a high-pitched giggle. Rapture was exactly what Mercy inspired in a poor, simple, sex-starved fool like her. She lowered her voice to one of coplike composure. "Yep. Let's do it."

They approached an intersection where several old washing machines almost prevented vehicles from passing through. Everywhere she looked, piles of rusting scrap metal and old appliances choked the sidewalks. An odd sight was a mound of smashed televisions and satellite receivers in the middle of the road. Various minivans and

SUVs jockeyed for position at high speed, as if the main street was an obstacle course built for their own version of NASCAR. Other than the transport, the place could have passed for a nineteenth-century movie set, with the women in pioneer garb and the men wearing plain shirts and long pants with suspenders.

Tulley halted at the stop sign. A woman with several small children stood at the side of the road, looking like she wanted to get across. Jude took in a round ruddy face beneath brass-toned blond hair, the bangs strangely waved so they bobbed high above her forehead. Tulley signaled to the woman to go ahead, but she remained rooted to the spot, glaring balefully at them, her children clutched to her bosom.

One of the youngsters broke away from his mother's skirts to hurl a stone at their car, yelling, "Apostates."

They were also attracting a more menacing audience. Several young males armed with shotguns emerged from behind a building and marched purposefully toward the vehicle.

"Think they've noticed we're not from 'round here?" Jude said.

They both unsnapped their holsters.

"Looks like trouble." Tulley seemed oddly pleased by the fact.

"We're passing through," Jude repeated the standard line they had discussed for this exact situation.

A hand thumped the car. Tulley lowered his window. A moon face occupied the gap.

"You folks lost?" The speaker looked about twenty, his beard a carefully combed straggle only an adolescent male would prize. Jude checked out his teeth. Nothing unusual there. But his eyes were a source of fascination, beady and deep set with no space between eyebrows and lids.

Tulley said, "Just passing through, sir."

The stony little eyes fastened on Jude, and contempt seeped into the youth's tone. "Keep your wife inside the car in her harlot's attire. We will not have this town corrupted by immorality."

Jude reminded herself that decking this little prick would be a good way to have the situation blow up in their faces before they got a single thing they wanted, but it was tempting all the same. She kept her hands in her lap and contented herself with a fantasy of dragging Epperson away from his harem in handcuffs. Maybe kicking him in the balls just once.

"Like I said, we're just passing through." Tulley wound the window up.

The youths backed off a few feet, but their shotguns, held casually at the hip, were still trained on the car. One of them spat, and a wad of saliva ran down the windshield.

"Now, that makes me mad," Tulley said.

Jude patted his shoulder. "Drive."

He jammed the car into gear and they left the clothing police standing around the woman at the intersection like dogs guarding a carcass.

❖

Summer stared at the grimy wall to one side of Nathaniel, her eyes fixed on a plaque that said: *Keep Sweet, No Matter What.* These were plastered up all through the house. As if anyone could forget. Summer thought she must have heard that saying every day of her life.

"Perfect obedience produces perfect faith." Her husband waved the *Book of Mormon.* "The greatest freedom you will ever enjoy comes from giving yourself to God in complete submission."

Summer wished she could lie down. Her heart was beating too fast and her skin felt clammy. The family meeting room was hot and smelled of baby shit, throw-up, and the sickly perfume Fawn Dew had on. Summer was shocked by this shamelessness. Even if she herself had been given perfume by the master, she would not boast her good fortune in front of all her sister-wives. Fawn Dew was also parading around in a brand-new, seamstress-made, green plaid dress with a white lace collar and big sash. She was the only wife Nathaniel had returned home with a gift for, and she wanted everyone to know.

Naoma said she wouldn't be the favorite much longer, but the other sister-wives said it had gone on like this for a year now. Fawn Dew was one of the new prophet's daughters. She and her Downs toddler had been assigned to the master after Mr. Jeffs took them away from one of the Barlows. He ran most of that family out of town not long after, the mayor included. Fawn Dew thought she was better than all the rest of them, and skipped her tasks. Anyone else would have been beaten till she couldn't walk.

"Give thanks that you will be lifted up," Nathaniel declared. "That you alone among the daughters of Eve will attain the celestial kingdom through living the sacred principle. Each of you must make a choice every day to keep yourself white and delightsome, otherwise you open a door to Satan."

This time Summer could feel his pale blue eyes burning into her. She dared a quick glance at his face and he shoved his index finger into her chest.

"Wife, I am asking you now, in the presence of our Heavenly Father, did you open that door to the devil? Did you release your sister?"

Summer swallowed bile. Fear had her by the throat. Her teeth chattered. She dug the nails of one hand hard into the wrist of the other to prevent herself sobbing. The master didn't like tears. Wives and children who wept were punished and if there was one thing she couldn't face at this stage of her pregnancy, that was having to hold her breath while Sister Naoma pushed her head underwater.

"No, I swear. I would never do that," she said.

"Then why were you in the barn on Saturday evening?" the head wife accused. Her face was aglow with anticipation and she ran a chunky hand up and down the thick leather belt she held.

Spies. Sister Naoma had them everywhere. Summer knew she'd been stupid to risk sneaking off to see Adeline.

Frantically, she said, "I went there to beg Adeline to submit herself. I told her that the only way she could find salvation was by living the principle as I do. I told her how honored she was to be chosen as the master's next celestial wife. I was trying to make her see sense."

Sister Naoma snorted, but the master placed his hand on Summer's head and intoned. "After a lifetime of self purification and sanctification, and of repentance and living the principle, I am now a Christlike man. My faith fills me and I am blessed by revelation, visions, and angelic ministrations. Lord, I your servant ask now for the ability to discern the truth of my wife Summer's reply." He paused and several of the wives dropped to their knees, adding their own exhortations to his.

The minutes ticked by with excruciating slowness. Summer felt sweat slithering down her back and her thighs. She wondered if she should mention the hiding place the boy talked about, but she held back. If they found Adeline, Summer could hardly bear to think about what they might do to her. And if Adeline still failed to keep herself sweet after being purified, Summer too would pay a price.

Just as she thought she might faint, Nathaniel flung his arms heavenward and announced as he always did when he received God's word, "If I dared to deny the Holy Ghost as it works in me, I would be committing an act of infamous perdition. If I trust in the arm of flesh more than in a revelation from the Holy Spirit, if I ignore the spring of living waters rising within me and the burning in my bosom, I will stumble from the paths of truth and righteousness, and I might as well become an apostate!"

Get on with it, Summer thought and shivered instantly, recognizing the tiny, derisive voice as the devil's, a cunning attempt to lead her away from the promise of salvation. Terror weakened her limbs. What if Nathaniel couldn't hear God today and decided she was lying? She would be cast out, and without the stewardship of her husband, she would be doomed for all eternity.

She clamped her teeth down on her bottom lip, filled with bleak despair at the thought of losing her home and place in the world. She might not be the master's favorite, but he had never used her harshly; only Sister Naoma had beaten her. Several of her sister-wives were great friends to her, especially Thankful, the sixth wife. Everything had been fine until Adeline came along with her apostate ideas and immodest ways. Wiping her hands on her dress, she allowed her husband's words to wash over her and prayed for God to help her hold fast to the rod.

Eventually Nathaniel made the pronouncement she was longing to hear. Patting her cheek, he said, "Summer is a good and obedient wife and a faithful servant of the Lord. Adeline has been led astray by her master, Lucifer. Let us ask in prayer that she may be returned and cleansed of her wickedness."

As Summer sank gratefully to her knees, she stole a sideways glance at Sister Naoma, who did not look at all pleased by this turn of events. Hastily Summer turned to face the Salt Lake City Temple, as they all did during their thrice-daily prayers. Eyes closed, she began repeating sentence for sentence after her husband.

"Lord, we present ourselves unto thee, thine humble servants on earth. Please hasten the day in which the blood of the prophets is avenged…"

As she mouthed the familiar, comforting lines, she added a prayer of her own. *Please God, protect Adeline, wherever she is, however foolish she has been.*

CHAPTER NINE

"Why did you do it?" Daniel asked.

Adeline ran a hand through her short hair, still amazed at how light her head felt with the waist-length braids cut off. "You said runaway wives always get caught. But I look like a boy now."

Daniel studied her for a moment, then his two front teeth peeped over his top lip. "You're real smart, Adeline."

She rolled up the legs of her denim overalls and marveled again at how free and comfortable she felt in men's clothing. She was never going to wear that sack of a dress and the long prickly underwear ever again. When she'd swapped clothing in the laundry, she'd wanted to burn everything, but she didn't have time and besides, someone would have seen the smoke. Instead, she'd stuck to her plan and stolen the scissors from Sister Naoma's bedroom. She still couldn't believe she'd made it in and out of that window without being caught, and that she and Daniel had reached the cave and survived the night.

She'd also stolen a saucer from the head wife's room and they'd used it to bake a couple of eggs in the sun once they were safe in their hiding place.

"I wonder how long it will be before they come looking," she said. "We need to get away from here."

"No." Daniel was adamant. "We should stay where we are. I don't think anyone knows about this place. We'll be safe, and when they stop looking, then we'll leave."

Adeline eyed their meager supplies. Daniel had a small stockpile of foods his mother had slipped him on the visits he'd made to the ranch before getting caught. Beans. Dried apple. Cans of soup. He also had a pocketknife with a can-opener tool. If they made everything last, they could probably survive for two weeks. Water was the problem.

"We've only got water for a few more days," she said.

"Once they've searched 'round here, we can go find some. They won't come back again."

Adeline wished she could feel so certain about that, but she had a feeling Mr. Epperson was not going to take kindly to their vanishing act. She wondered if he would tell her parents. Maybe they would go to Aunt Chastity's place and wait for her. What if she and Daniel somehow got as far as Salt Lake City only to be caught and brought back? She wished she was eighteen. When you turned eighteen no one could force you to live where you didn't want to live.

"How's your leg?" she asked.

"It's awful sore. I prayed but it doesn't feel any better."

"Let me see it."

He looked embarrassed. "I'd have to take off my overalls."

"I won't look." Adeline turned and climbed down toward the rear wall of the cave.

Their hiding place was not a large one. The cave had an entrance like a pair of slightly parted lips. To get in, they had to slide on their bellies. But it was cool and snaked back a ways into the wall of red rock. A fine film of moisture clung to the farthest part, which made Adeline wonder if there was water somewhere. She had felt around the rock and listened intently, without luck.

"You can look now," Daniel said.

He was lying on his front and Adeline almost threw up at the sight of his right leg. The thigh was dark purple and a long gash was trying to heal, but it had not knitted properly, no doubt because the wound was so swollen.

"What happened?" she asked.

"Some of the elders beat on me with a two-by-four. It had a nail in it. That got dug in and made the rip."

Cautiously, Adeline touched the messy area. It was hot and sticky with pus. "They punished you because you tried to see your mom?"

His head jerked in a nod and his shoulders started to shake. "She was going to give me money for a bus fare. She was set to steal it from the master. Maybe she got caught."

"You reckon that could be why she's—what'd you call it?"

"A poofer?—probably."

"Seems like anyone who acts half-decent 'round here gets thrown out."

"God makes the rules. He speaks through the prophet and we must obey or atone."

Adeline rolled her eyes. "If you believe that, you're dumber than you act. My Aunt Chastity says the prophet is not Christlike. She says his rightful place is in the state penitentiary."

A small hiss of air fizzed from Daniel and he snuck a look toward the mouth of the cave like he thought someone could be listening in on them.

"Boy, you're skinny," Adeline said. "I'm going to fix you another baked egg after I'm done with this."

She poured some of their precious water into the saucer and cut a strip from the funny-undie bag they'd carried the eggs in. Cleaning the wound as best she could, she asked, "Do you know if there's a doctor back in Rapture?"

"Nearest one is in Hildale."

"Then that's where we're going."

"No!" He seized her wrist. "We can't. They'll catch us for sure if we go there."

"What are we supposed to do? This is infected."

"Maybe if you pray, too—"

Adeline snorted. "Fat lot of good that will do. I did biology at school because I'm going to be a vet, and there's only one thing that'll fix your leg. Antibiotics."

Daniel propped himself on an elbow and squinted at her like he couldn't believe what he was hearing. "Are you talking about apostate drugs and the like?"

"I'm talking about regular type medicine that you get at the pharmacy."

He gazed blankly at her.

"Hello? The pharmacy, where they give you the prescription after you go to the doctor."

He had no idea what she was talking about, of course. He had never seen a doctor in his life. Neither had she until Aunt Chastity took her to one in Salt Lake to get all the shots she'd missed out on when she was little.

"Doctors are Satan's servants," Daniel informed her.

"Whatever. I'm still taking you to see one."

"It's a long way to Salt Lake. Where will we go first?"

Adeline had no idea, but she didn't want to let on about that. Even though she'd discovered Daniel wasn't as young as she thought, he still didn't seem like a thirteen-year-old. More like nine or ten. And he acted like she was his big sister—or, now that she was supposed to be a boy, his cousin. That was their story. They'd thought it all up while she was baking their eggs the day before. If anyone asked, she was going to say her name was Dell, like the computer Aunt Chastity had bought her.

As she squeezed out the rag and hung it over a rock, she wondered what Aunt Chastity would do if she was here. Adeline pictured her on the hiking trip they took last fall. She was really pretty, with her curly copper hair bunched up on top in a knot, her big smile, and her eyes so dark they looked almost black. She was so clever and dainty, Adeline felt like a clumsy idiot in comparison. One thing they had in common was they both liked gadgets and when they went on hikes, they always took a compass and fancy pocket knives with all kinds of tools. Aunt Chastity had showed her how to use the stars and the sun to plot their course, and how to make a fire without matches and find water. They'd hiked in some wild places, but nowhere like this.

Adeline peered out of the cave mouth looking for signs of moisture in the huge rocky desert. Creek beds. Cottonwood trees. Even bees had a story to tell. When the light started to fade, she would go gather some pigweed to supplement their food, and she would watch the birds. Most of the time they were just darting here and there, looking for food, but at dusk they went to their watering places, flying low and straight. If she could see where they headed, she'd know there was water in that direction.

Meantime, she had the plastic apron she'd taken from the laundry. She had intended to use it to sleep on, but now she had a better idea. Even in a place like this, the night was much colder than the day and that meant there would be morning dew. As soon as it started to get dark, she was going to set that apron up, hanging between some rocks. The way the temperature dropped in the desert, they could collect maybe a cup of water overnight.

She remembered something else Aunt Chastity liked to say— usually when Adeline was moaning about sleeping on the hard ground or having to remember the Morse code signaling her aunt wanted to use.

"All over the world, people live in difficult places," she would tell Adeline. "You just have to know how."

Aunt Chastity would not die out here in a cave, trying to get away from a creepy old man who wanted to marry her. Adeline knew that much. She would say, "When the going gets tough, the tough get going," and she would survive, no matter what.

That was exactly what Adeline planned to do.

"Chill, okay?" she told Daniel. "I'm going to have my own vet surgery one day and no crazy old man and his head wife are going to stop me."

Daniel drew his overall straps up and tightened them. "Do you think your aunt will let me stay for a while?"

"Sure she will. She's a real nice lady. She wants to adopt me."

"I wish I knew where my mother went."

"Is she nice, your mom?"

"She didn't want them to cast me out."

"Then she should have taken you away. That's what I would have done."

Daniel gave her an odd little smile. "That's what you *are* doing."

Adeline laughed. "Yeah. I guess I am."

❖

The Mohave County Sheriff's Office on the Arizona side of Rapture had been established after most of the Colorado City police lost their badges because they refused to give up their plural wives. It was a small outpost only a step up from the Paradox substation, but its existence demonstrated at least an attempt by the authorities to look like they were getting serious about the abuse problems rife in the polygamist nirvana on their doorstep.

"Child Protective Services cases don't go to the Colorado City Marshall's Office anymore," Sergeant Beau Gossett explained. "They come to me or go direct to CPS in our new building in Colorado City. Got a state attorney there, too."

"Sounds like an improvement," Jude said, thankful that even if Utah didn't have the will to police this area, at least Arizona was stepping up to the plate. "I guess you have your hands full."

"Not really. Victims are reluctant to come forward. They've never had a cop out here who wasn't part of their system, so they're suspicious. And afraid, of course."

"We're also talking about a class of victims who've been programmed to think their victimization is completely normal," Jude remarked.

"You got that right. Out here, polygamist and pedophile are synonyms. The sex abuse is not the only problem, either. These folks have been living this lifestyle for generations, marrying their own half sisters and what not. So, there's an issue with birth defects, water on the brain...Downs syndrome...fused limbs...that type of deal. They blame that shit on the mother not being obedient enough."

"Do they buy that?" Tulley could not hide his amazement.

"It's all they know. They've got no education and no contact with the outside world."

"Another reason children are easy pickings. Tell me something..." Jude had her mind on the prophet. If they were ever going to nail this creep on conspiracy charges, they were going to need a mountain of hard evidence. "I've heard rumors that there are kids murdered but they pass the deaths off as vehicle accidents. Know anything about that?"

"We have maybe the highest rate in the country of kids run over by motor vehicles. It can't all be bad driving."

"Are there any doctors I could talk to who would have medical records for these cases?" Jude didn't want to sound like she was questioning his competence, but if she could prove foul play in a single instance, they could be looking at whole new ball game.

"If you're thinking about an M.E.'s report, you're in the wrong town. If they actually report a dead kid, one of their pals writes it up as an accidental death and that's the end of it. There's all kinds of unexplained deaths, and that's not counting infants."

"What about medical treatment for abuse. Hospital records..."

"The plygs don't have any use for the medical profession. If a kid is sick or never woke up from the last beating, they pray and lay on hands."

"Heaven on earth." Jude shook her head in amazement. How could this be going on under everyone's noses on such a huge scale without so much as a peep out of the so-called family values lobby? Where was the outrage? Why wasn't the media camped out and running salacious exposé stories?

"I don't get it," she said. "Why isn't anyone held accountable? I know there's this hands-off policy in effect, but we're not talking about religious freedom here, we're talking about felonies."

"You're preaching to the choir. When Mohave first moved in here, we thought we could start a dialogue. We held a meeting with the mayor." Gossett's expression told the rest of the story. "Well, the guy's out of a job now, anyway. Jeffs expelled him."

Jude said, "This would be the Warren Jeffs who's on the FBI's Most Wanted list? The guy who said 9/11 was a 'magnificent portent and cause of great hope.' That freedom-loving American patriot?"

"Yep, that's our boy. The same one whose nephew just filed a lawsuit against him in Salt Lake, alleging Jeffs sodomized him when he was four."

Jude was intrigued. "I haven't heard about that. Is Utah pressing criminal charges?"

Gossett rolled his eyes. "Did I say anything about miracles? They're looking at him. That's a start."

"And it's put the spotlight on this place."

"That it has. Jeffs bailed like a rat off a sinking ship, soon as the heat was on. Left the troops in disarray. Last I heard he's holed up in Florida somewhere. So, we've got quite the power struggle going on now. Wannabe prophets up the wazoo. It's the plyg version of *American Idol*." He chuckled at his own joke.

"Where does Elias Rockwell fit in?"

Rockwell led one of the splinter factions in the FLDS sect and had originally proclaimed himself prophet after the death of Rulon Jeffs in 2002. Warren Jeffs had beat him out of the job, but now that Jeffs was a fugitive, Rockwell had stepped into the power vacuum. He had even announced his godlike status to the press.

"He's leading the charge," Gossett confirmed. "Got his soldiers out there on every street corner, calling him the One Mighty and Strong. The Lion of Israel. Yadda yadda."

"I can see why it's the job everyone wants." The FLDS sheltered their financial assets in a trust called the United Effort Plan, which owned all the property and businesses in the twin towns, as well as valuable compounds in Canada, Texas, and Colorado. The trust was supposedly worth about $150 million, and the Utah government had recently frozen its assets to try and stop Jeffs and his lieutenants from stripping them. "I mean, we're not just talking about a spiritual position, are we?"

"No, we are not." Gossett unclipped a ballpoint from the breast pocket of his gray uniform and slapped it down on the notepad in front of him. "We're talking about a dictatorship. The prophet owns this town and everyone, and everything, in it."

He looked like a good ol' boy, Jude thought as he was talking. Tall and beefy, flat top, football ring, fully optioned belt, *God Bless America* emblazoned on his wall between a couple of taxidermied bass. And so far, he didn't seem to be aligned with the Fundamentalist Latter Day Skunks.

Just to be sure, she asked, "Are you a personal acquaintance of Mr. Rockwell's?"

"If you're asking me if I have a couple of spare wives stashed away somewhere, the answer is, 'Do I look like a crazy man?' My missus would cut off my balls—if you'll pardon the expression—if I started yammering about celestial marriage and the likes. No..." He grinned. "I think Rockwell's waiting for me to get struck down by lightening. He asked his buddy, God Almighty, to take care of that after I arrested some of his personal militia last month. They were looking to lynch an African American trucker. The guy made an emergency repair stop. Thought he'd stretch his legs while he waited. Damn fool idea."

Tulley made a small sputtering noise and Jude paused to give him room to speak. He shrugged helplessly and looked so uncomfortable she resumed talking, observing to Gossett, "Nice town you got here."

"Those jokes about living behind the Zion Curtain...they're all true."

She laughed. "Do you see things improving now that Jeffs is out of the picture and we're finally seeing some action from the state?"

"It's hard to say. My wife reckons it couldn't get any worse, but I don't know about that. The rival prophets could start murdering each other, then we'd have a civil war going on. I can't see Arizona or Utah wanting a piece of that."

"Well, we'll do our best not to rock the boat."

"Uh-huh." Gossett gave a small, wry smile. "So, don't keep me in suspense. What can I do for you, Detective?"

Jude took Darlene's file from her satchel and slid it across his desk. "We've reason to believe a Rapture man—Nathaniel Epperson—

abducted this girl in Cortez. She was subsequently murdered. Body showed up back in our jurisdiction."

"Help yourselves to coffee." The sergeant indicated a kona machine. "Or there's soda in the fridge." He opened the file and scanned the paperwork. Eventually he said, "You're going after Epperson and that pit bull he calls a wife?"

"Yes, sir."

Gossett closed the file and said his last big case involved a topless dancer who tried to cut off her husband's organ. "The thing with the tongue. That's what put me in mind of her," he explained.

"Obviously we'll need a search warrant," Jude said.

He frowned. "Not a good move. If we initiate a warrant, we'll be shut down before we can make first base."

"What are you saying?"

"The judge is a big-time buddy of Rockwell's, and Epperson's a key ally. They'll phone him and he'll clean house before we get there."

"Great. So, what do you recommend?"

"You have your witness statement. Naoma Epperson cut this girl's tongue out. Bring her in."

"You're okay with us questioning her here?"

"I'd pay money to watch."

"What about Epperson?"

"Want my advice?—let him sweat. Most of these first wives hate their old man's guts. Specially the ones that weren't reared plyg. He'll be shitting himself if you've got her here and he can't talk to her."

"You think we can turn her and cut a deal? Her testimony against Epperson in exchange for reduced charges?" Jude wasn't counting on it, but she was relieved that Gossett thought they were in with a chance.

"The way things are, that's your best option."

"If we can get a confession, they'll have to give us a warrant." Jude glanced at Tulley. He was trying on his handcuffs.

Gossett made a noncommittal sound. "You have to get a hold of her first. How would you feel about going in alone? You might get further if I'm not tagging along."

"Sure, if you're fine with that."

"I'm fine with anything that'll put that jerk-off behind bars where he belongs."

"I want Jeffs, too," Jude said.

The sergeant barked a guffaw. "I want box seats at the next Superbowl. No one's gonna find that shitweasel."

The phone rang and he picked it up. A few moments into the call, he flicked it onto speaker so they could hear the discussion.

A woman said, "There's a search party out there now."

"Who's the girl?" Gossett asked.

"The sister of one of his wives. Fourteen years old. She was supposed to be sealed to him on the weekend, but they're saying she ran off with one of his sons."

"How old is the boy?"

"No idea. Could be Daniel, the one they chased off a while back. He's maybe thirteen."

"Okay. Thanks for the call, Brenda."

He replaced the phone and stood up, straightening his overloaded belt. "We caught a break. Epperson's wife-to-be ran out on him."

"She was being forced into the marriage?" Jude asked.

"Round here they're not big on long engagements, or female consent," he replied dryly. "The prophet orders a marriage and it happens right away. It's not like they're legal marriages. They don't have to obtain a license or anything."

"Makes marrying underage girls a whole lot easier. How are these so-called marriages performed?"

"Basically the prophet says a few words and it's a done deal. They call it a sealing."

"So what's happening at the moment—are any of these sealings taking place?"

"In theory they're on hold because Jeffs is still officially the prophet and president of the church and he's the only guy who can perform them. But Rockwell isn't wasting any time. He was supposed to be sealing Epperson and his latest victim."

"Which would make him an accessory to child molestation."

"Hey, don't get me started. The guy has thirty-something wives. Some of them were only twelve when he married them."

"You have proof of this?"

"Only hearsay. The lady who called—Brenda Barlow—she was forced to marry her uncle when she was thirteen. Got fed up with her situation after eight kids. Nowadays she lives outside the town and helps us out with information."

"Her uncle," Tulley noted with distaste.

"Are you in a position to bring charges if I collar Rockwell?" Jude asked.

"We'd need at least one of those underage wives to testify against him. If you can find one, the state attorney would be all over it."

Jude could imagine how difficult it would be to persuade a brainwashed, terrified, uneducated girl to testify in court. "Well, this runaway bride is underage. So, at least we can detain Epperson on suspicion of attempted child molestation."

"He'll claim he wasn't going to marry her until she turned sixteen, and you won't get a statement from anyone disputing that."

"Not even the girl's sister?"

Gossett's shrug said it all. If they wanted Epperson, they would have to persuade his wife to implicate him.

"What's the situation out there?" Jude asked. "Do you know the place?"

"Big compound. Fifty acres. The menfolk will be out searching for her when you show up."

"Excellent. I take it they're all armed."

Gossett laughed. "Oh, yeah. The plygs have been shipping weaponry and ammo into this place by the truckload for the past twenty years."

Jude unholstered her Glock 22 and inspected it. "Can you let us have a few extra rounds?"

"You got it." Gossett unlocked his firearms cabinet and took out a box full of .40 S&W magazines. "That all you're carrying?"

From the tone of the question, Jude surmised they were probably crazy to be going to the Gathering for Zion Ranch short of a SWAT team. On the other hand, they had the element of surprise in their favor.

She said, "I have a backup snubbie and a Model 19 in the vehicle."

The Smith & Wesson was an old favorite her father had passed on to her when she'd graduated from the Academy. Even now, she seldom went anywhere without it; she preferred it to her Glock, the peace officers' duty weapon of choice in Montezuma County. The Model 19 handled like a dream and always seemed to lock effortlessly on target. Jude loved the lethal elegance of the six-gun with its four-inch barrel, classic nickel plating, and smooth wood grip. She loved the serrated trigger and the very slight stack at the end of the pull-through, just enough so you could measure each shot. The 19's action was like buttered silk, and the earsplitting reports would scare most criminals shitless.

Beau Gossett must have caught her small sigh. "Now that's a real handgun. None of your polymer and titanium crapola."

They shared a moment's silence, aficionados contemplating the passing of an era. Was there anything finer than seeing the sky shimmer across your barrel and hearing that magical kiss as the case heads went flush with the cylinder?

Tulley said, "I'm in the market for a Sig P220."

Gossett considered this. "I could see you with a 1911, a Les Baer maybe."

"Nice, but they cost," Jude said. "I looked at a Kimber Tactical a while back. Pretty good and half the price."

Tulley frowned. "Isn't the 1911 kind of…old fashioned?"

"If you mean it comes from the days when they designed sidearms to win fights, not avoid product liability lawsuits, sure it's old fashioned," Jude responded.

Gossett said, "No kidding. We're out there with popguns and they lift the ban on assault rifles. Put those morons on Capitol Hill in a peace officer's uniform for a week in Washington Heights and see if they can keep their pants dry."

Jude was a little surprised to hear this good ol' boy criticizing the government. On the other hand, he was surrounded by wackos who carried shotguns in the main street.

"Maybe I'll try a 1911 on the shooting range before I make my decision," Tulley said.

"Good plan." Jude returned her Glock to its holster. "I mean, how often do you buy a sidearm? Might as well be the right one."

"Are we going to go look for those kids?" Tulley asked.

"Kind of hard to do that officially when they haven't been reported missing," Gossett replied. "How about I swear you both in and you go take care of Mrs. Epperson? Then we'll see about the search."

"I knew we should have brought Smoke'm along," Tulley said.

"He's a K-9 handler," Jude told Gossett.

"No kidding? What kind of dog you working with?"

Tulley whipped out a photo of Smoke'm. "He's not top of his class in agility, but he's one heck of a sniffer hound, sir."

"I'll bet he is. Man, those are some jowls." Gossett examined the picture with the air of a man who knew the real McCoy when he saw it. "We run a few K-9 units ourselves. German Shepherds and Belgian Malinois."

Tulley slid the picture back into his breast pocket. "Smoke'm could find those kids, no problem."

Jude said, "Guess you'll be bringing your own dogs in once the search is official, Sergeant."

"If we get that far. The plygs used to report their runaway wives to the marshall, and he'd go find them and bring them right on back to the compound. Nowadays they're supposed to report missing person cases to me. Fat chance."

Jude gathered up the spare ammo, suddenly impatient with the talking. "We need to be moving along."

After they were sworn in, the sergeant walked them to their car. "Any trouble, you know where to find me."

Chapter Ten

"There's a house full of bored-shitless women out here who've never seen a movie and are married to an ugly old fart," Jude declared as she and Tulley bounced along the narrow, potholed road to the Epperson ranch. "All we need is to entice one of them to agree, and we can take a look around."

Tulley listened earnestly, but he wasn't getting it.

Jude clarified, "That's your job, Mr. Smooth Talker."

A rosy glow illuminated his ears and he hastily moved the discussion along. "You want me looking for the crime scene. Right?"

"Right. I doubt she was murdered this far from the body dump site, but anything's possible. We're looking for blood, a hammer, more of those tree spikes, a knife, and the owner of the attractive teeth, of course. We also need to check all vehicles and collect trace."

"I packed extra latex gloves."

"Good." Jude was starting to wish she'd packed an assault rifle.

Gossett's flip remarks about plygs and their weaponry had come as no surprise. She was already uneasy about the whole scenario. Two officers alone on the property of a group of paranoid lawbreakers who think they are God's chosen and have the weapons to defend themselves—definitely not a walk in the park. She could see the sense in making a low-key approach, and she could see why Gossett thought they might be better off going in without him. But this was a volatile situation. No question.

They had two big advantages and she didn't want to squander them. The first was surprise, the second was the search for the missing teenager, which hopefully meant only women and children would be present on the ranch. They would only catch the Epperson clan off guard once, and they needed to capitalize on that. Her primary objective was simple—Naoma Epperson in custody. A thorough search for evidence could happen later if it became unwise to proceed this morning.

"I wouldn't want to be those kids." Tulley had his window down a notch and a hand out, testing the breeze or lack thereof. "It's gotta be a hundred out there."

"Don't worry, we'll join the search as soon as we have Mrs. Epperson in a holding cell. They can't have gotten far on foot. They're probably sheltering somewhere to stay out of the sun."

"We could get one of the other deputies to fly down with Smoke'm."

"Rapture's maybe not the best place for dogs," Jude said. "Sounds like they shoot first and ask questions later."

Tulley blanched. "I'd kill anyone that hurt a hair on my dog's head."

"An incident with Utah—Sheriff Pratt would be thrilled."

Tulley huffed.

"Any more thoughts on that number they found in her stomach?" she asked.

They'd tried phoning it. There was no such number. What else had ten digits? She'd worked her way through all the usual suspects. Bank deposit box—when would Darlene have been able to get to a bank, living out here in the middle of nowhere? Floor safe—most did not have ten-digit codes. Computer password—did these people have computers? The Universal Product Code and Standard Book Numbers had ten digits. Ciphering—if the numbers related to letters of the alphabet, they spelled out: BCBIAEIIAI. Jude had gotten nowhere treating this as an anagram and had so far resisted the urge to phone her boss and hand it over to the cryptologists. She figured she'd take that liberty only if she didn't get a break on the case by arresting the Eppersons.

Tulley consulted a slip of paper he kept in his pocket. With the measured deliberation of a monk reciting a Gregorian chant, he read, "2329159919."

They reflected in silence.

"Amazing she could remember that whole string," Jude said.

"It must have meant something to her."

"No kidding." It was bound to end up being something blindingly obvious. In the meantime, they could waste hours gnashing their teeth on a fruitless quest for the esoteric. "We need to put ourselves in her shoes if we're going to decode this. It has to be linked somehow to her environment."

"Maybe it's birthdays," Tulley suggested. "Important dates."

Jude hit the brakes. Directly ahead, a huge sign proclaimed *Gathering for Zion Ranch* in lime green lettering. This was emblazoned above a montage in sunrise hues, which depicted what Jude took to be the faithful assembled for the lift-off to heaven. Puzzled by some odd black blotches on the canvas, she got out of the vehicle for a closer look. Seven of the radiant, upturned faces had been painted out. It also seemed new figures had been added periodically; some looked fresher and brighter than the others.

"Check it out," she said. "I have a feeling this is meant to be the Epperson family."

Tulley joined her, camera in his hand, and took several photographs of the painting. "That's a big family."

They both counted.

"Looks like fourteen wives and forty-seven kids and that's not counting the blacked out ones." Jude was troubled by the faceless few standing among the awestruck throng. "I wonder what's up with that."

"Dead people maybe? Or excommunicated like Zach."

Crossed off the list for the celestial kingdom? "Good theory," she said. "The question is, how many of them ended up like Darlene?"

"Three of them are women." Tulley moved closer. "This could be Darlene."

He pointed to a woman whose hair was silvery blond. Most of the others had hair the same shade of reddish gold Jude had noticed on the woman back in Colorado City. Bummer that the faces were concealed. She studied the other two female figures, trying to discern a likeness to Poppy Dolores in either. It was impossible to say.

"I guess we'll be wanting to ask Mrs. Epperson who they are," Tulley said, adjusting the camera for a close-up.

"Indeed."

"Some of the males are just kids." Tulley noted darkly. "Wonder how many of them got hit by cars."

Jude shifted her focus to a man who still had a face, if you could call it that. The mouth was horribly twisted. And that wasn't his only problem. She asked Tulley, "Does this guy look like a hunchback to you?"

"Sure does. And what's up with his face? You think maybe he had a stroke?"

"Seems a bit young for that." Jude called to mind Sergeant Gossett's comments about birth defects. She had a feeling they were looking at a case of spina bifida and who knew what else. The guy certainly looked like a poster child for dental issues.

Tulley read her mind. "You're thinking Mr. Snaggletooth?"

"Could be. And if he's still got his face, maybe that means he's still around." She pointed at a white-haired patriarch at the epicenter of the painting. He was taller than everyone else and bathed in a golden glow, arms raised above his head. "Wild guess—Nathaniel Epperson?"

Tulley grinned. "I see how come you made detective."

"Yeah, well, let's find out if I'm any damn good." Jude unfastened the Eppersons' wide steel gate. "We'll leave this open. I don't see any livestock around, and we might want to expedite our departure."

Tulley looked sideways at her. "You think they'll do something crazy?"

"The deal in this type of situation is to take precautions, just in case."

The approach to the Epperson's house was a long, red dirt road. On either side, a few sad junipers eked out an existence amidst the pigweed and silvery scrub that clung to the hillside. An assortment of barns and outbuildings cluttered the front of the property. Beyond these lay a sprawling, whitewashed stucco structure with various additions that lacked windows. *L*-shaped, it extended back into what looked like several different dwellings interconnected by walkways.

"Well, it's not Tara," she remarked, earning a quick, puzzled glance from her colleague. "That's the plantation from the movie *Gone With the Wind*. Just thought I'd flaunt my age."

"I keep meaning to rent that," Tulley said in a tone of polite deference. "I'd like to know more about the Civil War."

"Uh-huh. Where are those binoculars?"

He reached into the backseat. "Got 'em."

"Okay, take a look around and see if you can spot the search party. We could do without them showing up in the middle of the proceedings." She halted behind a barn that screened them from the house, and turned off the motor. They got out of the car.

Tulley pointed north and handed the binoculars to her. "That's gotta be them over there on that hill."

She aimed the binoculars northwest. Sure enough, twenty or more tiny figures were fanned out across the hills a few miles away. Hopefully Nathaniel Epperson was among them, running his unwilling child bride to ground. With any luck it would be a while before the posse returned to the house. She gazed up at the sky. A delicate cloud cover diffused the sun's harsh rays, a small blessing for the missing kids. Rain looked unlikely, and she wondered if the runaways had access to water. In this heat, they would not last more than two days if they didn't.

They were about to get back into the car when a young, heavily pregnant woman emerged from the barn, pushing a wheelbarrow. She stopped and lowered her barrow at the sight of them, staring with startled deer eyes. Like most teenage girls in this neck of the woods, she wore a homemade dress down to her ankles and long braids bound into a bun at her nape. A wisp of snowy hair fluttered from these confines and tangled across her eyes. She tucked it discreetly away and dropped her gaze to a spot somewhere in front of Jude's feet.

Tulley spared her the immodesty of speaking first to a man she'd never met. "Morning, ma'am. I'm Deputy Sheriff Virgil Tulley, out of Montezuma County, Colorado, and this here is Detective Jude Devine. Would this be the Epperson ranch?"

The girl snuck a disconcerted look at Tulley's face. A handsome man was almost as much of a novelty in these parts as a woman in pants. And tall, dark, lean Tulley would make any straight woman look twice. Which is exactly what the girl did before blushing wildly. Jude dug her colleague in the ribs. An impressionable young female who mistook him for a Greek god was exactly what they needed.

Tulley caught his cue and flashed a movie-star smile when the girl glanced up again a millisecond later.

"Outsiders are not allowed here," she asserted, but her tone lacked conviction, and this time she did not lower her eyes, instead gazing transfixed.

Tulley cocked his head slightly and managed a look of such unadulterated country-boy charm that Jude wondered if he practiced it in his bathroom mirror. This certainly worked on the girl, who babbled a breathless justification of her previous pronouncement.

"The gentiles mean us harm, so we are not permitted to talk to anyone that does not share our beliefs."

"We're not here to harm you, ma'am," Tulley said softly. "We need to speak with your father."

"My father doesn't live here."

"Do you know a Nathaniel Epperson?"

"That's my husband." Her voice held an odd mixture of pride and defensiveness.

Tulley shot a look at Jude, who refrained from saying: *Congratulations on being some dirty old man's sex slave.* Instead she said, "Would you please inform him we're here to speak with him."

Silence.

"If he's busy right now, we'll wait." Tulley hit her again with the matinee session smile.

The girl shifted her weight from one foot to the other. "He sleeps in the afternoon."

"This is important," Tulley persisted winningly. "We'd sure appreciate it if you'd let him know we're here."

"Before you do, could you take a look at this photo for us?" Jude moved a little closer, took Darlene's picture from her shirt pocket, and held out it.

Without touching the photograph, the girl darted a quick look at it and made a tiny, fractured sound like a suppressed whimper.

"Do you recognize her?" Jude kept her breathing shallow in the face of the wheelbarrow piled high with horse manure.

The girl shrugged and slid a hand over her big, round belly. Jude guessed that by staying silent, she was avoiding an outright lie.

Tulley took another step forward and murmured like he was coaxing a timid cat from a hiding place. "It's okay. We know you can't tell us. But, there's something I want to ask you."

The girl dared a look at him from beneath her blond lashes.

"Did Diantha ever do anything to hurt you?"

Before she could stop herself, the girl began to shake her head. Flustered, she immediately suppressed the giveaway movement.

"She was a friend to you, wasn't she?"

After a long moment, the girl nodded very faintly and Jude realized that by enabling her to remain silent, they could get some answers. On a hunch, she asked, "Is it your sister they're out looking for?"

Another small nod.

"She's what—fourteen?"

Again, an affirmative. This time her brow creased in worry and she looked close to tears. She rubbed the small of her back and Jude was abruptly conscious that they were keeping a very pregnant teenager outdoors in fierce heat. Shrouded in that all-encompassing pink dress, she had to be miserable.

"I think Mrs. Epperson would like a bottle of water from the car," Jude told Tulley.

The girl gave her a grateful look. Jude wasn't sure if that was for the water or the respectful use of her married name. She held out the photo once again, and said, wanting to gauge the reaction, "Diantha is dead."

The hand resumed its caress of her belly, this time in an agitated tempo. She looked completely terrified.

"You didn't know?"

She shook her head emphatically. Tulley returned with the water and the girl took it and drank.

"What's your name?" he asked.

She wiped the excess water from her lips and vacillated for a moment. "Summer."

"Summer, that's pretty. My name's Virgil but everyone calls me Tulley."

A nervous smile.

"How about if I wheel that for you?" He indicated the barrow. "Where are you headed?"

She pointed at a fenced-off enclosure twenty yards from the barn, out of sight of the house. They started walking, Tulley pushing the manure.

He said, "I grew up on a pig farm. Eleven kids in my family."

A quick little nod. A platoon of siblings was obviously something Summer could relate to. She opened the gate and they entered the enclosure. Large piles of horse and chicken manure festered in the heat. Tulley emptied the barrow on the mountain the girl pointed out.

"I used to shovel the pig shit, so I know all about this. Some days I'd skip my chores and go hide out behind the barns to read books." He grinned and Summer seemed to fight off an answering smile. "My ma always caught me and beat on me with the pig paddle."

Also something Summer could relate to. She cast another look toward the house, then returned her attention to Tulley, transparently eager to listen. Jude kept silent, intrigued by her colleague's instincts. He was finding a way to reach out to this girl. She guessed something in his own life enabled him to put himself in her shoes. It was more than Jude could do.

"Oh, boy. She whipped me good," he said. "Beats me how she knew what I was up to."

"Sister Naoma always knows," Summer disclosed in a mumble. "That's the head wife."

"Bet you're in a load of trouble on account of your sister," he said ruefully.

Her shoulders tensed. "Mmm-hmm."

They left the foul-smelling enclosure and headed back to the barn.

"I sure hope they find her," Tulley said. "You must be pretty darn worried."

"My husband forgave me."

Jude counted to ten so she wouldn't say exactly what she thought about that magnanimous gesture.

"Sounds like he's a real fine man," Tulley said earnestly.

Apparently taking that at face value, Summer shared, "People say he is one of the most Christlike men they've ever met."

Jude didn't recall ever seeing it mentioned in the gospels that Jesus Christ married a bunch of schoolgirls and ordered his wives' tongues to be cut out. But what did she know? She said, "I need something from the car," and left them talking about what a prince Epperson was.

Back in the car, she located the plaster teeth and slid them into her pocket. She knew Summer would instantly clam up if they pushed their luck, and she wondered how to broach the subject of Darlene's "silencing." The girl had to have seen it happen. According to Zach, the whole family was forced to watch. No doubt the example was intended to terrorize anyone who might be tempted to disobey rules. Summer knew she shouldn't be talking to them, that much was obvious. Yet, despite her well-grounded fears, she was responding to the interest of a handsome young man as any normal teenage straight girl would. Summer was not so completely lost to herself that she functioned as an automaton—not yet, anyway.

Thankful for this, Jude closed the car door and strolled back toward the pair, formulating a plan. "I was thinking about your sister," she said in a sympathetic tone. "I know you're worried about her, but maybe it would be easier for you if they didn't find her."

Summer clasped her hands together. "Adeline will always be a problem."

"Are you worried she'll come back and make things difficult for you?"

A reluctant nod.

"Well, you have to think about your baby." Jude glanced at the pregnant belly. "When are you due?"

"Next week."

"That's wonderful."

"I think it's a boy," Summer volunteered.

Jude detected an ambivalence in her tone and contemplated its source. Any first-time mother would be anxious about the birth, she supposed. And Summer was just a kid. She would also be giving birth without a doctor, not that she would know this nineteenth-century approach was anything unusual.

Carefully, Jude said, "You know, if Deputy Tulley and I found your sister, we would have to take her away from here."

A flicker of interest registered in Summer's face.

"Yep. That's state law," Tulley added with conviction.

"We live by God's law, not the law of man," Summer pointed out.

"Your sister ran away," Jude said. "So she has to obey man's law now. Of course, if the folks from your church find her, she'll be brought back here no matter what."

"Any idea where she went?" Tulley asked. "'Cos if we knew, maybe we could get to her first. That way, she'd be safe but you wouldn't have to deal with her coming back here."

Summer took her time thinking on this. The idea clearly appealed, but the risk of her role being discovered weighed.

"No one will know you told us," Jude said.

Finally Summer pointed mutely east to a distinctive mesa-like red cliff stratified in black. "They talked about a hiding place up there."

"Have you told anyone else?"

Summer shook her head.

"Okay, so we'll do our best to find her. Now will you do something for us?" Jude took the teeth from her pocket and displayed them on the palm of her hand. "Have you ever seen anyone with teeth that look like these?"

Summer lifted a hand to her mouth, muffling a telltale gasp. Agitated, she said, "You must leave now."

"Summer, wait," Tulley began, but she was already walking away, signaling for them not to follow.

He called her again and she turned around. Rooted to the spot, she took her full measure of him, then it was as if a terrible realization dawned. Her face crumpled, and frantically wiping tears, she blurted, "Thank you for being nice to me," and fled toward the house.

Jude placed a detaining hand on Tulley's arm. "Leave her be."

"She knows more than she's saying," he protested. "She recognized the teeth."

"Yes. But, if we push her any harder, she'll fall apart. I don't want her telling Epperson where her sister is."

"Do you think he's really asleep in there?"

"Let's find out."

They headed back to the car and waited a few minutes to give her some time to get indoors.

"Did you hear her talking about him like he's some kind of saint?" Tulley marveled.

"What's she going to say—that he's an asshole? No. She has to believe in him or the whole house of cards comes down." On an impulse, Jude removed her belt and switched her Glock for the Model 19.

Watching her, Tulley said, "I think she likes me."

"Let's hope this Sister Naoma individual is equally undone by your charms." She tucked the Glock into the back of her belt when she was done, then checked the tactical holster on her right leg.

"You expecting trouble?" Tulley released the safety catch on his own sidearm.

Jude shrugged. "Stranger things have happened."

❖

A hand-painted sign hanging above the Epperson's front door declared: *And No Unclean Thing Can Enter Into His Kingdom.*

"You sure about me doing the talking?" Tulley asked.

"You're the man, and these people are programmed to see males as authority figures." Jude had nothing to prove. Everything was about outcome, and she'd learned a long time ago that ego had no useful role to play in strategic thinking.

Tulley gave an awkward nod and Jude was suddenly conscious of her hands sweating. *I am the law*, she reminded herself. Sliding her identification into her palm, she signaled Tulley to ring the doorbell, which was quite literally a bell with a string attached. Jude could hear voices inside the house and figured that she and her companion had been inspected, identified as outsiders, and the women of the house were now trying to decide whether the gentiles would leave if ignored.

Eventually the door swung open and to Jude's dismay a tall, white-haired man in a somber black suit stepped onto the threshold. He was carrying a pump-action Remington and was the spitting image of the patriarch from the montage at the front gate.

"Drop your weapon, sir." Tulley showed his badge and identified them.

Grandad Moses looked him up and down. "Speak your business, then leave."

"I said drop it, or I'm going to arrest you for obstruction of justice."

Jude was impressed with the gritty resolve in Tulley's voice. Who knew he could channel John Wayne?

"I don't answer to the laws of the beast." All the same, the older guy handed the Remington back to someone behind the door.

"Nathaniel Epperson?" Tulley asked.

"What's it to you?"

"So, you are Nathaniel Epperson?"

"Yes, and I'm ordering you off my land."

"We'll be happy to oblige just as soon as you look at this." Tulley held up Darlene's photograph. "We're investigating the murder of this young woman. Do you know her, sir?"

Epperson ignored the picture, instead staring at Jude, eyes glued to her pants. Saliva collected in one corner of his mouth and, muttering something, he spat on her shoes.

"I'd be obliged if you'd look at the photo, Mr. Epperson," Tulley said. "Have you ever seen this girl?"

Epperson lifted his eyes to the heavens. "Verily, I say unto you, the names of the wicked shall not be mingled with the names of my people."

Tulley consulted his notepad. "Last count your people would be sixty or so women and children collecting welfare and food stamps, right?"

"I don't know her," Epperson snapped. He still hadn't looked at the photograph.

"Darlene Huntsberger. Colorado girl. Last seen getting into a white minivan just like that one." Tulley pointed toward the cluster of vehicles parked around the yard.

"I do not know of any woman who goes by that name," Epperson grated.

"Do you know her by another name?"

"No."

"We have a witness that says she was your wife, sir."

"What witness? Name the son of perdition."

"I'm not obliged to do so at this time."

"You got any young males here?" Jude interrupted.

As she'd expected, Epperson reacted to her temerity with a nonplussed stare.

She cast a pointed look toward a couple of barns. "Maybe working on the ranch?"

"No."

"I find that hard to believe. Are you telling me you manage this spread by yourself, a man of your age?"

"I guess he has his womenfolk doing men's work," Tulley suggested with amused contempt.

Jude smiled inwardly. They had rehearsed their approach during the flight from Durango to Las Vegas, and the subsequent two-hour drive to Colorado City. Tulley had worried that he would not be able to say the right things when the time came, and he'd been so quiet in the meeting with Sergeant Gossett, she'd more or less expected to find herself alone in the hot seat. But she could sense his growing confidence and guessed he had probably surprised himself.

Epperson's face took on the same tomato-tinted hue as the landscape. "Be silent! On this ranch we are governed by the laws of God, not the laws of men."

"Well, that's good news. We'll go ahead and take a look around, then." Jude gave Tulley a nod and he set off toward the outbuildings.

"Wait up, boy." Epperson descended the verandah steps, eyes wrathfully ablaze. "You have no right. Where's your search warrant?"

Tulley halted. "But you just said the laws of men don't apply here."

Epperson looked like he was ready to explode. "Beware. The Lord is not mocked."

"We'll leave when Deputy Tulley has spoken to every male thirteen or older on this ranch," Jude said. "If you fail to cooperate, I guess I'll just have to file that welfare fraud report we're working on, and you can explain your situation to the state and federal government." Cheerfully, she informed Tulley, "While Mr. Epperson shows you around, I'll wait here in the shade."

"Yes, ma'am."

Epperson treated her to a poisonous stare, but could not resist hurrying after Tulley. As soon as the two men vanished beyond one of the outbuildings, Jude knocked loudly on the front door. She heard footsteps and mumbling from inside the house, but no one answered.

"Mrs. Epperson?" she called. "May I trouble you for a glass of water? It's mighty hot out here."

The door opened a crack and Summer peeped out, her face tight with apprehension. "You should not have come here," she whispered.

"I have no choice, ma'am," Jude said formally. "This is an investigation. The sooner our questions are answered, the sooner we'll leave your family in peace."

The door opened a little wider and an older woman wearing a super-sized version of Summer's pastel frock said, "We're entitled to everything we receive."

Had she not overheard her husband being asked about Darlene, or was she so preoccupied with keeping those welfare checks coming, it was all she could think about?

Jude fanned herself for effect. "We can discuss your entitlements once I've had something to drink."

Suspicious blue eyes glinted from a sagging face. There was not a sign of generosity or happiness in the bitter line of the woman's mouth. She shoved the pregnant teenager next to her. "Get some water, Summer."

Jude moved slightly closer. "According to our information, a number of single women and their children live at this address. Are you one of them?"

"I'm legally married." With malicious satisfaction, the woman added, "The rest of them are not."

"So, you're Naoma Epperson?"

"If you say so."

"Do you deny it?"

Naoma shrugged. "I do not answer to you. Only to my husband and the Lord."

"Neither of whom appear to be providing adequate financial support to the members of this household," Jude said, briskly bureaucratic. "However, if that's your position, I can report back to my superiors that you have declined to cooperate with representatives of the taxpayers who put food on your table. I'm sure this ranch will fetch a decent price in the asset sale."

"What are you talking about?"

Jude smiled. "Defrauding the government and the IRS…Trust me, Mrs. Epperson, they'll want their money back." As Summer appeared with the water, she waved it away and backed up like she was about to leave. "Thanks, but I'll be going. I have a mess of paperwork to complete and since I can't speak to Mrs. Naoma Epperson to verify her status, I—"

"You are speaking to her and don't pretend you don't know it!" Naoma stuck her hands on her hips and declared, "I am the legal wife of Nathaniel Epperson."

"Tell me something," Jude said softly enough that Naoma instinctively stepped closer to hear her. "Do you obey your husband in all matters?"

Naoma's eyes registered confusion. "I submit as God commands."

"That would be a yes, then?"

Before the big woman had time to respond, Jude caught her off guard, seizing one arm and twisting it behind her back. Pinning her against the wall of the house in an arm lock, she found her cuffs and said, "Naoma Epperson. You are under arrest for assaulting Darlene Huntsberger."

As she read Naoma her rights, glass smashed in the doorway. Summer stood with her mouth open, the hand that had held the tumbler still outstretched. Several other women appeared next to her, their expressions equally stunned.

One of them, a plump bottle blonde wearing a blue dirndl dress, complete with frilly white apron and petticoats, stepped out onto the stoop and demanded, "What's going on?"

"What's your name?" Jude asked.

"Fawn Dew Rockwell Epperson." She tilted her head. "I am a daughter of the true prophet."

"You don't say."

Jude had several more sets of restraints in the car. It could be interesting to arrest this self-satisfied Swiss Miss as an accomplice. Would Rockwell intervene on behalf of one of his offspring, assuming he could remember who they all were? Probably not. Ignoring Fawn Dew for the moment, she hustled a vociferously protesting Naoma down the steps toward the car and honked the horn, her prearranged signal for Tulley.

As she locked the door on her captive, she heard a distinctive metallic click and dropped automatically to a crouch, scrambling around the car.

"Let go of her!" Fawn Dew wielded the Remington.

Jude grabbed for her weapon, and yelled, "Drop it, or I'll shoot."

To her horror, the younger wife fired several rounds into the air and with that, shouted, "Take your posts. They've come to destroy us!"

She backed into the house and ten seconds later a manual siren sounded.

Aghast, Jude pictured twenty crazed elders abandoning the search for the runaways to respond to the alarm. Where in hell was Tulley? She climbed into the front seat of the car and trained her gun on Naoma.

"Call them off," she said.

"Shoot me," Naoma invited.

"Do you really want to give your life to protect a man who brought his girlfriends into your home?"

Jude peered past Naoma out the back window, seeking Tulley. The seconds were crawling by. A movement in the front windows of the house captured her attention. They were being boarded up. The Eppersons were preparing to shoot it out.

Disbelieving, she tried to reason with Naoma. "Don't allow this. People are going to get hurt. You have a house full of women and children. Please. Tell them to sound the all clear."

Naoma laughed. "You think I care about those whores and their brats?"

A figure ran toward the car. Tulley. Alone. He dived for the ground behind it and, keeping her head down, Jude reached across and swung open the door for him. He scrambled into the passenger seat. Blood ran down one side of his face from an open gash.

"Jesus. What happened?" Jude asked.

"He hit me with a shovel and ran off. I can't find him."

"Perfect." Jude started the motor. "Keep your heads down. We're out of here." As she jerked the car into motion, a bullet ricocheted off the bonnet. "I said get down!" she yelled at Naoma.

The head wife laughed and began reciting scripture. A hail of bullets fell short of them as they accelerated away from the house. It wasn't worth shooting back. There was no one to shoot at and Jude wasn't about to open fire on a house full of innocent civilians.

She swung hard on the wheel and they made a one-eighty, hit the road beyond the gates of the Gathering for Zion Ranch, and laid rubber turning for Rapture.

CHAPTER ELEVEN

"Oh, my Lord," Sergeant Gossett said after they'd locked Naoma in a holding cell. "This is going to get ugly."

"Tell me about it." Jude pulled a can of ginger ale from the fridge and tossed a Coke to Tulley. "We need to turn it over."

Gossett rolled his eyes. "There's gotta be some way we can defuse the situation. If we bring in the feds, we'll have another Waco on our hands."

Jude groaned. So much for her stellar career and unblemished reputation. She'd go down in the annals of the Bureau as an agent who dragged them into a shitstorm. She'd be hauled in front of the Office of Professional Responsibility and she'd never work in the field again, let alone undercover. They would transfer her to a training post at Quantico, or worse, she would be demoted to mindless wiretapping stakeouts for some two-bit field office.

Angry at herself, she took a slug of soda. How could she have misjudged the situation so badly? She'd seen it coming, yet she'd been so focused on bringing Naoma Epperson in, she'd decided the risks were worth it. Picturing, at worst, a few shots fired, she'd underestimated the escalation potential. The targets of her investigation were not just religious extremists who were armed to the teeth and might shoot if provoked, they were actually hoping for trouble. Cults like the FLDS fostered a siege mentality among their members and stockpiled weapons in readiness for the day of reckoning they thought was just around the corner.

The Eppersons would see the arrest of their head wife as the beginning of the end. It was tailor made for their paranoid fantasies. They were expecting the government to attack them at any moment, and not only that, their leader had proclaimed dates for the end of the world on more than one occasion in the past year or so. The true believers had duly maxed out their credit cards and spent money like there was no tomorrow, because that's what they expected. They had arrived at the place where their prophet said they would be lifted up, only to find themselves up to their ears in debt the next day and told Armageddon had been postponed because they were not faithful enough. They had to be chomping at the bit to get things rolling. She should have taken that into account.

"I blame home schooling," she said.

This ill-timed levity earned a funny look from Gossett and a worried stare from Tulley, who suggested, "Maybe we should just wait it out. They can't stay holed up in there forever."

"I should have taken early retirement," Gossett said.

"Is there anyone we could ask to go talk some sense into them?" Jude asked. "A local bigwig—the mayor maybe?"

"He'd only encourage them."

"You're telling me these people want a bloodbath?"

Gossett pondered this briefly, and confirmed, "Yes."

"We'll have to go back for Epperson eventually," Jude said. "And there's the missing kids to think about. We need a plan."

"We need a friggin' army."

Jude chewed over their options. There really was only one. Notify the FBI. By now Sheriff Pratt would also be looking for an update. She decided to phone him later, once they'd settled on the plan. Maybe she would have better news then. Maybe she would have a confession.

She signaled Tulley. "I think it's time we had a chat with Mrs. Epperson. Then we'll work up a strategy."

Gossett set about cleaning his guns. "Good luck. You'll need it."

❖

"When did you first meet Darlene Huntsberger?" Jude asked.

Naoma Epperson didn't bother to look up. "Never heard of her."

"We both know Darlene went by the name Diantha and that she was one of your husband's spare wives, so let's not play games. He seems to like them very young. Has it always been that way?"

No response.

"Some women would feel pretty uncomfortable having their husband sleeping with girls younger than their own children," Jude said.

The gray head finally lifted and Naoma smoothed the tidal wave of hair that loomed several inches above her forehead. Jude wondered if this elaborate coiffure was mandatory for polygamist women, or if they'd adopted it because they thought it was captivating. Naoma was staring at her like she would love to practice her tongue excision technique, right here, right now.

Jude referred to her notes for a moment or two so her subject could enjoy the fantasy, then asked, "Is it true that one of your husband's wives is also his daughter by another wife?"

From all accounts, polygamist family trees were like a bad soap opera, girls marrying uncles who were also their stepfathers, half brothers and sisters marrying, then their progeny marrying the grandfather. The Eppersons were no exception.

Naoma sipped the water she was holding. Her face was stubbornly set, her attitude one of martyred disgust. "The Lord's elect have a duty to keep our bloodline pure of contamination. Anyone who mingles their seed with the seed of Cain loses all right to priesthood blessings."

"You're telling me people of other ethnicities are inferior and God thinks incest is a good idea?"

"I would not expect you to understand the higher goal that we must aspire to as the chosen people."

Jude realized she was going to get nowhere fast trying to make this woman feel ashamed. Naoma Epperson firmly believed her lifestyle was mandated by God and that she was being victimized by the servants of Satan. Changing direction, Jude took several photographs of the Gathering for Zion montage from her file and laid them out on the table.

"This is an amazing piece of work. Wonderful detail."

Naoma's pudding face registered an expression Jude couldn't quite read. It lay somewhere between embarrassment and gratification.

Hoping she was interpreting this correctly, Jude summoned a trace of awe and asked, "Did you paint it yourself, Mrs. Epperson?"

"Yes."

Jude's mind raced. Naoma was proud of her painting. She had an ego. Amazing, given the life she must have led. Wondering how she could best capitalize on this chink in the head wife's armor, she said, "I'm impressed. You have a real talent."

"I apply my gift to the glory of God."

Jude pointed to the white-haired zealot in the center of the image. "Your husband, right?"

It seemed Naoma couldn't help herself. She followed the progress of Jude's finger with a faint nod.

"And here's you when you were younger, holding the hand of a little girl. Is that your daughter?"

"Yes."

"She's really beautiful. I suppose she's married now with kids of her own."

Jude wondered if she imagined a very slight tremble in Naoma's hand. The head wife poured some more water into her glass from the plastic pitcher at the end of the table. "She's far away."

Shipped off to Bountiful, Jude deduced. According to the material she'd been reading, numerous American girls were dispatched by their families to the large polygamist settlement in British Columbia. The traffic in youthful brides went both ways, with Bountiful girls shipped across the border to marry Utah men. It was one way to freshen up the gene pool, she supposed.

"How many children do you have, Mrs. Epperson?"

"Three."

Intrigued by this modest number, Jude said, "That's interesting. You know, most people on the outside have this idea that women in plural-marriage situations usually have many more."

"God chooses when to bless us with children."

"You never took birth control?"

Naoma gave her an odd look, doubtless trying to second-guess where this line of questioning was headed. "It's a sin to interfere in God's business."

"So all the members of your church simply trust that God will make the right decision about when babies should be conceived?"

"Of course."

With slight puzzlement, Jude said, "You see, I'm wondering— if that's the case, why would your menfolk keep fertility charts for their wives? If conception is entirely in God's hands, why are they interfering?"

"I don't know what you're talking about."

Jude shrugged. "I can show you. It's all over the Internet...men from your lifestyle sharing information about how to be sure they'll impregnate their wives. Charts. Mucus. Female cycles. You'd think they were talking about cattle breeding." Laughing, she added, "I guess they don't trust God to make the decisions about what is right for a woman. They think they know better."

Naoma blinked.

Deciding she had given her subject something to think about, Jude pointed to the painting again. "This woman. Fawn something...the one in the milkmaid costume."

"Fawn Dew." Naoma spat the name. A short, neatly manicured nail stabbed the picture. "And that's her brat."

No love lost there. "Downs syndrome?"

Amazingly, his condition was evident from the image. Naoma was no slouch. Out in the real world she could probably have made a decent living painting portraits.

With a short, disdainful grunt, the head wife said, "He's not my husband's child."

"I see." Jude studied the picture a moment longer, then as if she'd only just noticed the grotesque hunchback, she said, "And this guy. Is he really contorted like this or did the paint melt or something?"

"I paint as I see," Naoma snapped, clearly affronted by the suggestion of sloppy craft.

"I'm sorry. I didn't mean to offend. If he's your son, I—"

"He's not."

"He's still alive?"

"Yes."

"Amazing. Does he work or is he an invalid?" When Naoma didn't answer, she continued, "It must be a terrible burden caring for someone with such disabilities, medical treatment costing what it does. And of course there's the stress. His mother must be very patient."

A small sniff. "His mother is mentally handicapped. I brought him up myself."

Jude processed that information and tried not to leap to any conclusions. Had Naoma trained an obedient and grateful "son" rejected by all but her? Anxious to please? Mommie Dearest's hit man?

"I guess sharing the load is one of the advantages of the larger family structure," Jude said. "It must be a relief to know you won't be missed the way a mother would normally be. In a typical family. I mean, where she's the one everybody depends on."

Naoma worked her jaw.

Blithely, Jude directed a question at Tulley. "Deputy, would you say judges tend to be lenient with mothers who commit a first offense because they don't want to punish the children?"

"I've seen it happen. This would be different. For a start, you've got all those other wives just waiting to step into her shoes."

"I think you're right about that," Jude said.

"They're probably in her bedroom right now, dividing up her stuff," Tulley continued. "Times like this, you see what folks are made of. Anyone with a grudge—man, they'll be dancing on her bed."

Jude nodded sagely and leaned a little closer to Naoma, mixing a trace of sympathy with her satisfaction. "They're going to put you inside and throw away the key, Mrs. Epperson. We don't even need a confession. We got ourselves an eyewitness, and he can't wait to testify that he watched you cut Darlene Huntsberger's tongue right out of her head."

"You think this will go before a court? You're sadly mistaken." Naoma dripped smug disdain.

Jude laughed and turned to Tulley. "Go find out if the sheriff's faxed over those extradition papers yet."

Confusion wiped the smugness from Naoma's face. "What are you talking about? You can't try me in Colorado for something that happened in Utah."

"Sure we can," Jude said cheerfully. "The thing is, we're bringing kidnapping and conspiracy charges against you, and the kidnapping happened in Colorado."

"I didn't kidnap anybody."

"Know something? I believe you. But my boss—he doesn't care who we put away, just so long as someone pays. You know how that goes. He needs to get himself reelected, and this case has them all riled up back in Colorado. They're looking to make an example."

She paused as Tulley reentered the room. He gave a thumbs-up.

"I was telling Mrs. Epperson what she can expect," Jude said. "Reckon Sheriff Pratt will go for the death penalty?"

"You bet. He wants that family values vote real bad."

"Yeah, those pro-lifers are busting for an execution," Jude said. "It's been a while in Colorado. Nineteen ninety-seven, I think. Was that the gas chamber?"

"Nah. They hanged him," Tulley lied cheerfully, playing up their Wild West credentials.

"What?" Naoma sat forward, flushed and breathing heavily.

Jude hoped she wasn't going to have a heart attack. She contemplated backing off a little, but the clock was ticking. They needed a confession so they could get a search warrant and have a statement that implicated Nathaniel Epperson.

In a businesslike tone, she informed Naoma, "If we'd liberated Darlene alive, the death penalty wouldn't apply. Unfortunately for you, she turned up dead."

"But I didn't kill her," the denial tumbled out.

"That's not our problem. I recommend you see a lawyer once we get to Colorado. You'll be needing the best defense your husband can buy for you."

"Kidnapping." Tulley swept his black-Irish bangs away from the plaster on his brow. "That's a class one felony. A hangin' offense."

"Lethal injection, nowadays," Jude corrected.

"I heard they look quite peaceful afterward," Tulley said. "That's nice."

Naoma could struggle all she liked to keep her face impassive, but fear and fury flashed from her small blue eyes. In a voice like wet gravel, she grated, "I can pay for my own lawyer."

"Uh-huh." Jude gave a disbelieving smile.

Like a trapped rat, Naoma insisted, "I have money." She groped around beneath her skirts and produced a credit card. Slapping this down on the table, she said, "I want my own lawyer. Not one my husband hires."

"I think you're making a mistake," Jude replied like she had no idea why Naoma might not want an attorney who'd be looking after Nathaniel's best interests instead of hers. "Your church has a ton of money. I'm sure they'll hire a good defense team for you. I could make a call right now to Mr. Rockwell and let him know of your dire situation."

"No!" Naoma banged her fist down next to the credit card. "I said I'll pay."

"Defense attorneys are expensive," Jude continued dubiously. "How much money do you have?"

"Over a million dollars." Naoma bristled. "More…I don't know."

"Don't jerk me around. Where does a woman like you get a million bucks?"

"I manage my husband's business activities."

"And he pays you that kind of money? I thought most of the people working in your church earned less than minimum wage."

"I pay myself."

"What kind of business activities are we talking about here?"

"We sell investment shares."

"In what—an oil well?"

"In the ranch. For the gathering. People pay twenty thousand dollars so they can witness the full glory of the Second Coming on the last day."

Jude glanced sideways in time to see Tulley's jaw descend. "Wait. You're telling me Jesus Christ is coming to your ranch, and you're selling tickets?"

She tried to imagine what kind of person would be taken in by a scam like that. Presumably the same kind who bought that shit about FLDS prophets being immortal and getting advance notice of the date for Armageddon.

Tulley said, "Tickets to the Second Coming. Wait till I tell my ma. She'll probably want to buy one."

Satisfied that she'd made her point, Naoma tucked her Visa card away and reiterated her demand for a fancy attorney.

Jude said, "I'll make some calls for you. But first, because I believe you didn't kill Darlene, I'm going to do you a big favor. I'm going to offer you a chance to help yourself."

Naoma folded her arms as if she wasn't interested, but her eyes were intent.

"After we're done here, I'll be heading back to that ranch of yours to arrest your husband. Now, I could be wrong, but I think he'll bring in those high-price lawyers right away. Then he'll say whatever it takes to get himself out of here."

Naoma exhaled slowly and shakily. "My husband is above earthly trials. He is a high priest and can only be judged by God."

"Be that as it may, he's not going to want to go to jail in the meantime. In fact, he is going to do whatever his lawyers tell him to do. And guess what? They're going to tell him to blame everything on you." As Naoma turned her head away, Jude said, "C'mon, Mrs. Epperson. Don't pretend you don't know what I'm saying. How long have you been married to this man? You know exactly who he is."

"My husband will not speak of these matters."

"You think he's going to be loyal to *you* when he's got Fawn Dew waiting out there in her pretty dress?" Jude mocked. "You think he's going to go to jail to save *your* ass?"

Naoma reached for her glass. Water spilled from one side as she lifted it.

"Listen to me." Jude softened her tone. "You have one chance to tell your side of the story. If you wait, your husband is going to cut a deal and walk out of here, and you'll be left facing murder charges. Trust me. I've seen it a thousand times." Leaning on her a little harder, she said, "Once I walk out of here, your chance goes away. I'll be talking to his lawyers and taking down his statement. If you think he's going to protect you, then that's your funeral. Like I said, my boss doesn't care who gets the needle for this."

She got to her feet and Tulley unlocked the door. As Jude began to walk away, Naoma blurted, "Wait."

Jude stood still. "I'm listening."

"What do you want to know?"

"Everything. For starters, who killed Darlene?"

"Not me."

"Do you know who did?"

Naoma nodded, tight-lipped.

Jude returned to the table. "Are you willing to give me a statement about what happened without a lawyer present?"

Naoma said she was, and Jude reminded her again of her rights, then slid a waiver form in front of her and read it aloud before handing her a pen. After mentioning again that the interview was being recorded, she said, "Mrs. Epperson, I'm showing you a photograph. Do you recognize this girl?"

"Yes. She was my husband's twelfth wife. We called her Diantha."

"Do you know her real name?"

"Darlene Huntsberger."

Looking past Naoma's shoulder, Jude met Tulley's eyes. He was doing his best to act like he routinely extracted murder confessions. Only his strenuous gum-chewing and propensity for rocking back and forth on his heels gave him away. Jude had asked him if he wanted to sit at the interview table, but he'd elected the spot by the door, maintaining that handsome would buy them nothing with Naoma. He was right. All the head wife wanted to do was survive so she could spend some of the cash she'd looted from her husband's ill-gotten wealth.

"When did you first meet Darlene?" Jude asked.

"Two years ago. My husband came home from a trip to Colorado with her." Naoma's face was stony. "He said God had instructed him to take her as a wife."

"Did Darlene agree to this marriage?"

"No."

"How old was she?"

"Sixteen."

"Did she try to leave?"

"Yes. She wanted to go back to her family."

"What did your husband do?"

"He told us to purify her so that she was worthy to be sealed to him. She was under the influence of Satan."

"How did you purify her?"

Naoma gulped some water down. "We had to beat the evil from her."

"I see. Did she then agree to marry Mr. Epperson?"

Something flickered across Naoma's face. "Yes."

Jude gave her a hard look. "Well, that's not the whole story, is it? What are you leaving out?"

Naoma's eyes darted back and forth from Jude's face to the tabletop. Like most subjects, she had no idea how transparent her body language and minute facial movements were to a highly trained detective. As a consequence, she was easily disconcerted.

Grudgingly, she said, "God revealed that she should marry one of my husband's sons instead."

"And did this marriage transpire?"

"Yes."

"What was the name of the groom?"

"Hyrum Epperson." Naoma drew the family portrait closer and stuck a finger on the hunchback with the twisted face. "Him."

Hello, Mr. Snaggletooth. Jude stole a glance at Tulley. His arms were folded tightly across his chest. No doubt he could smell the ink on his commendation letter.

"But you said Darlene was your husband's twelfth wife. Was she married to both men at the same time?"

"No. She was assigned to my husband later, once she had a baby on the way. God told him it was time to take her as a wife."

The father takes the unattractive son's pregnant wife away from him. No search party needed to find a motive for murder in a sick triangle like that one. "How did Hyrum feel about that?"

Naoma shrugged. "It was the fulfillment of prophecy."

"What prophecy?"

"Before the end God will choose from among his servants one who takes the burden of his son's wife, she who multiplies his son's seed."

Jude renewed her efforts to keep her face and voice free of expression. "We'll need to confirm your story. Where can we find Hyrum?"

"He lives on the ranch."

Tulley made a covert hand signal and pointed toward his teeth. Jude shook her head slightly. Flashing the plaster teeth at Naoma would only make her add two and two. If she thought they were in possession of evidence that could pin the murder on this Hyrum individual, they would lose their leverage.

Jude pondered her theory about the well-trained human pet once more. "You were saying you brought Hyrum up because his mother couldn't manage him. Was this because of his physical disabilities?"

"Yes, but he was also possessed by demons."

"How did you know that?"

"He could not be still, and when he read the scriptures he went into fits and foamed at the mouth."

"Was he violent as a child?"

"No more than usual. I knew how to handle him."

"Did you ever take him to a doctor for his condition?"

Naoma scoffed. "You gentiles think doctors have all the answers. The Lord giveth and the Lord taketh away. My husband laid his hands upon Hyrum and our prayers were answered."

"God healed him?"

"Not on the outside. But my husband received direction and he put Hyrum to work serving God instead of Satan."

Jude wondered if Naoma really believed this. The woman didn't strike her as an idiot, more likely a survivor, with a survivor's adaptability and cunning. "What kind of work?"

"When my husband receives commands, Hyrum helps him carry them out."

Jude took that to mean Nathaniel used his maimed son to do anything he didn't want to dirty his hands with. She asked point blank, "Did God command that Darlene should be killed?"

"He must have."

Jude slowly released a breath and kept her face carefully impassive. "Because your husband carried out the killing?"

"Yes. He received word from the Heavenly Father that Darlene had betrayed us and would have to atone by the spilling of blood. She had to be eliminated before she gave birth to an innocent who would be corrupted."

"I heard that in your community babies are taken from unfit mothers and raised by others."

"That happens," Naoma conceded. "But God wanted this baby returned to him in heaven before Satan claimed it."

"When did you last see Darlene alive?"

"Sunday, a month ago."

"Tell me about that day. Where did you see her? What happened?"

"We were in the great room, praying and reading the scriptures together like we always do on the Lord's day. That was when my husband received the revelation. When he proclaimed it, Darlene rejected God's word and tried to run away."

"Too pregnant to get far, I'm sure."

"Yes. We brought her back so she could pray for the salvation of her soul."

Jude nodded. What was wrong with these people? "What happened then?"

"After prayers, my husband took her away and I never saw her again."

"Where was she killed?"

"I'm not sure."

"Do you know how she was killed?"

Naoma hesitated. "Was her throat cut?"

"I'm asking you."

"I said I wasn't there. My husband didn't tell me what they did."

They. "Then what makes you think her throat was cut?"

Naoma was suddenly agitated. "You're trying to trick me into saying something that makes me look like the guilty one."

Jude studied her in silence. Over the years, she'd learned that amateur criminals were typically unnerved by prolonged scrutiny and would attempt to fill the uncomfortable silence. She played chicken with Naoma for several minutes, the head wife getting increasingly red-faced and restless.

Finally Jude allowed herself a sympathetic smile. "Let's face it, Mrs. Epperson. You haven't given me a thing. So far, it's your word against your husband's. Who do you think the jury is going to believe? A man prominent in his church, who has a house full of wives—it's not like he needs to kill one to marry another. Or a head wife jealous of a young, beautiful woman who's taken her place?"

Breathing hard, Naoma blurted, "I can prove Nathaniel did it. I kept the proof!"

"Go on," Jude feigned boredom.

"He gave his raiment to me to wash. It was soaked in blood and there was a knife in the pocket. That's why I thought they cut her throat."

"What did you do with the clothing and the knife?"

Naoma eyes glittered with malice. "I put them in a trash bag and hid it in one of the barns."

Jude felt her fingers curl into her palm and, for a moment, she kept the fist closed. A smoking gun. Naoma could parrot the submit-yourself crap all she wanted, but Gossett was right. This first wife hated her husband with a passion, and she was not as brainwashed as she made out. Not only had she siphoned a million bucks from his Armageddon scam, she'd kept herself an insurance policy in case she ever needed something to hold over him. Proof of his involvement in a murder—it didn't get any better. Like a prisoner investing twenty years in digging a tunnel to freedom, Naoma had her eyes on the future, and she'd done whatever it took to survive in the meantime.

"I'll need that evidence to prove you're innocent," Jude said blandly.

"If you let me go, I'll tell you where it is."

"Not an option. I'll talk to the state attorney about reduced charges. But without that trash bag, I can promise you, you're going down."

She hoped Sergeant Gossett could obtain a warrant without going through the prophet's tame judge. The ranch was on the Utah side of the boundary, and from what she'd ascertained, Mohave County had arrest authority, but who knew what would happen if the Utah powers-that-be caught a sniff of trouble brewing.

"Diantha was better off dead," Naoma said with a trace of belligerence.

Jude bit back an angry retort and reminded herself that this woman was a victim too. She would serve time, and she would help nail the men who were the real criminals. It had to be enough.

Schooling her expression to one of unruffled tranquility, she slid a notepad across the table and said, "Draw me a map."

The head wife looked her dead in the eye. "How long will I be in prison?"

"My guess? Five years." As Naoma began sketching, Jude asked, "Where were you planning to go?"

Naoma didn't pretend not to know what Jude was talking about. "Mexico."

Jude summoned Tulley over and said, "Would you bring in some refreshments for Mrs. Epperson. Maybe a sandwich and a soda…"

Naoma looked up. "I'll take a Turkey sandwich and Pepsi. And fetch me some ice cream. Ben and Jerry's Karamel Sutra flavor. You can find that at the supermarket in Colorado City. Get two of them."

Before Tulley could articulate a response, Jude said, "You heard the lady. Karamel Sutra."

She stared at the bland beige wall as Naoma drew her picture. She would give a month's pay to slap this woman's face, but there was prima facie evidence to collect and a pair of handcuffs with Nathaniel Epperson's name written on them. She could live with that.

CHAPTER TWELVE

This is a problem," Sergeant Gossett said. He handed his binoculars to Jude.

They were parked about seventy-five yards from the Epperson house, Gossett standing next to his Ford pickup, Jude and Tulley beside a spare Mohave County black-and-white, and several deputies providing backup. It was not going to be enough. The place was barricaded, wood nailed over the windows, the barrels of rifles protruding from narrow gaps. The door had been fortified with a heavy iron grille bolted into place and, making as much sense as anything else about the cult, a Confederate flag was flying. Said charming touch aimed at the inevitable media, Jude supposed.

Her every instinct screamed. The situation had trouble with a capital *T* written all over it. "I think we should back off. It doesn't look good."

"Epperson won't hang around," Gossett said. "If we don't pick him up now, he'll be in Canada next time we come knocking."

"I want to nail him too." She didn't add that she also wanted to get out of Utah without a major incident. "But for now, my priority is securing that evidence."

"This can work as a distraction." Gossett was full of bright ideas. "We'll keep them occupied while you search that barn."

"Let's just notify Epperson of the search and get on with it. Then we should leave."

"I hear you," Gossett said. "But since we're out here, we might as well try to bring him in. You never know. Sometimes people just want a way out."

Jude shrugged, unwilling to overstep and risk their ability to do business in Gossett's jurisdiction. If she was going to screw up their working arrangement, she needed to wait until after she had the murder weapon. She could see where Gossett was coming from. Cops like him spent their whole lives fighting the good fight, invisible and taken for granted, never getting a sniff at a glamour case. If Gossett was looking to make his mark before retiring, this was it. No matter how badly it panned out, there would probably be some fat in it for a guy like him, maybe even a book deal.

"It's your call," she said.

Gossett picked up a bullhorn, identified himself, and announced, "Nathaniel Epperson. We have a search warrant for the buildings and vehicles on this ranch. My staff will now proceed with the search. Should you wish to view the warrant, please lay down your arms and step out of the building with your hands on your head."

The rifles remained in position, their barrels moving slightly until they were trained on the four police vehicles.

Gossett continued, "We don't want anyone getting hurt here. Come out with your hands on your head. I personally guarantee your safety."

The tableau remained inert, then, in a crackle of static, Epperson's reply boomed contemptuously from a bullhorn of his own. "My safety is guaranteed by God. Yea, I will dwell forever in his heavenly sanctuary, where the crown, the heart, the seed, the feet, are unified into the most precious metal, paving the very streets with gold. Thus is the alchemy of the doctrine."

"I left D.C. for this?" Jude muttered.

"I don't think he's coming out." Tulley fidgeted with his bulletproof vest. Lowering his voice, he murmured to Jude, "What are we doing here? Why didn't Gossett call the FBI?"

"He's trying to avoid an escalation."

"Could have fooled me." Tulley cast a pointed look at the beefy sergeant.

He was dishing out orders to one of his deputies. "Call the state patrol. We need road blocks before this turns into a circus, 'cos it's going to." Catching a frown from Jude, he explained, "Don't want to take any chances. If this goes out of control, the plygs will swarm in from the twin towns."

"Terrific." He had the fever. Jude had seen it before. Adrenaline could divorce the sanest people from their common sense and situations could suddenly gather a momentum of their own. It was on the brink of happening here.

"I'm calling Kingman," Gossett went on. "We better get the Tactical Operations Unit out here."

"Good plan." Jude was aware of the clock ticking. She needed to get that evidence and extract herself and Tulley before this went south in a big way.

She scanned the outbuildings until she spotted the one that met Naoma's description. Her objective was a small barn in poor repair, the farthest of three southwest of the house. Part of the building was charred from a fire. Jude figured she could make it as far as the large new barn nearest it without being seen. Then there was a stretch of about fifty yards in the open, completely visible to anyone watching from the north-south wing of the house.

There was always the possibility that the outbuildings themselves were staked out. Jude could see no sign of the search party on the surrounding hills. It seemed more than likely that they were holed up with Epperson, busting to defend his right to break any law he wanted on the grounds of "religious belief."

She said, "That's the objective. Farthest building to the right."

"You could take one of the cars," Gossett suggested.

"No. We need to group the vehicles for a shield."

Three Ford PLs, a pickup and seven officers. Not exactly a show of force. There had to be at least thirty adults in that house, all of the males armed. And, if Fawn Dew was anything to go by, Epperson's wives were gun-friendly too.

Jude studied the outbuildings closest to them, looking for protruding rifles or signs of movement. The windows and vents were too high for easy access. Any prospective snipers would have to be hanging from the rafters. But she had a feeling no one was out there. Epperson wanted a Waco. That much was obvious. He would have everyone assembled in that house, so if the whole thing went up in smoke the body count would be as high as possible.

"I'll come with you," Tulley said.

Jude sized things up and decided Gossett needed the extra man more than she did. "No. Stay here." The gentle command earned a whipped-puppy look. Ignoring it, she addressed the sergeant. "How long before the TOU makes it?"

"Assume an hour. The boss says they'll bring a chopper."

"We don't want to be stuck here without a SWAT team for that long," Jude said. "So I'm going in to collect that evidence, then we're backing off."

Gossett seemed to be having second thoughts about his Rambo role at last. "Yeah. We'll only get our humps busted if these screwballs want to blow themselves up and blame the government."

Jude thought about a house full of children whose parents would probably bc willing to let them die to score points against the authorities. They couldn't allow this to escalate into a showdown. Once she had her evidence, they could leave and do nothing for a few days. Let Epperson cool off and get distracted wondering what his head wife was saying. Keep the place under surveillance and wait for the plygs to drift away. They could escort Naoma to Cortez and come back for her husband at a later date with the right personnel. There was a sane way to get the desired outcome. All she had to do was collect that trash bag and they could take Epperson when the time was right.

"You're right about that diversion," she told Gossett. "How about if you move the vehicles in closer and exchange a few more words with Epperson while I make a run for the barn."

"You got it."

They piled into the cars, Tulley looking like his firstborn just died.

Weapon in hand, Jude moved away from the group and skirted the first barn, her back to the wall. The second had a grain silo on top. In a matter of seconds, she covered the distance to take refuge in its shadow. She allowed herself exactly a minute to calm her breathing and survey her surroundings once more for signs of activity. In an odd way it was like a training exercise at Quantico. She felt cold and detached, yet tightly coiled, adrenaline charging her muscles with tension.

Taking a quick, deep breath, she stepped out into the sunlight and ran. Within seconds she heard the familiar pop of a gunshot. She hit the ground and crawled on her elbows, thinking the whole time, *it really is like Quantico, only the bullets are real.* Her blood group leapt to mind. AB-negative with a few unusual antigens, rare enough that she made extra donations to the blood bank. She kept meaning to freeze some, just in case. Even though she could accept blood from a good proportion of the population, she supposed in a transfusion it was always better to use your own.

Gossett's voice echoed through the late afternoon torpor. "Hold your fire. Mr. Epperson, you are placing your family in danger. Lay down your weapons."

Predictably, the reply was a short barrage, but none of the shots came Jude's way. She scrambled to her feet and bolted the final twenty yards to her target.

The barn was hot and dark and smelled disgusting. Jude tried to codify the choking stench. Urine, feces, putrifying flesh, rotting vegetables, burnt timber. Shafts of light from fissures in the roof cast zebra shadows across the dirt floor. As her eyes adapted, she saw what Naoma had described, a wooden ladder leading to a loft. She was a few feet away from it when she began hearing sounds other than the rush of blood coursing through her arteries. A grunt, low whines, a faint wheezing noise like a chuckle. Animal sounds, their source perhaps ten feet away, coming from the deep shadows beneath the loft. She froze and aimed in their direction. The rasp of rapid, heavy breathing made her fingers tighten on the pistol grip.

Her instincts urged her to shoot. Her mind reasoned that anything could be cowering there in the darkness, a frightened woman, a sick animal, a youngster like Zach. She had not been attacked. There was no justification for her to open fire. The smell was overpowering, burning her nose and throat.

Gagging, she identified herself and said, "I won't hurt you. Step away from the wall. Put your hands on your head. Come out where I can see you."

The wheezing grew louder. Something shifted and the outline of a figure came into view. He was virtually naked, hunched and drooling from a terribly misshapen mouth. As far as she could tell, he was also unarmed.

"Hyrum?" Jude asked.

The man made a gurgling sound.

"I'm glad I found you. We need to talk." Jude reached slowly for her handcuffs and took several steps closer. Gently, she said, "I want you to come with me. I have food and water. First I need for you to lie down on the ground."

He dropped into a crouch. Feral eyes glimmered a warning at her and between one breath and the next, Hyrum Epperson uttered a low, guttural howl and sprang at her, clasping her around the legs, throwing her off balance. Pain shot through her thigh as his teeth sank in. For such a mangled human being, he moved with power and agility, pinning her down, clawing at her throat, resisting her frantic attempts to throw him off.

The barrel of her gun was wedged to his chest. Jude shouted, "Get off me or I'll shoot."

He ripped her radio away and tore at her shirt with his teeth, then found her shoulder, gouging viciously into her flesh. His hands tightened around her throat and Jude understood she was not going to be able to fight him off unless she dropped her weapon to free her right hand. She could not even move the gun away from his heart; it was the only thing stopping his weight from descending completely. One last time, she fought to break his grip and roll him off her, but he was crushing her windpipe.

She had no choice.

Jude pulled the trigger, and the hands around her throat instantly relinquished their grip. His body was thrown back, blood spraying. She hurriedly elbowed herself away and scrambled up, her gun still trained on him. His eyelids fluttered and he released a single deep sigh. Then his gaze was unseeing. Gun gases and smoke stained the air. Jude tapped the barrel of her 19 against her shoe and a small clump of gore plopped onto the hay. Fuck, she thought. The same human tartare was all over her face and through her hair, too.

With one foot, she nudged him. Then she knelt and took his pulse, the 19 hard against his temple. Hyrum Epperson was dead. She had killed a person who belonged in a mental hospital, a suspect she'd hoped would help make the case against Epperson. Shaking violently, she lurched to her feet and leaned against the wooden ladder. Her blood-soaked clothing reeked of iron, and adding to the general foulness of the environment, Hyrum had emptied his bowels. Now she had to climb into the loft and find the trash bag.

"God damn these people," she croaked, clutching her injured throat. "Fuck you, Nathaniel Epperson. Fuck you and the horse you rode in on."

❖

"That was a gunshot," Fawn Dew said. "Sounds like it came from over there." She pointed at the barns on their side of the house.

Standing beside her, Summer clutched her belly. Liquid gushed from between her legs and an agonizing pain made her double up. "I think I'm having the baby," she sobbed.

"Fetch the master," Fawn Dew ordered.

One of the women cleaning weapons on the floor scrambled to her feet and ran from the room. Another, Thankful, stood up and came to Summer's side. "Looks like your waters have broken," she said, leading her to the bed.

Terrified, Summer lay down and curled onto her side. The pain intensified like a rubber band tightening around her middle.

"What are we going to do?" Thankful asked Fawn Dew, who was looking through binoculars.

Without turning around, Fawn Dew replied, "Get some water and keep her quiet. Birth pain is the price we pay for the blessing of children and the master expects that we bear it sweetly and silently."

Summer had heard it all before and she wanted to scream anyway. How was this huge baby ever going to get out of her body? Part of her was desperate to be rid of it, another part was eager to see her child after all these months. But mostly she was afraid. And thirsty, so thirsty her tongue felt like it was glued to her teeth.

Thankful placed a hand to her brow and said, "Don't be afraid, sister. I'll fetch a cool washcloth."

"And water. Please."

Thankful was her best friend among her sister-wives. She was not one of Nathaniel's favorites, which meant that she seldom shared his bed and was landed with some of the worst chores. She and Summer often helped one another out with their workloads and Summer made sure to watch out for Thankful's eight kids.

"What's happening?" she asked Fawn Dew as the pain eased. "Why are the police here again?"

"I knew that fat old bitch couldn't keep her mouth shut," Fawn Dew spat. "She's told them a pack of lies, just like I said she would."

"I don't understand."

Fawn Dew cast a swift, scornful look at her then gazed back out the window. "She'll pay for it. She will atone in blood for her betrayal."

As Fawn Dew continued her tirade, Summer felt a tightening just below the hot heavy lump of her belly. Pain amplified from front to back, stealing her breath. She turned her face into the pillow to muffle the sharp cry she could not arrest. How long would this go on? Since she'd been living at Gathering for Zion, four babies had been born. Thankful had popped her newest daughter out in two hours, but one of the other wives had been in labor for almost three days, then the baby was born dead. Everyone said her lack of faith was the cause and that God had found her unfit to be a mother.

Summer felt a crawling fear that she too might be found wanting and punished. With all her heart, she prayed, silently assuring the Heavenly Father that she submitted herself completely unto His will and would keep herself sweet, no matter what.

❖

"You hear that?" Tulley asked, frantically zooming the binoculars in on the door of the broken down barn. He reached for the door handle.

In the driver's seat, Gossett said, "Give it a minute, son."

"No, sir. I'm going in. That was a single shot."

He pictured a crazy guy squeezing his trigger, Jude Devine in his sights. He'd probably shot her in the back. That was exactly the cowardly shit you'd expect from people who'd slaughter innocent dogs in cold blood. Zach had told him all about that terrible day when they'd killed his dog, Sam. Tulley wanted to find those guys and see how they liked being rounded up into a pen and shot to pieces. If there was one thing he couldn't stand, it was animal cruelty. The other thing was the thought of Jude lying wounded in that barn.

Gossett had a hold of his shoulder. "Fifty bucks says that was a model 19 we heard. If she didn't fire again, that means her target's down. You ever seen what a .357 Magnum does to a guy?"

"There's nothing moving out there." Every second counted if the sergeant was wrong about the gun. "I'm going in."

"Suit yourself."

What the heck was that supposed to mean? Tulley gave the guy a look. "Sir, a shot has been fired and we're not getting any communication."

Gossett shrugged. "She told you to stay put is all." But he backed up his truck so they were screened by the other vehicles. "Okay, Deputy. Get in there. We got you covered."

Tulley didn't wait around. He dived out of the pickup and made a run for it, reaching the first barn in Olympic record time. Nothing was moving and he glanced back toward the truck. The sergeant waved him on and he sprinted to the next big barn, holding his gun extended in front of him with both hands. This made running kind of awkward and when he reached the corner of the barn, he paused for a few seconds to catch his breath and take a look around.

Ahead of him lay the open expanse of dirt he would have to cross. They could see it from the house, that's if they were looking. He wondered if he should crawl across it instead of running. Or maybe he should run crouched with his pistol in one hand. It wasn't like he was under fire. Not yet, anyway.

He peered around the corner of the barn trying to make out if there were rifles jutting from the boarded up windows along the south facing elbow of the house. He was too far away to be sure. An image flashed into his mind—himself standing in front of the entire Cortez PD and Sheriff's Office at the annual ceremony, getting the medal for valor. That would mean a promotion, for sure.

He darted across the open space, but only made a few strides when something whizzed past him and he heard the pop pop of shooting. Dust sprayed at his foot where a bullet hit the ground. The barn door swung open and Jude stood there drenched in blood.

"Get down!" she yelled.

Which was exactly what happened. He fell. Flat on his face. But it wasn't an intentional dive. His legs were knocked out from under him. Pain erupted and he grabbed his left thigh. Blood spurted between his fingers. He loosened his bulletproof vest so he could move better.

"I'm hit!" Did that squeal belong to him?

Jude pointed to the large barn behind him and shouted, "Go back! Go!" She picked up a black trash bag. Clutching it to her, she ran.

"No! Get down," he begged, but she wasn't listening.

Tulley tried to shuffle backward toward the barn, hanging on to his leg. Dust sprayed in his face where another bullet earthed. His heart pounded in his ears and he hurled himself around and managed to get to his feet, balancing on his good leg. Bullets zinged and hissed. A laser pierced his side, and he felt his flesh curdle. Pain and sweat blinded him and he sagged to his knees. He knew he should have tightened that vest again.

He heard Jude yelling like a slave-driver, "Move!" and "Go, Tulley!" then a stampede of feet.

The trash bag soared past him and landed somewhere ahead. A hand caught hold of his arm beneath the shoulder and the wind was knocked out of him as Jude hauled him into a fireman's lift and staggered the remaining yards.

Seconds later they were both on the ground in the shade of the barn and she had her shirt off, ripping at it with a pocket knife. Underneath it, her white T-shirt was glued to her body, soaked in blood.

Panicking, Tulley asked, "Where'd he get you?"

"I'm not hit. But you should see the other guy."

Tulley didn't have the strength to laugh like a normal person. His teeth were chattering, and a sound like a girly hiccup rose from his throat. He covered his mouth, frightened he was about to throw up.

Jude touched his shoulder. "Okay, buddy?"

He nodded, not trusting himself to speak.

"I'm going to fucking kill him," she announced with dark calm as she fastened a tourniquet around his leg.

"I thought you already did." Tulley craned to see the barn. Was there a second assailant?

Jude took the radio from his shoulder and got Gossett on the other end, "Officer down. I repeat, officer down. Get your truck over here. Now."

Her voice was scratchy and uneven and she placed a hand to her throat. It was red and purple with bruises.

Tulley stared at the injury. He could make out the imprint of fingers. "Your neck...what happened?"

"I behaved like an amateur. We need to get this off." She removed the vest, then unbuttoned his shirt and helped him shrug out of it. The whole time she was mumbling the kinds of cusswords Tulley could only say in his head. "If I have to use my bare hands, I'm going to take him apart," she noted as she drew Tulley's T-shirt up and examined the wound to his side. Her hands dripped blood. She stared down at his midriff with a frown.

Embarrassed, Tulley said, "I got bullied real bad in school."

"Are those from cigarette butts?"

"Yes, ma'am." He touched a familiar scar above his heart. "And this one is where a guy carved his initials."

"I see." Her expression didn't change. "How's the pain?"

"Pretty bad."

The Ford pickup jerked to a halt a few yards away and Gossett jumped out. He was carrying an HK MP5 like he knew how to use it. Amazed to see a peace officer with the kind of close-quarters battle weapon you'd normally expect to find in the hands of a SWAT team member, Tulley said, "I don't think he won that in a poker game."

Jude placed Tulley's hand firmly against his ribs and instructed with grim humor, "Try not to bleed too much." She stood up and greeted Gossett. Indicating the submachine gun, she asked, "Got another one of those in the truck?"

"As a matter of fact, I do. You tactical weapons trained?"

"Yep."

He grinned. "I kinda guessed that."

"We need to get him to the hospital."

"No point waiting for a bus. Deputy Gonzales better take him."

"Where's your first aid kit?"

"I got it." He headed back to the truck, talking into his radio.

Jude crouched down next to Tulley and said, "They both look like flesh wounds. You'll be fine."

He glanced down at his wet red hand, surprised at how composed he felt now that the urge to vomit had passed. "Do you think I'll get a promotion?"

Jude's sleepy stone moss eyes swept his face and she cocked her head like she hadn't heard right. "Okay. Now I get it. You weren't rushing to my assistance like Sir Galahad. You were shopping for a bullet so you could increase your take-home pay."

She was teasing, Tulley decided. Sometimes it was hard to tell with her. She kept a straight face like she meant every word. The eyes were flat, the mouth hard and not too feminine either. She had a mulish look about her—that's what his ma said after they met at the ceremony for Smoke'm. Tulley wasn't sure if he'd go that far, but the detective wasn't soft or pretty and she didn't wear lipstick. Some of the guys said she was probably a lesbian, but they only made their dumb remarks behind her back. Too scared to say it to her face was Tulley's guess. She had that effect on people. He saw it all the time.

He thought maybe it was because she didn't smile that much, and Steve Abbott down at the shooting range said she shot like she was born with a six-shooter in one hand and a Winchester in the other. She could put three bullets in the same hole at 300 yards and never went over 0.5

MOA. Abbott said she must be sniper trained. No one at the MCSO had a scorecard like hers.

She didn't say a whole lot, either, and Tulley didn't ask too many questions, even though the boys in Cortez were busting their asses to know why she'd left the FBI and who she talked to on her cell phone. Since Tulley had gotten himself assigned to Paradox, he'd gone up in the popularity stakes, which wasn't that big of a deal. When you're at rock bottom, things can only get better. The sheriff's office reminded him of school sometimes, only these days no one called him a faggot or stole his clothes, and he didn't get beat up in the john.

He had thought everything would be different if he moved to a place where no one knew him and no one would ever hear about his humiliations in high school. He didn't stutter anymore; he'd spent a year curing himself of that before he went to the police academy. Yet he wondered if people still heard some trace of his speech defect. He spoke slowly and sang any complicated sentences in his head first, but sometimes he caught them staring at him all weird or smirking when they thought he couldn't see. He never knew if it was his imagination or not.

He felt his hand pulled away from his ribs and Jude poured some medical-smelling fluid into his wound, then taped gauze over it front and back. She sat him up and wrapped a bandage around his middle, saying, "I want your abs, pal."

Tulley laughed, then winced, and Jude ran a gentle hand over his hair, moving it back off his face with the absent-minded tenderness of a mom like the ones on TV. The gesture took him by surprise.

"I'm truly sorry to have put you in harm's way, Detective. You shouldn't have rescued me like that."

She said, "Jesus, Tulley, I was rescuing myself. I just happened to haul your ass out of there at the same time."

He looked at her damaged neck again. It was even more purple. "What happened in the barn?"

"I met Hyrum."

"Mr. Snaggletooth?" Tulley wished he could go see.

"Otherwise known as the deceased." She looked at his leg wound but let it be, then took his pulse.

"You took him out?"

"He got up close and personal. I don't appreciate that in any man, let alone one who stank like him."

Tulley wanted to say something about the attempted strangulation that wasn't insulting. Obviously she was sensitive about what had happened and was playing it down. Her pride was at stake, he thought. Best thing he could do was make like it was no big deal.

Cheerfully, he said, "Guess the dust was the last thing that mutant'll be biting."

This drew one of her rare smiles. "Think you can walk to the truck?"

❖

"Sounded like gunshots," Adeline said.

They both hung out of the cave mouth and stared around the valley. The figures they'd seen drawing closer that morning had retreated to the ranch a few hours back. Daniel said maybe they'd given up, but Adeline wasn't so sure. In the distance she could make out the same cluster of vehicles parked in the Epperson's yard. No one had gone home. Maybe they were just resting up in the heat of the day.

"You want to get going?" Daniel asked.

Adeline had been trying to decide whether this was the time to make their move. They couldn't stay in the cave forever with Daniel's leg the way it was. But it would be crazy to leave if the searchers were going to come back at any moment.

"If they don't come back, we'll leave tomorrow morning," she said.

"Where will we go?"

"We have to find a road. Then we'll follow it north and when we're clear of this place, we'll hitch a ride."

Daniel looked uncertain. "Everyone's looking for us."

"Everyone's looking for *me*. A girl. Two boys trying to get a ride out of this place—you think they'll try and stop us? I doubt it."

Several more of the distinctive cracks sounded in the distance and Daniel said, "I reckon they're coming from the ranch. Look, there's lights flashing." He pointed slightly away from the house.

"They've called the cops." Adeline said, shocked.

"Go!" Daniel urged. "I'll stay here and when they find me I'll tell them we split up and you went the other way."

She tried to decide. Without Daniel slowing her down she could probably hike ten miles by nightfall. She had no idea how far they were from the road she'd traveled along a week ago, but it couldn't be more than a couple of days' walk. But what if the police didn't find Daniel? What if he waited another day, then tried to make it out of here alone?

"Let's wait and see what happens." She shielded her eyes against the light. If old man Epperson had called in the cops to look for her, why weren't they out here already? Why were they parked away from the house with their lights flashing? Who was shooting?

She had an idea. "I think there's something going on down there. Maybe I'll go see."

"Are you crazy?"

She fidgeted with the pocketknife. He was right. It was a dumb idea. "I had my own cell phone when I lived with Aunt Chastity," she said, knowing he'd be impressed. Women and kids weren't allowed to use phones in any plyg family she knew. "My daddy took it off me when they brought me back here. Wish I had it now."

She slid back down into the cave and worked open a can of beans with the attachment on Daniel's knife. She was about to discard the lid when a shaft of light hit the metal and beamed onto the rear wall of the cave. Adeline stared at the illuminated spot, then wiped the lid clean and placed it on the cloth bundle that held her most important possessions. Once she and Daniel started their long hike, they would need a way to signal one another if they got separated for any reason. That was something else she'd learned from Aunt Chastity. A tin can lid could act like a mirror. She scavenged the litter pile in the corner of their hideaway and located another one.

As she cleaned it off, Daniel moved gingerly down from the lip of the cave and settled on the cool rock next to her. They shared the can of beans in silence.

Adeline couldn't stop thinking about her phone. It was the obvious answer to their problems. How come she hadn't thought about it sooner? Irritated, she mumbled, "I am so dumb."

Daniel said, "What?"

"We don't have to hitch rides all the way to Salt Lake City. All we have to do is find a phone and call Aunt Chastity, and she'll come pick us up!"

Daniel's forehead crumpled into a puzzled frown like this was a really bizarre idea. "Where can we find one?"

"I don't know, but I need to go see."

Daniel's expression grew nervous. "You want me to wait here?"
She took his hand. "I promise I'll come back for you. Okay?"

"Take the knife."

"No. You need it to open cans." Adeline assessed their dwindling
water supply. "You remember how to get water from the dew?"

He nodded, and she took their last full bottle, leaving him with
one that had enough in it to get him through the night. She packed the
water in her cloth kit along with a few eggs she'd left out in the sun to
cook inside their shells the day before. Then she started back up to the
cave mouth.

"Good luck," Daniel called after her.

He sounded so worried, she stopped and turned around. He was
crying, his hands over his face. Adeline put her kit down and went back
over to kneel next to him.

It was forbidden to hug a boy, but she held him tight anyway and
said, "When all this is over, we'll have as much food as we can eat and
we'll get to sleep in beds with soft pillows made of feathers."

He drooped against her, making her shoulder moist. "I'll pray for
you."

Adeline wished she could feel comforted by that, but she knew it
wasn't God who was going to save her. She had to do that for herself.

CHAPTER THIRTEEN

After Gonzales drove off with Tulley, Jude stowed the evidence in a cooler in the back of Gossett's truck, climbed into the passenger seat and retrieved the spare MP5 from behind it. She and the sergeant shut their doors, hit the aircon, and sat in silence as the adrenaline tide washed out.

"You better get those bites seen to," Gossett said after a time. "They give you a rabies shot when the biter's human?"

"Right now, I'm more interested in morphine." Jude studied the painful dentition on her shoulder. It looked like a pretty good match for the marks on Darlene's swollen body. "Could you take a photograph of this, Gossett?"

Not that it mattered anymore. Hyrum wouldn't be standing trial. Even if he had lived, he would have been found mentally incompetent; she was certain of that. But he could have led them to the murder scene and given his version of events. He could have testified against Nathaniel Epperson, and any jury would have been able to draw some conclusions about a man who had never sought medical help for his disturbed son and had instead used him as an attack dog.

Again Jude berated herself for failing to take appropriate precautions. What in hell was wrong with her? It was not like she hadn't added two and two the moment she set eyes on the drooling hunchback. He was obviously the man who had semi-cannibalized Darlene. Did she think he was going to behave rationally and allow her to cuff him without putting up a fight? Had she lost her edge living in the slow lane—playing the part of a small-town sheriff's detective, was she now thinking like one?

No, Jude realized. She had pitied Hyrum. She had seen a tortured soul and for a lethal split second she had thought: what if it were Ben? Angry with herself, she located her viscera-coated shirt and fished around in the breast pocket, retrieving the small Olympus camera she kept there. Gossett aimed it at her shoulder. Incredibly, it still took photos after its baptism in blood.

He said, "Want the one on your leg, too?"

"Sure. Why not." Jude ripped her pants away a little more and held her leg where he could get an angle on the wound.

"Make sure they test for HIV," he advised after handing the camera back. "You look like you partied with a vampire."

"Sure feels like it." She opened her cell phone and bleakly reviewed her options. It was time to call Sheriff Pratt and fill him in on the good news that the case was pretty well solved. Admittedly, she had killed one of the lead suspects, almost lost a deputy, and was now involved in an armed standoff, but hey!

Jude winced as she pulled her T-shirt sleeve back over her shoulder. Maybe she should put off talking to Pratt until after they'd notified the FBI.

Gossett read her mind. "What do you reckon? Time to bring in the big guns?"

She nodded. "Want to make the call?"

They would need to follow protocol and go through Kingman. She could just imagine how that was going to play out. A couple of Colorado cops show up and cause all kinds of trouble then head home, squeaky clean, leaving the Mohave County Sheriff to take the media heat and explain himself to the Utah cadre after calling in the FBI. This was exactly the kind of potential career-destroyer no cop in his right mind wanted to deal with.

Reading Gossett's faint hesitation, she said, "We can't delay until the TOU gets here. These people aren't going to play by the rulebook."

Gossett picked up the radio. "One thing I don't understand. What the heck is it about religion that makes people pull this crazy shit?"

"Answer that, and they'll give you the Nobel Peace Prize."

Jude wondered how long it would take Gonzalez to get to the hospital. She wished she could have gone, but Tulley's wounds were not critical and she could not leave Gossett here to deal with a problem that was largely of her making. She had to call Pratt. But first, she would need to speak with her FBI handler.

"I need to make a call," she told Gossett and cautiously got out of the truck, heading for the deep shadows behind the barn. A few yards from the vehicle, she crouched down with her back to the wall of the building and rehearsed a calm statement as she dialed.

Her contact said, "What's happening?"

"It's coming down."

"Utah?"

"Yeah. It's a standoff. Subjects barricaded in a domestic dwelling. Maybe twenty armed adults plus an unknown number of civilian women and children."

"Who's dealing?"

"We're calling in federal support now."

A faint pause. "Get your ass out of there."

"Sir, I can't leave until support arrives. We only have five officers present."

"Copy that. But Hawke watches TV. As soon as the situation is under control, you're back in Paradox."

"Got you."

There was no way Harrison Hawke would take her to his saggy bosom if he thought she was involved in an operation like this. At the first sniff of another Waco, he and his buddies would be wetting themselves in anticipation of a federal government screw-up. Surrounding the home of some white, Christian patriots who were merely exercising their constitutional right to bear arms and exercise religious freedom was an act of tyranny and treason as far as the Aryan nation was concerned.

She said, "I'll lay low and keep you apprised of any developments. Can we run some interference?"

"Got it covered."

Jude let go of the shallow breath she'd held too long. Her masters would see to it that her name never hit a newspaper. The sheriff at Kingman would receive some mysterious orders and instruct Gossett accordingly. So long as she didn't get her face splattered across the TV screen, she could slide out from under this with her cover intact and her disheartened ex-fed story unblemished.

As she signed off, she realized this mattered to her. She didn't want to leave Paradox. She'd invested a year in this surveillance op and things were getting interesting. The FBI could no longer check the names of gun purchasers against terror watch lists after changes that pandered to the gun lobby—one of the major success stories in the white militia movement. Thanks to former Attorney General John Ashcroft, sales records for guns were not kept for ninety days anymore; they were now pegged at a laughable twenty-four hours. So much for national security.

Despite this hurdle, the team investigating Hawke had tied him, via Internet transactions, to the purchase of twenty semiautomatic 82A1 rifles. The Barrett .50 caliber battlefield weapon was in a class by itself. David Koresh had turned one on the FBI at Waco. The sucker had a 2,000 yard range and, even using standard ball ammo, it could take out a vehicle and destroy an aircraft with a single well-placed hit.

In their wisdom, the authorities treated these as hunting rifles, so Hawke's purchase was not illegal, merely suspicious. What would anyone want with a stack of BMG armor-piercing sniper rifles? Hawke had never so much as hunted a chicken, unless you counted his midnight drives to the KFC in Montrose. There was nothing unusual about a neo-Nazi hoarding weapons. What had the Bureau interested was the nature and quantity of Hawke's purchases, and how they were being funded. They were now almost certain Saudi money was involved, top-secret intelligence that could see their investigation shut down.

Disturbing whispers of links between extreme right militias and Islamic terrorists were growing louder. Since 9/11 several neo-Nazi websites had listed links to Islamic sites, and the American Front and a few other hate groups had lauded Osama bin Laden as an enemy of Zionism. To complicate matters, the dangerous Central American crime gang the Mara Salvatrucha was thought to be smuggling al Qaeda operatives into the U.S. from across the Mexican border. A few intelligence reports were suggesting neo-Nazi involvement in hiding these sleepers.

Over the past several months, Hawke had been trying to obtain illegal Raufoss high-explosive rounds, and Jude's masters were now toying with the concept of a sting operation. First, they wanted to know what he was up to. If he had a target in mind and had started planning, there were probably other domestic terrorists involved. They could not risk shutting him down before they knew enough to thwart the attack.

Jude wanted to see this one out. She also wanted to put some roots down. Having cut herself adrift from her past, she felt strangely unanchored, yet out here, far from the world she had once inhabited, she could also breathe easier, and she wanted to stay awhile.

There was also Mercy. She rejected the thought instantly. Mercy was not a consideration. None of her casual encounters had ever figured into her thinking and Mercy Westmoreland was no exception. They were two adults who had engaged in a mutually gratifying physical transaction. Period. There was no relationship, and no pretense that the desire for one existed. They would never be more to each other than occasional sexual partners. Mercy had made that abundantly clear and Jude appreciated her honesty. In a situation like theirs it was important to be on the same page or someone could get hurt.

She swapped to her work cell phone and fortified herself with rationalizations in readiness for her next call. She had nothing to apologize for. They'd found Darlene's killer and had evidence that would hopefully tie him to the crime. All she had to do now was bring him in. Admittedly that might require the National Guard, but in the end, Sheriff Pratt would be able to look Clem Huntsberger in the eye, just like he wanted.

She hit her speed dial and told herself to keep her cool. Pratt was not going to be happy about one of his deputies getting wounded and that was understandable. Jude wasn't happy either. He was also going to hear from her boss and that would make him jumpy. Jude decided to give him a heads-up about that, so he wouldn't be taken by surprise.

"Jude?" The voice was not Pratt's.

"Mercy?" Jude lowered her phone and stared at the pad. She must have mis-keyed. "I'm sorry. I meant to call the sheriff."

"He can wait. It's good to hear from you. Are you still in Utah?"

"Yes."

"Any progress?"

"One arrest. One dead. And Deputy Tulley is wounded."

"Damn. Is he okay? Are *you* okay?"

"He's going to be fine. He took one in the leg and one in the side. Both bullets exited."

"You must be feeling like shit."

Jude didn't want to go down that track in case she burst into tears like a rookie. She glanced across at the truck. Gossett was still talking into his radio. "How are things with you?"

"I'm at the hospice. It won't be long, now."

What was there to say that wasn't completely trite? Mercy was about to lose a parent. "I can't imagine how hard that is."

"He's ready, I think. We've said our good-byes." Mercy's breath seemed to catch in her throat. "He's been a great father to me and he was a good husband to my mom."

Jude could believe that. Mercy exuded the confidence of a person whose parents had nourished her in every way and the self-esteem of a woman cherished and encouraged by her father. In the very best sense, she seemed like a daddy's girl. This loss was going to be a huge blow to her. Jude's first instinct was to get in her car and drive nonstop until she reached Grand Junction, just so she could be there for her. As if Mercy would want that.

Feeling foolish, she said, "I'm so very sorry."

"Thank you." A long pause. Jude heard her blow her nose. When she started talking again, she changed the subject, asking with a brittle edge, "So, when will you be back?"

"Pretty soon. Maybe tomorrow."

"Okay."

Wondering if she'd imagined trace of relief in that reply, Jude asked, "Is your friend still with you?"

"Yes. Why?" A teasing note entered her voice. "Are you jealous?"

Yes. Jealous as all hell. Jude remained silent for a beat, getting a grip. She had no right to be jealous. Apart from being irrational, it was immature. All the same, she said, "I don't like sharing."

Mercy laughed. "How frank of you to admit it."

"What do I have to lose?"

"You tell me," Mercy said softly.

"That's another conversation."

"Perhaps we could have it some time."

What was Mercy saying? Jude frowned. This was not the time or place to ask. She got to her feet, shuffled along the wall to the far end of the building and peeped around the corner. There was nothing moving. The Epperson house was so still, it looked almost unoccupied, yet there was a brooding menace about it. Jude shivered. She needed to get back in the vehicle, not stand out here delaying the inevitable good-bye.

"Are you still there?" Mercy asked.

"Yes, but I need to get going."

"You didn't answer me."

"What was the question?"

"It was more of an invitation."

Dryly, Jude said, "I don't do love triangles. Or threesomes."

"And I don't do jealous partners."

"Well, I'm glad we got that out of the way."

"You have a temper," Mercy said.

"And you're a tease."

"Will you come see me when you get back?"

Jude rolled the dice. "That depends."

An audible intake of breath. Eventually, Mercy said, "I can't change who I am."

"No one is asking you to. You're...perfect."

"I bet you say that to all the girls."

"Give me some credit."

"I wish you were here. Tonight...now." Mercy sounded drained suddenly.

Me too, Jude thought, sliding her way back along the barn wall toward Gossett's truck. Mercy Westmoreland's delicious, if elusive, self versus a house full of religious extremists hoping for Armageddon. No contest, really.

"I wish I could do something to help," Jude said in neutral tone.

"That wasn't what I meant."

Pushing the envelope a little more, Jude replied pointedly, "Give me a call after your friend leaves."

Mercy was silent for a long moment, then she said, "Pass my best wishes on to Deputy Tulley."

"I'll do that." Jude had a feeling this was Mercy blowing her off. She looked up at the sound of a chopper approaching and heaved a sigh of relief when she saw the dark figures within. The Tactical Ops Unit hadn't wasted any time.

Mercy lingered. "Take care of yourself."

"You, too."

"Jude..." The tone was regretful. A bad sign. "I really do like you."

"I like you, too, Mercy." Jude vacillated, unwilling to end it there.

But by the time she came up with some suitable wording, Mercy had ended their call with a wistful good-bye.

❖

"It's a helicopter." Fawn Dew aimed her rifle higher and fired a couple of shots, then instructed a boy standing next to her, "Go tell the master it's time to get that grenade launcher set up."

Summer groaned and tried to see if Thankful was in the room, but she could barely lift her head. Pain squeezed her like a giant hand until she could feel fluid dripping from her pores. She was drenched, her nightdress clinging to her skin, the bedding soaked with sweat and blood. The spells between her contractions were so short now, she could hardly catch her breath before her body was trapped once more in that merciless grip.

Sobbing, she called Thankful's name and Fawn Dew turned to her with a look of irritation. "Thankful is busy."

"Please. I need some water."

"You'll keep."

"Why won't God help me?"

"Ask *him*."

Summer wept anew. "I think I'm going to die."

"Every woman thinks that when she's having a baby."

Something tore at her and Summer screamed and reached down between her legs. Her fingers met a smooth foreign wet lump. "There's something there," she cried. "Please, Fawn Dew. Help me."

With a loud sigh, Fawn Dew left her post at the window and flounced across the room, her stiff petticoats bristling against her pink gingham dress. Summer would know that sound anywhere. She was the one who had to starch and iron Fawn Dew's clothes.

Her husband's favorite swept back the bedclothes, lifted Summer's nightgown and inspected her. Something in her face changed and Summer could tell she was shocked. "What is it?" she asked in a panic.

"I think it's your baby's foot."

"So he's coming? Oh, praise the Lord."

But Fawn Dew said nothing. She looked under Summer's nightgown once more then marched to the door and yelled, "Thankful! Get your fat ass in here!"

One of the children hanging around the doorway, a girl of around ten, pointed at a sign on the wall and said, "Keep yourself sweet, Sister-Mom."

Fawn Dew cuffed the girl around the head and yelled for Thankful again. This time a man stuck his head in the door, informing them, "We need this room."

"Yes, sir," Fawn Dew simpered. All eyelashes and coy smiles, she stuck her bosom out and said, "I'd be so grateful and I know the Heavenly Father would guide you, if you could come over right now and deliver this baby. Then we could be out of your way in a minute."

"Er..." He cleared his throat. "We can wait a bit longer."

Even as he backed out into the hall, she followed him, insisting sweetly, "Please, Brother. The birth is slow and there is a problem."

"Then we must speak with Brother Epperson," he said.

"Yes, my husband will know what to do."

Several minutes later, they returned with the master, who laid his hands upon Summer's head. At his touch, a warm tide washed through her and her pain was miraculously relieved.

"The spirit is with me," she breathed, filled with hope. God spoke through her husband and she trusted He would now save her.

Nathaniel continued in prayer for a little longer, then announced, "I will speak to the prophet," and took out his cell phone, moving to the window.

A hushed awe descended on the room, broken only by the moans and gasps Summer tried to stifle. When Nathaniel returned he stood in the middle of the room, surrounded by his wives and the men who had been out on the search party, each with a rifle in his hand.

He raised his arms and said, "God has spoken. We will wait for Summer to bring forth her child. If she has not done so by dawn, that will be a sign from God that she must atone for the grave sins she has committed."

Summer's head spun. What was he saying? She caught Thankful's eye and made a silent plea. Pale faced, Thankful came to her bedside and stroked the hair back from her face.

They both listened as Nathaniel concluded with some good news. "The child is blameless and he is worth ten of the mother. When the time comes, he will be spared."

CHAPTER FOURTEEN

Chastity Young surfaced from a deep sleep and squinted at the digital display next to her bed. Two in the morning and someone was banging on her door. She turned on the lamp and swung her legs over the side of the bed, sliding her feet into a pair of fluffy mules. The doorbell rang some more, followed by a volley of loud knocks. She stumbled to her bedroom window in panicky confusion, assuming there had been an accident nearby or maybe something terrible had happened at a neighbor's house. Lifting, her blackout shade, she peeped out at the front driveway and frowned at the sight of an old Chevy pickup.

Her thoughts instantly jumped to Adeline. Could her niece have run away and come back home? Had she caught a ride with a stranger? Elated at the possibility, Chastity hurried from her room to the front door. Through the peephole she saw a young man in his twenties wearing the plyg uniform of dark pants with suspenders over a plaid shirt. He looked vaguely familiar, and it seemed safe to assume he was one of her sister's many offspring, but she made sure her security chain was secure before she opened the door.

Her nocturnal visitor did not waste any time on small talk. "Mrs. Young?"

"And you are?"

"Woodruff Fleming."

Chastity tried to place him. "The fourth son?"

"The third, ma'am." The reply was courteous but barren of warmth. "My daddy sent me. Is Adeline here?"

Chastity's heart leapt but she was careful not to show her emotions. Schooling her tone to one of bland indifference, she said, "Your father took Adeline away about a week ago, remember?"

He craned past her to see into the house. "Has she been here since yesterday?"

"Why would she be here?" Chastity had to bite her lip not to spit the next question out like she was ready to punch someone. "Isn't she married?"

"She went missing."

"Missing?" Chastity caught her breath.

With an impatient snort, he said, "Thanks to you, she desecrated the good name of our family by running away before she could be sealed."

"Nice of you to drop by and let me know."

He was speechless for a few seconds. "If you take her in, you will atone."

"Oh, I see." Her temper got the better of her. "Your father was too chicken to come and threaten me himself so he sent you? What a piece of work."

Woodruff handed her a piece of paper with a phone number scrawled on it. "If she comes here, call this number."

Chastity laughed. "Your sister won't be coming here. This is the first place your father would come looking for her, so she'll be headed in the opposite direction. She always used to talk about California, come to think of it. If I were you, I'd look there."

He surveyed her dubiously.

"Seriously, er…Woodruff." Chastity adopted a sincere, almost sympathetic tone. "Even though your family and I don't see eye to eye on a lot things, I don't like to think of Adeline out there by herself. A fourteen-year-old girl should be at safely at home where she can't come into harm's way. You know—end up molested by some disgusting pervert five times her age…that type of thing. Who did you say she was supposed to be marrying?"

Woodruff's face was frozen in self-righteous affront. "God is watching you," he warned, and strode off toward his pickup.

"Hey, Woodruff," Chastity yelled after him. "God is watching you, too. And guess what? He said you shall have no other gods before Him. Think about that next time you break a commandment following orders from that self-appointed prophet you all worship."

After she'd made this announcement to the entire neighborhood, she slammed her door and slid the security chain in place with shaking fingers. She should have felt a sense of satisfaction about making her point, but her older sister Vonda's family was a lost cause. The Flemings had broken away from the mainstream Mormon church a few years after they married. Tucker, her sister's husband, had started reading polygamist literature and decided that the only way to the celestial kingdom was through plural marriage. He duly announced a revelation from the Heavenly Father that Chastity should become his second wife, which, given he could barely keep his hands off her ass, seemed remarkably opportune. When she declined this honor, he moved his family to Hildale where he could find more submissive young women.

In the fifteen years since then, he and Vonda had added ten more kids to their brood and he'd married two other women, the minimum to ensure his place as a god in the celestial kingdom. Chastity often wondered how Vonda coped without the antidepressants she'd been addicted to before the move. The last time they saw one another was when she'd showed up with Adeline three years earlier. Chastity had been shocked to open the door to a prematurely ageing woman unrecognizable as the funny, adventurous big sister she grew up with. Vonda was a mere shell of herself. She had a chronic cough and a bladder infection and said she could not cope with Adeline. Somehow she'd talked Tucker into handing her over to Chastity instead of marrying her off on her twelfth birthday to one of his brothers.

Despite the rationalizations Vonda trotted out about her illness and the need to make Adeline more feminine so she didn't disgrace them when she was married—an argument that had apparently won the day with her husband—Chastity sensed an underlying desperation. Her sister had not yet surrendered the final vestiges of her own decency; she didn't want her prepubescent daughter to be raped by her own uncle.

This small act of rebellion was the only sign Chastity could find of the woman she had once looked up to. She played her role in the necessary farce, assuring Vonda that she would help ready Adeline for decent wifehood at some later date, and there would be no dating, no haircuts, and plenty of scripture reading. The entire time they spoke, Adeline was silent and downcast, one hand toying with her tight braid, her gaze never leaving the floor.

As soon as the Flemings had left, Chastity said, "The first thing we're going to do is get you out of those ridiculous clothes." She led Adeline upstairs. "Let's find something more comfortable for you to wear tonight. Tomorrow we'll go to the mall and you can choose some new clothes."

Within minutes, Adeline was standing in her closet with her, looking through racks of pants and tops. In the end she picked out a pair of old Levis and said, with trepidation, "Am I allowed to wear these?"

"I wear pants most of the time. And God hasn't struck me down yet."

Adeline wavered, glancing back at forth between a row of skirts and the jeans she obviously found more appealing. In the end the jeans won and she chose a rugby shirt to go with them.

After she'd taken a shower, she emerged, wrapped in a toweling robe, and nervously asked, "Sister, do you have a hairbrush I could use? I left mine behind."

Chastity pulled out the chair from in front of her dressing table and said, "Sit down. I'll comb out the knots for you. And I'm not your sister, I'm your Aunt Chastity. Okay?"

Halfway through the painful process, Adeline said, "I wish I had hair like yours. It's really beautiful."

"Thank you." Chastity smiled. "I don't know where the auburn came from. Everyone in the family is blond like you."

"I'm not a proper blond. You should see my sister, Summer. Her hair is almost white."

"Is Summer older or younger than you?" Chastity felt sad to think she knew only the oldest of her nieces and nephews, those born before Tucker Fleming had latched onto the perfect way to justify his infidelities.

"She's thirteen. But I'm taller than her."

Chastity smiled, remembering how important that once was to her. She'd been the shortest in her family until she was twelve, then she'd shot up four inches almost overnight. She still had long legs, no hips, and almost no breasts. Adeline had the same coltish build. Something about the girl reminded Chastity of herself as a kid, and it wasn't just her physique. Adeline had an air of defiance even her nineteenth-century clothing could not disguise. It announced itself in the stubborn set of her jaw and the piercing intelligence of her gaze.

Her dark brown eyes sought Chastity's and she said, "How long will I be staying with you?"

"Quite some time. Perhaps a year or so."

"Where's Uncle Orrin?"

"I threw him out a year after we were married."

Adeline quickly lowered her head but not before she'd emitted a startled giggle. "Do my parents know?"

"I suspect not."

The Flemings had attended her wedding seven years before, and the funerals of both her parents, but had not been in contact since. Chastity knew they would not have been so quick to leave Adeline with her had they known she'd not only divorced Orrin but had left the church, as well. Her temple recommend was automatically rescinded after her marriage ended, a fact that had rankled much more than Chastity expected. It bugged her that a blameless divorced women was deemed unfit to enter the temple, but a lousy ex-husband could come and go as he pleased.

She was so irritated by this that she refused to obtain a cancellation of sealing so she could get her recommend back. Instead, she started thinking about the way women were treated in the church, her anger giving way to an exploration. She'd spent months reading and thinking about the beliefs she'd taken for granted her whole life. The more she learned, the less she clung to the familiar, until the time came when she realized she was happier outside of the church than in it.

She stopped feeling angry and became aware of a strange sense of relief. For many people the church provided security, comfort, support, and certainty, and she could respect that. But she wanted to discover who she could be unfettered by the fear of failure that had dogged her adult life.

She didn't discuss her journey of discovery when Vonda and Tucker arrived with Adeline. Her sister and brother-in-law saw mainstream Mormonism as lacking the fullness of the gospel, and the LDS leadership as traitors to the priesthood, but it was still better than living entirely outside the church. Chastity had the impression they expected her to see the error of her ways momentarily and catch the first Greyhound to Hildale, eager to abandon her business and her freedoms for life as a baby factory.

"Why did you throw him out?" Adeline asked, plainly fascinated by this radical concept.

"He was an arrogant, cheating maggot and he hit me."

Chastity figured she'd just described what passed for acceptable behavior in her niece's world, so it was little wonder that Adeline processed this information with a confused frown. The very idea of a woman holding a man accountable had to be a novelty.

"You threw him out of his own house?"

"The house is mine."

Barely a day passed that she didn't thank her parents for this blessing, and the sizeable nest egg they'd left behind for their two daughters. Vonda's share had gone straight to her husband and the coffers of the FLDS. But for Chastity, financial independence and the absence of children had made ending her marriage a relatively painless process.

"Where did he go?" Adeline asked.

"I don't know and I don't care." Chastity still marveled that she had married Orrin Young at all. What had she been thinking?

Lately she'd been working on forgiving herself for that decision, able to see how skewed her judgment had been at the time. Orrin had shown up when she was feeling increasingly guilty about being a dreaded single adult. A woman unmarried at twenty-five was almost unheard of in Salt Lake City. To compound matters, her parents had been in a serious road accident, leaving her father in a wheelchair and her mother in poor health. Unable to return to the activities and joys of their normal life, and with nothing to do all day but worry, they obsessed over finding a prospective husband for Chastity.

She could understand their anxiety, even if she didn't share it. They lived in fear that some accident would befall her and, without a husband to assure her admission to the highest levels of heaven, she would be lost to them for eternity. Chastity had always had trouble buying official Mormon doctrine on that subject. The idea that a wise and loving God would admit any nitwit who married at eighteen, yet would turn away an unmarried woman like Mother Teresa, simply didn't hold water. All the same, she'd found the relentless pressure hard to cope with.

She had not fallen in love with Orrin; rather, she had succumbed to the imperatives of her upbringing and the stress of trying to deal with her parents' situation alone. Chastity remembered feeling a weird sense of resignation the day she'd agreed to Orrin's proposal. It was as if in that moment she had folded her true self away, understanding she might never feel whole again. Even before the wedding ceremony, she'd known she was making a huge mistake, but she was determined to go through with it, to prove herself worthy of her parents' love.

They deserved that much. They had been good and generous and kind their whole lives, and she could not bear to disappoint them. She wanted to give them a reason to live and something to look forward to. A wedding to plan. The promise of grandchildren they would see grow up. Vonda had caused them great anguish by isolating herself and her children from them when she and Tucker moved south. Chastity could never forgive her for that. She could not understand how her sister could have shut them out after the childhood they had given her.

She and Vonda had never wanted for anything. Chastity was aware that many people on the outside thought Mormons were narrow, humorless, and authoritarian. Her father had been the opposite. He was an erudite, sweet-natured man with an insatiable curiosity about the world and a great sense of fun. At the same time, he was immensely faithful and proud to belong to what he called "the one truly American religion." He had married Chastity's mother after returning from a mission overseas, and they were made for each other. Like him, she was good hearted, hardworking, and gentle. She adored her children and had made their family's home life as close to perfect as Chastity could imagine.

A great deal had changed since then, but looking back, Chastity could not honestly say she would have wanted it any different. She felt extremely fortunate. And bereft. She had many aunts, uncles, and cousins, but not a day passed that she didn't feel the loss of her parents keenly. They'd been so thrilled by her marriage they'd put her name on the title of their house as a wedding present. Ten months later they were both dead and she was living with a man she loathed.

In retrospect, she could see she'd made Orrin just as miserable as he'd made her. Just like her, he had struggled to do what was expected of him. She couldn't stand him in her bed, and had been relieved when he started secretly drinking alcohol and cheating on her. The trouble was, he had still expected his matrimonial "rights" and seemed hell bent on getting her pregnant.

She had tried to be understanding about this obsession, aware that the status of Mormon men, on earth and in heaven, depended on the number of children they fathered. Her uncooperative womb cast Orrin into a deep depression which alternated with rages in which he would shove her to her knees, ordering her to recite her sins and ask the Heavenly Father's forgiveness. When she could think of little to admit to, he would seem almost mad with frustration, insisting that God was punishing her and she needed to make herself white and delightsome once more.

After tolerating a year of this, Chastity had finally lost her temper one evening and suggested he could be the infertile half of the equation. Orrin had lashed out at her, an act for which he'd since apologized profusely. But that was the day she'd ended their marriage.

"Let me tell you something, Adeline," she said. "In life there are choices. My husband thought I would put up with his bad behavior because a wife is supposed to obey and accept. But I chose not to be with someone who did not love or respect me. Do you understand?"

Adeline nodded. "I chose too. Daddy told me I was going to marry Uncle Loudell but I said no."

"Good. You did the right thing."

"Daddy says he doesn't want a daughter that's Satan's whore."

Disgusted, Chastity didn't comment on Tucker Fleming's moral compass. Instead, as she combed and blow-dried Adeline's long hair, she said, "In this house we don't use the word "whore." It's disrespectful. Okay?"

"Okay, Aunt Chastity." Adeline indicated a photograph on the dressing table. "Is that you?"

Chastity smiled and handed her the framed picture for a better look. "Yes, that's me climbing in the Himalayas. The mountain behind me is Annapurna."

"Is that in Canada?"

"No, Nepal." At Adeline's blank expression, Chastity crossed to her bookcase and took an atlas from the shelf. She opened it at a map of the world and invited, "Come see. It's just a little country but it's famous because it has the highest mountain in the world. Mount Everest."

Adeline pored over the map. After a moment, she said, "One day, I'd like to go to a faraway place like that."

"Then one day you will. It's your life and you can do anything you want with it."

Like her, Adeline had a sense of adventure, and over the next two years they'd made the most of it. Every time Chastity could take a few days' vacation from her job in geriatric nursing, they'd gone to the countryside. Recently, she'd moved into private care, starting up her own agency. It was hard work but she had more flexibility as her own boss. She'd been planning their first overseas trip when Vonda and Tucker arrived unannounced, demanding that Adeline accompany them and telling Chastity that their daughter's celestial marriage had been arranged by the prophet.

In the few moments they'd had to hug before Tucker dragged her away, Adeline had whispered, "I won't do it. I'd rather die."

"I'll find you. Don't worry," Chastity murmured in her ear. "Don't give up."

"Everest," Adeline called as Tucker bundled her toward the waiting SUV.

Chastity blew her a kiss, then went around to the passenger widow and told her sister, "You don't have to do this, Vonda. Get out of the car now. You and Adeline can stay with me. Please."

Vonda would not look at her. She seemed even more shrunken, and this time there was no flicker of rebellion. She had given up, Chastity thought. She had accepted the unacceptable and had traded her spirit in doing so.

One last time, Chastity tried to get through to her. "Please Vonda. Don't allow your husband to pimp your child."

Tucker got into the car and started the motor. He looked past Vonda with ill-concealed glee and informed Chastity, "Pray for direction from God. Your salvation is at stake, Sister."

Each day since had dragged by with no word from her niece and a frustrating series of calls to the authorities who said they needed proof of a crime before they could investigate. After making a fruitless trip to Hildale, she'd started looking into hiring a private detective or one of those cult rescue guys. It hadn't crossed her mind that Tucker would inadvertently end up giving her exactly what she needed—hope and new direction. What now? With so much adrenaline in her system, Chastity knew she would never get back to sleep. Mind working overtime, she strode down the hallway to the kitchen and made a cup of strong coffee, thankful as she often was that she no longer abstained from caffeine. Hildale was a five-hour drive. If she got on the road now, she could be there around eight in the morning. Someone had to know about a missing girl. Tucker and his buddies must be organizing the search. All she had to do was take a drive near her sister's house and look for the action. She carried her coffee upstairs, got dressed, threw some clothes together for Adeline, then stared at herself in the mirror.

A woman in jeans and a T-shirt would attract way too much attention where she was headed. She went to her closet and rifled through her most conservative outfits. By contrast with the pioneer chic seen on the Arizona Strip, the mid-calf length skirts and twinsets she'd kept from her church-going days looked like the trappings of a scarlet woman. She closed the closet door despondently, then pulled it open again, struck by a brainwave. She hauled an old suitcase down from one of the storage shelves. Inside it were the drab garments Adeline had been wearing the day she arrived.

Thrilled, Chastity peeled off her clothing and buttoned herself into the shapeless gray dress. It was only slightly too small for her, having been far too big for eleven-year-old Adeline, but no one was going to notice the extra few inches of leg and the slight tug across her chest. Hastily she French plaited her hair, pinned it up at the back, and tied a headscarf on. No one would know she didn't have the long, tight braids every woman in Southern Utah seemed to wear. At a glance she looked just like any other young plyg wife.

She drained her coffee, wrote a note with her cell phone number on it, and stuck it on the fridge just in case Adeline made it to the house before she got back. Then she put a spare key inside the carved-out rock a few feet from the main entrance, looked around to make sure no one was watching, and opened the garage doors. It was almost four and the air was at its coolest. Heady with relief that she could finally *do* something, she opened the back of her minivan, threw her overnight bag in, and checked that her new off-road Honda CRF450X was tightly secured.

This time she would not come back without Adeline. She didn't care what the lawyers said. She should never have let Tucker and Vonda drive off with her niece. That had been her biggest mistake since her marriage. With a shock, she realized that she had been an idiot and a coward. She was always worrying that she would never find a man she could truly love, and never have the kind of partnership her parents had, yet she had placed at terrible risk the one relationship that really mattered to her. She had allowed the most important person in her life to be taken away as if neither she nor Chastity had any rights in the matter.

The fact that, legally, they didn't was beside the point. By any moral standard, and according to the Declaration of Independence,

Adeline was endowed with certain inalienable rights, among them liberty and the pursuit of happiness. That the law failed to reflect this in her case was a failure of the law. As such, was there any obligation to respect it?

Feeling resolved about what she was about to do, Chastity got into the van and backed out of her driveway. As she accelerated down the quiet suburban street, she made a solemn promise to herself. Whatever it took, she would find Adeline and keep her safe.

CHAPTER FIFTEEN

The six-man Mohave County Tactical Ops Unit staking out the
Epperson place had been joined in the middle of the night
by an FBI crisis management team from Denver, comprising hostage
negotiators, SWAT and SOR teams, and various support staff. They
hadn't brought in the Bradley fighting vehicles yet, but they were on the
way. This was now a Bureau-led operation, the objective to negotiate,
watch, and contain. The shift that came on at six a.m. was commanded
by a quietly spoken man with duck down blond hair and gray eyes too
flinty for his closely shaved baby face. Special Agent in Charge Trent
Farrell from the Phoenix division treated Jude and Sergeant Gossett with
the patient disdain his breed reserved for small-town law enforcement.

He referred to the events of the previous day as a "failed tactical
effort," and said he would have to put on record his concern that they had
delayed calling in the FBI, who were now saddled with the unenviable
task of "coming in backward to salvage the situation." Endearing
himself even more to the Mohave County team, he had immediately
stood down the deputies who'd been at the scene since the beginning,
effectively denying them the chance to be associated with the positive
outcome everyone hoped for.

They now had the house completely surrounded. Farrell had set
up the command post inside the northernmost barn, having his team
remove hay bales and farm equipment from the wooden platform that
ran below the high ventilation windows. From this vantage point,
they had a bird's eye view of the house and its surroundings, which,
during the strategy briefing that was underway, Farrell had termed "an
operational advantage that will enable us to avoid unfortunate errors

during this little picnic outing, gentlemen." He had positioned snipers at key junctures along the platform.

"See why I held off," Gossett muttered. "You realize if this goes sideways, they're going to point the finger at us."

"I'm not hanging around. My boss wants me out of here today," Jude responded, adjusting her bulletproof vest.

Gossett rolled his eyes. With good-humored sarcasm, he said, "Sure he does. Come on my turf, raise some Cain, then haul ass back home leaving you know who to take shit from the er...elite, here."

"Yeah, we sure livened things up. You'll be thanking me in your retirement speech. Just wait and see."

Gossett snorted. "I'll be thanking the big guy upstairs if I get out of this without being demoted."

"We have the most capable men and women in the business," Farrell wrapped things up on a positive note. "We have the tactical advantage and the firepower, and we have all the time in the world to sit these individuals out. No one acts in haste. Deadly force is a last resort. An all-out assault is a last resort. Do I make myself clear? You will all play a vital role in keeping this operation disciplined, strategic, and lawful."

No one mentioned Waco. They didn't need to. It hovered in the ether, an unspoken presence grating on nerves like ghostly fingernails sliding down a pane of glass.

The negotiator was about to commence phase one of their plan, an attempt to engage Nathaniel Epperson in dialogue over the bullhorn since he wouldn't answer his cell phone. The initial aim was to defuse the hostility by asking if everyone in the house was safe and well and offering to send in any food or other supplies needed. Meantime, they had dispatched a couple of senior agents and one of the sheriff's people to Elias Rockwell's compound in Colorado City, hoping to persuade him to instruct his followers to put their weapons down. The negotiator claimed this had all the makings of a protracted standoff. If they wanted a good outcome they would have to be patient and gradually shrink their perimeter.

This seemed like the right time to get out of Dodge. The first thing Jude wanted to do was document and submit the evidence, ensuring integrity and a continuous chain of custody were preserved. She got a headache thinking about it sitting in Gossett's truck, even though the cooler was locked and, as custodian, she held the only key. She would only rest easy once everything was packaged and labeled and transported to Grand Junction for examination.

The nearest lab was in Cedar City, not far from the hospital where Tulley was being treated. She could visit him, then return to Rapture and escort their prisoner to the Four Corners. With any luck, by the time she was back, Gossett and his team would have located the two missing kids and she would be able to take their statements. She cleared her departure with Farrell and left the barn, heading for the brace of vehicles parked beyond the exterior perimeter. She had barely made twenty feet when a flash blinded her momentarily and an explosion shook the ground. Diving for cover, she gazed back over her shoulder to see what was hit and whether anyone was down. Frantically, she crammed the speaker back in her left ear and elbowed her way to a group of agents taking cover behind an armored car.

"Rocket-propelled grenade!" someone yelled, and Farrell's voice issued instructions over the radio in a steady stream.

I am never getting out of this goddamned place, Jude thought.

❖

Summer felt a hand slapping her cheek and opened her eyes. She no longer had the strength to push or the energy to pray. A numbing despair had taken hold of her. God had found her unworthy, and had not answered her prayers. She had no idea what she had done to disappoint Him so greatly that He would punish her this cruel way.

"Wake up." Thankful shook her. "You have to come with me."

"Come? Where?"

Loudly, Thankful said, "We are going to a different room where we will not be in the way. Can't you see, Sister, that there are more important things going on than your childbirth?"

Summer blinked and gazed over toward the window where several men stood with Fawn Dew. All around them, on the floor, rifles were stacked.

Fawn Dew turned and said, "Good idea. You can put her in Naoma's room until Nathaniel is ready to deal with her."

"Thank you, Sister." Thankful slid her arms beneath Summer's shoulders and lifted her. "Swing your legs over and get up."

"I can't." She had barely uttered the protest when Thankful slapped her face, earning an approving look from Fawn Dew.

Thankful's low, urgent voice hissed in Summer's ear. "Listen to me. Once all this shooting is over, they are going to exorcise you to get rid of your demons, then cut your throat. You need to come with me now or you will die and so will your baby."

As Summer started to speak, Thankful placed a washcloth over her mouth and hauled her to her feet. Arms through Summer's, she half dragged her from the room and they shuffled down the hall until they reached the walkway that led to some half-built rooms at the back of the house. Thankful rushed Summer even faster along the unfinished wood floor until they came to a room at the far end, blocked off by a large timber board. Only then did Thankful release her and ease her to the floor.

Gasping for breath, Summer wailed, "What are you doing?"

"Be quiet," Thankful said.

With a stifled grunt, she lifted the large board and propped it against the wall, then she hurriedly pulled Summer inside and deposited her on the floor. The room was without drywall or glass panes in the windows, and in the corner nearest the window frame, Thankful's children sat in a tight little knot, their arms around one another, big frightened eyes gazing from pale faces. Fawn Dew's son, Jareph, peered out from behind the oldest girl.

After Thankful had dragged the board in front of the doorway once more, she summoned a couple of the children, saying, "Each of you pick up a leg and I'll take the other end." Between them they carried Summer to a quilt on the floor below the window.

Summer felt strangely cold and her heart was beating so fast she thought she was going to pass out. "Why are the children here?" she asked.

"Because we're all leaving."

"What?" Fear clamped her throat together.

"You heard me. I'm not letting our husband kill my children so he can get his picture in the newspaper."

Shaking violently, Summer grabbed Thankful's skirt. "No! We can't. We will be cast out. We will reap eternal damnation."

Thankful dropped to her knees and seized Summer by the shoulders. "I trust in the Heavenly Father, and he sent me a vision last night. In it, my children and I were safe and I saw this house. It was lifted up and sitting in the palm of the devil's hand."

"What if that's a false vision? What if it's Satan, testing your faith?"

Thankful brushed tears away. "What's happening here is not about faith. I've taken all I'm going to take, Summer. This is just too much."

"They'll come after us. We'll never get out of here. Remember what they did to Diantha?"

"Do you think God wants you dead?" Thankful shook Summer hard and gestured toward her kids. "Do you think he wants them dead? They're just babies."

"I don't know."

"He doesn't. And that's why He is going to lead us out of here."

"I can't do this. I'm in so much pain." Summer buried her face in Thankful's large bosom. "Go without me. I'll only hold you back."

"You're coming." Thankful let go of Summer and moved to the window, standing to one side and peering out. "I think they're going to be shooting out front for a while. The prophet wants them to keep the government agents pinned down until the Colorado City militia gets here."

"Is this Armageddon?" Summer asked, stunned by her bad luck.

Of all the days to have been found lacking, why did it have to be the day of Christ's return? There was still time for her to repent and be purified. The prophet said if a women told her priesthood head—her husband—everything, and he forgave them and punished them as he saw fit, they would be resurrected and live forever as his celestial wife on a far-off planet.

Thankful snorted. "Let me tell you something. If the prophet says this is going to be the last day, then we know for sure it isn't, since that's one prediction those idiots get wrong every time."

Summer did not get a chance to react to this heresy. She clutched her lower body and moaned in pain as a powerful contraction tore through her.

Thankful squatted next to her and took her hand, signaling the children to draw closer. Once everyone was in a tight huddle, she said, "Listen carefully. As soon as I tell you, we're going out that window and we're running. There's a white minivan not too far from the house. Run to it and hide behind it. Everyone understand?" Thankful tapped her oldest daughter on the shoulder and said, "You're in charge of Jareph."

"Are we going to live among the gentiles?" The girl seemed mortified.

"We can worry about that later. Right now, all I want you to do is get to the white van. Okay?"

The children nodded and Thankful hugged each one. "I love you very much, and one day all of you will tell your children about this," she said. "Now let's pray."

❖

If anyone wanted to know where the middle of nowhere was, this was it, Chastity thought. No one gets to Hildale and Colorado City by accident. It's not on the way to some bigger, better place, unless you wanted to count heaven like the locals did.

This was her second visit in as many weeks. She'd hired an attorney the day after the Flemings took Adeline, paying a lot of money to find out that there was nothing she could do. Adeline was only fourteen. If Chastity wanted guardianship she would have to go before a judge and prove her sister and brother-in-law were unfit parents. If she took Adeline against their wishes, she would be breaking the law, no matter what her niece wanted. It went without saying that an arrest would not help her cause.

The attorney had advised her to wait until Adeline was forced into the marriage, then report the case to Child Services so she could be legally removed from her home. She would have to testify against all the adults involved. He didn't think much of their chances. The authorities in Utah had spent fifty years ignoring the activities of their polygamist hatchlings.

Frustrated, Chastity drove to Hildale with all her savings—twenty thousand dollars—in a locked briefcase. This she'd offered to Tucker in exchange for legal guardianship of Adeline. All he and Vonda had to do was sign the papers she'd brought with her.

She could tell he was tempted, but in the end he backed off, claiming the marriage was God's will. The One Mighty and Strong had spoken and Tucker had to show his allegiance. Adeline had already been taken to the home of her chosen husband. Tucker wouldn't give the groom's name and after Vonda had refused to see her, Chastity had returned home, afraid to be gone too long in case Adeline tried to contact her.

She shifted in her seat, impatient with the cars in front of her. Everyone had slowed down to drive through the town of Hurricane, a small hamlet that felt like the last outpost of modern civilization before the steep two-lane highway overshadowed by the cliffs of Canaan Mountain. The route was like a passage to another world, another time. Chastity had never been on drugs but she thought it probably felt like this—weirdly disorienting. Every time she came here she worried that she might somehow be sucked into the vortex of irrationality and doomsday thinking that kept her sister blindly obedient to an amoral dictator.

It astounded her that no one seemed to reevaluate their beliefs in the face of reality, as she had after her divorce. For as long as she could remember, Tucker and Vonda had cited the immortality of the last prophet, Rulon Jeffs, as proof that theirs was the one true faith. Jeffs had claimed not only that he would he never die, but he would live to see the return of Christ. He had picked various dates for the lifting up, none of which came to pass. Undeterred, he gathered his flock in a field in the year 2000 to await the parting of the clouds. When Jesus stood them up yet again, Jeffs blamed lack of faith, the usual explanation for prophecies that failed to transpire. He died two years later, not immortal after all.

Chastity could not understand how anyone could still believe the various FLDS prophets were the mouthpieces of God when none had turned out to be immortal and their most lofty prophecies were nonevents. Was the Heavenly Father really so quixotic and petty-minded that He would plan to end the world, inform His elect of the date and time, then change His mind on the day because a few individuals didn't feel that burning in the bosom? It made no sense.

She had tried to have this discussion with Vonda, pointing out that Jeffs was just another emperor with no clothes. But her sister clung to the fairy tale that justified her painful existence. The prophet had to be right and her beliefs had to be true or that made her a gullible fool who had thrown her life away on a scam. Impossible. Chastity supposed ego had to play a role in such determined self-deceit. True believers would rather ignore reality than accept they were wrong. Some people called this "having the courage of their convictions." Chastity thought it was cowardice. How any mother could sell her own children down the river for the sake of a senseless and evil mutation of religion was beyond her comprehension.

Hildale and Colorado City loomed ahead and Chastity slowed down to take in the depressing sight of the strangely barnlike half-built plywood houses and unpaved streets, and the dull sienna pall that hung over the town from the wood-burning stoves. High above this, plumes of black smoke rose from the asphalt plant that employed the last vestige of child labor in the country.

She would never change Vonda's mind, she thought sadly. Obeying rules and not thinking for herself was easier than having to take full responsibility for her life. Cults counted on people like her, and certainly the FLDS would disintegrate if women began to question their indoctrination. That's why they pulled girls out of school before eighth grade, if they ever went at all, and prevented their members having radio, TV, the Internet, and any books other than scripture and doctrine.

It was amazing that Adeline had still had a functioning mind at eleven, she reflected. She doubted that her niece would have run away had she not known there was a bigger world out there, one that offered so much more than the circumscribed existence FLDS girls endured. Adeline knew she would not be denied salvation simply because she chose a different path from her mother. She had discovered that her dreams and hopes were nourished by the so-called Babylon her church decried, and she'd discovered how it felt to be happy. She would never surrender that willingly.

It had taken Chastity herself a long time to accept that the sky would not fall if she stopped going to temple, to step back from the beliefs she took for granted and examine them for what they were—religion. No better or worse than any other, but no substitute for life in the real world with all its joys, risks, and uncertainties. She could never go back, and she knew it would be the same for Adeline.

Once in Colorado City, she headed for the supermarket. Of all the places in town, this was virtually a male-free zone and the one where she would be most likely to overhear useful gossip. A runaway wife was hot news, and if it had reached anyone in the town, the women shopping for groceries would be talking about it. Chastity straightened her headscarf and practiced the look of dopey innocence Vonda wore perpetually. Lowering her head, she followed a woman through the entrance doors, picked up a shopping basket, and wandered past bulk containers of beans and dried apple.

Signs around the walls advertised fresh milk and various nutritional aid programs for women and children. Chastity paused at a vast assortment of lubricant jellies and pregnancy testing kits and listened carefully to a quiet conversation between two other women. As they spoke and herded their children, she lifted tubes of cream and read the ingredients as if engrossed.

"...I haven't heard anything since yesterday," one of the woman said.

"They'll find her. Stupid girl."

Chastity did not allow her head to pop up. Instead she dropped a pregnancy test into her basket, moved a pace closer to the women, and said in the most timorous tone she could muster, "My cousin says she ran off with a boy."

The women stared at her for a moment and the older of the two said, "I haven't seen you at a meeting."

Chastity smiled guilelessly. "I came down from Bountiful with my husband only a few weeks ago, just before the prophet cancelled Sunday meetings."

Their faces lifted. The younger one said, "Welcome. Will you be staying?"

"With the prophet's permission."

"Who are you visiting with?"

"Tucker Fleming," Chastity lied. "His second wife is my double-cousin." Lowering her voice to a fretful whisper, she added, "It's difficult there right now...with the trouble. That girl's embarrassed the whole family."

This earnest disclosure was accorded sage nods. Eyes glinting, the older woman said, "My husband is going this morning to join the search."

"I'm on my way over there now with some extra food." Chastity heaved a sigh. "I'll have to go back and ask my cousin for directions again. I don't know this area."

"Oh, Gathering for Zion is easy to find," the older woman said. "Once you get through Rapture, there's a right turn onto a one-lane road. The ranch is about two miles along. You can't miss it. Just look for the sign."

Chastity smiled. "Thank you. I'm sure I'll see you both when meetings begin again."

She headed for the counter where a notice at the register instructed shoppers to have their welfare cards ready. She paid in cash and brushed past a group of men gathered around a pickup truck not far from where she'd parked. Acting like she was fumbling around for her keys, she stopped a few feet away and tuned in to the raised voices.

"Only way past the roadblocks is on foot through the canyon," one man said. "The area is swarming with the servants of Lucifer."

"The day is upon us," cried another.

"What does Uncle Elias say?" asked a young man carrying a shotgun.

"The prophet has spoken with God," a man with a bushy salt and pepper beard answered. "We are commanded to organize. Your wives and children must remain in the home. Assemble every able-bodied man. This is the moment we have been awaiting. We will seize back the kingdom of God and avenge the blood of the prophets."

No wonder laughter was forbidden for FLDS women, Chastity thought. If she had to listen to baloney like that all the time, she'd crack up. Head lowered, she moved past the men and got into her minivan. When she pulled away from the curb, she let her tires spin long enough to throw a cloud of red dust over the zealots.

Adeline buried herself in the cool sand in the shadow created by a north facing overhang in the canyon wall. It was slightly damp there, the rock wall at least thirty degrees cooler than the air. When you were stuck in a dangerous environment, the thing to do was watch how wildlife behaved. Small mammals didn't try to move, they sought shadows, content to wait out the extreme heat in the middle of the day. To survive, Adeline knew she would have to do the same thing.

She spat the pebble she'd been sucking and took a small sip of water, then she gazed across the shimmering red desert to the Gathering for Zion Ranch and wished she'd stolen binoculars while she was in the house. There was no sign of a search party and she was beginning to think she'd made a terrible mistake leaving Daniel alone in the cave. She'd been traveling west, toward the area where they'd last seen the searchers, convinced they would not return to ground already covered.

While she'd been hiking that morning, she'd seen helicopters land near the compound and she kept wondering when the police would start fanning out. She was so hungry and thirsty she almost wanted them to find her. Naoma could whip her all she wanted; she would escape again. She stared at the pale buildings glittering in the distance, still puzzled over the gunfire.

What if the police weren't there because of her and Daniel? What if something else was going on? They would have phones. Maybe she could steal one while they weren't looking. Adeline checked the level in her water bottle. She could make it to the ranch in about two hours if she started now. And if everyone was cooped up indoors because the police were parked outside, no one would notice her, and even if they did, she looked like a boy now.

The more she thought about it, the more it seemed like a good idea. Adeline was sure she didn't have sunstroke or such bad dehydration her mind was affected and she was making a stupid decision. She felt okay. Taking her time, she wriggled back out of her damp sanctuary and scrambled to her feet. She was going to do it. She would find a phone, call Aunt Chastity, and she and Daniel would be saved.

CHAPTER SIXTEEN

H oly cow!" Gossett swung around as a sleek red motorcycle emerged from the scrub northwest of their position. Ignoring the swarm of agents in assault gear who converged on it, the driver bounced up the steep slope and halted behind the police vehicles.

"Hold your fire," Farrell commanded, as if anyone was doing more than stare in shock at the sight of a plyg woman, in *Little House on the Prairie* drag, climbing off a trail bike. She kicked out the side stand, propping the bike like she did it in her sleep.

"It's one of *them*," Gossett said as the young woman removed her helmet, hitched up her skirt, and strode purposefully past her stupefied audience, making a beeline for Farrell.

"Perhaps they've sent an emissary," Farrell murmured.

Somehow Jude couldn't see the patriarchs of Rapture dispatching a young woman to negotiate on their behalf, but she was willing to keep an open mind. The shooting had slowed down to the occasional stray bullet; maybe they were out of ammo and wanted to discuss surrender terms. She took a mental snapshot of the rider: burnished copper hair, a small oval face and a confident white smile. Even her unflattering dress could not fully disguise a slender, athletic body. How depressing, Jude thought, she was probably married to her own grandfather.

Surprisingly, the woman made direct eye contact with Farrell. "Are you in charge here?" she demanded.

He nodded curtly. "SAC Trent Farrell of the FBI, Phoenix. How may I be of help, ma'am?"

Piercing dark eyes swept their small group. "I'm Chastity Young. I'm here about my niece, Adeline Fleming. Are you conducting the search?"

The SAC cast a silent query in Jude's direction, and she reminded him, "The two children thought to have escaped on Sunday."

"I've come to take her home," Chastity Young asserted.

Startling the troops even more, she began to undress, stripping down to a white T-shirt and khaki hiking shorts. She kicked her discarded dress, petticoats, socks and sandals into a small pile, and said, "Could you add these to your trash, please."

Gossett glanced sideways at Jude and raised his eyebrows.

"What can you tell us about the circumstances of your niece's disappearance?" Jude asked when it seemed Farrell was lost for words.

"Only that she was living with me in Salt Lake City until a week ago." Chastity took a pair of hiking boots from her backpack. "Then her parents came and took her. They said she was going to be married. She's fourteen."

Jude said, "We met her older sister yesterday. Summer."

"You met her here?" Chastity sat down and set about methodically getting into her boots.

"She's one of Mr. Epperson's wives."

Chastity shook her head, clearly shocked. "I had no idea."

"She thinks your niece may be hiding in those hills." Jude indicated the towering red and black rock formations about ten miles northeast of the ranch.

"Ah. The Seeds of Cain."

Puzzled, Jude said, "I'm sorry?"

"That's what they call those hills 'round here." Chastity was on her feet again. "I don't think you'll find that on any of the maps…in the interests of good taste."

Jude finally got it. The Mormon church had been a whites-only club for most of its history, asserting that African Americans were cursed with dark skin so that they could be identified as a caste apart. Referred to as the seed of Cain, they were excluded until the late seventies when Africa became a target for missionaries. At that stage, the president of the church recanted the racist doctrine, claiming to have received new instructions from God.

Since then, the mainstream church had worked hard to dissociate itself from its past. However, the breakaway fundamentalist sects rejected this abandonment of the original doctrine and still saw African Americans as "inferior." This pronouncement coming from a bunch of people who married their own siblings and had most of their wives and children living on welfare.

"Ma'am, you can't remain here," Farrell told Chastity.

"I'm not planning to. And by the way, those plygs back in Colorado City are forming some kind of army and they're on their way out here to have a showdown with you people. Just thought you should know."

Farrell's eyes narrowed. He seemed to be torn between patronizing disbelief and stunned speculation when he asked, "How many men would you say are forming this vigilante squad? And what kind of weaponry did you see?"

Chastity shrugged. "I don't know anything about guns, but 'round here, if it shoots they want to own it." She fell silent and gazed slowly around. Comprehension filtered into her eyes. "You're not here to search for my niece, are you?"

"No, ma'am," Farrell said.

"Then what's going on?"

"We're not at liberty to discuss the operation."

"Well, it looks like you have your hands full." Chastity headed back to her bike. "I need to get moving while the sun is still low."

"You cannot remain in the area," Farrell said. "Sergeant Gossett will escort you to Rapture."

"That won't be necessary." Chastity fired up her bike and rocked it off the stand. "I'll be sure to stay out of range. If you see a flare, don't worry. It means I've found them. Two flares, and I need help at the location. Okay?"

"Ms. Young. I really must insist—"

"No. I must insist." Chastity was completely unmoved by the voice of authority. "I am here to find my niece. Period. Stay out of my way, and I'll stay out of yours." She put her bike into gear and negotiated a path around the cars.

"Wait." Jude ran after her. She scribbled her cell phone number on a piece of paper and handed it to the feisty woman. "If you need to communicate, call me."

She wasn't sure how she was going to help, given she was planning to make her getaway now that the guns had fallen silent. But she'd promised Tulley she would follow through on the missing kids and she wanted to interview them once they were found.

"Thanks." Chastity smiled broadly and glanced down at the number. "You didn't give me your name."

"Jude Devine. I'm a detective with the Montezuma County Sheriff's Office."

"Colorado?" Chastity's dark eyes swept her up and down with interest.

"Yes."

"I love hiking in that area. Your wildflowers are just spectacular."

"Well, if you're ever in Paradox, stop in at the sheriff's office there. That's where I'm based."

"Be warned, I'm the kind who takes people up on offers like that."

Jude grinned. "And I'm the kind who never expects that to happen." Now that they had established a rapport, she said, "Oh, and by the way, would you mind leaving your contact details with the sheriff's office in Rapture? I may need to talk to Adeline. I'm investigating the murder of a young woman."

"By these people?" Chastity gestured in the general direction of the Epperson home.

"Yes."

"About time. I'd be happy to help."

"Good luck with your niece," Jude said.

Chastity thanked her and turned the bike toward the desert. "Good luck with the crazy people," she called and with a brief wave, she kicked off down the slope handling the off-road like a professional.

Jude managed about ten paces toward the forward staging area when Farrell flagged her down. "Hold up, Devine. We need all available personnel. Looks like they're releasing a bunch of civilians at the rear of the dwelling."

"Want me at ten o'clock?"

"Yes. I've issued instructions to give the civilians any cover necessary and facilitate extraction."

As they walked briskly, she asked, "Do we have telephone contact with anyone inside yet?" There was no land line in the house, and Epperson had not been answering his cell phone.

"He's still not picking up."

They parted company at the barn and Jude ran along a barricade of hay bales, shields, and SUVs, then down the slope to the exterior perimeter, heading for the rear of their northeast position. As she moved toward a group of agents staked out behind a rock formation, she could see several small children standing at the corner of a half-built extension to the rear of the house.

Ten agents were grouped around the rock and a support team was situated on the exterior periphery well below the position, surrounded by banks of ammunition, tear gas canisters, def-tec grenades, and additional weaponry.

Jude joined the agent at the point farthest north and said, "Detective Jude Devine, Montezuma County Sheriff's Office."

"Special Agent Patrick Kelly." He eyed her MP5 dubiously. "Ever handled one of those before, Devine?"

"I'm FBI sniper and tactical weapons trained," Jude replied without expanding.

"In that case." Kelly indicated a foothold a couple of feet up the rock formation. "Wanna take up position there? I have a more suitable weapon for you."

He spoke into his headset and a support staffer showed up with a hefty M40A1. Jude had encountered the sniper rifle at Quantico; it was a lot like a Remington 700. She could make a clean shot dead on target at a thousand yards. Their rock barrier was a little over a hundred from the house, the closest point on the interior perimeter. The weapon was overkill for a scenario like this one.

"Child's play," she mumbled.

"Poor visibility and brief windows of opportunity." Kelly flagged the significant issues just in case she hadn't noticed.

Jude surveyed the SWAT team members around her. Each held an MP5 in gloved hands, the stocks tucked against their shoulders, their right thumbs resting on the safety selector switches above the pistol grips, index fingers just outside their trigger guards. Every weapon was mounted with retina-searing gun lights and loaded and bracketed with thirty-round magazines. In their left ears, tiny radio speaker buds conveyed their orders. The pockets of their tactical vests were weighed down with spare magazines, each filled with 10 millimeter bullets designed to stop any opposition within seconds.

They were ready to storm, if the order was given. Each had practiced the maneuvers a hundred times at Quantico, yet no situation was ever the same as another and there were real people inside the house, and the pale faces peering from behind the stucco wall belonged to real children.

Jude could measure the adrenaline hitting her system by the sudden increase in lung capacity, the urge to run, the sharpening of perception. She could feel her heart pumping blood harder, her muscles tensing, time slowing down. The children started running, heading for a white minivan parked about thirty yards from the house. It was a mistake.

"Oh fuck," Jude muttered. "They should have gone straight out the back."

Through the telescopic sight, she watched barrels shift along the north-facing flank of the house. The people inside were aiming at the fleeing figures. In disbelief, Jude heard the pop of gunfire. A child fell. Another crouched over him, her hands covering her head.

In her ear, Farrell's voice ordered, "Cover them!" and the agents opened fire.

Jude dropped to the ground, swapped the M40A1 for the MP5 Kelly had left propped against the base of the rock. Grabbing a shield from the spares stacked next to it, she yelled, "Kelly, let's roll!" and darted along the base of the rise until she could see the white minivan looming. Bullets whizzed over her head.

"Extract!" Farrell ordered. "Get in there and carry them out if you have to."

She and Kelly shimmied up the rise until they could see over. There were two women and about eight kids pinned down at the edge of the house. Jude was stunned at the sight of Summer, wearing a bloodied nightdress and looking like she was in a state of near collapse.

"That woman's giving birth," she told Kelly.

The plygs were returning fire, hitting the rock position with everything they had.

"You take the two kids," Kelly said. "I'll get to the group."

Jude looked back over her shoulder. Agents were streaming along the exterior perimeter toward their position. "Go!" she cried and she and Kelly bolted over the rise, to the rear of the minivan.

They had only seconds before the plygs caught on. She could hear Kelly yelling at the women and children to get down as she ducked in front of the two children huddled on the earth. Bullets struck her shield and she fired back. A steel hailstorm infused the air with the smell of gunpowder. She knew from the deafening rat-tat that reinforcements had arrived and they were doing their best to draw the plygs' fire. Jude snatched the wounded boy into her arms. He was maybe three years old. The little girl with him looked six or so and gazed at Jude like she was an apparition.

"Stay with me," she said, tucking the girl's hand in hers, horribly aware that she had no way of firing with any accuracy while trying to hang on to a gun, a shield, and two small children.

She sent a message to Ben—*if you're already an angel, please help me.* Then she sprang up and ran. She felt weirdly light and fast, the world passing her by in a rush of blue sky and red earth. The ridge loomed faster than she'd expected, and she threw herself and the little girl over, rolling and hugging the bleeding boy to her. They landed in a heap at the feet of several fully armored men who instantly seized the children and ran them down the line.

Panting, Jude checked herself out for wounds, almost unable to believe she hadn't sustained any. She realized she was being clapped on the shoulders and an agent was handing her a water flask. She took a single, rapid slug and checked in with Farrell.

"Are we going in, sir?"

"No. I want minimum casualties."

This had to be a tough call. They had enough firepower to storm the building. Sledgehammer the windows, drop in a few flash-bang grenades with delayed fuses, breach the front door with charges—a battering ram wouldn't cut it. They could be inside within ten seconds, but the body count would be high.

She watched Kelly lower Summer to the ground and thought, poor bastard. FBI SWAT training did not include delivering babies in the middle of a siege. Over the radio, Farrell ordered a couple of vehicles in as a diversion, a high risk strategy. These people had a rocket propelled grenade launcher and they knew how to use it. They'd already taken out a car.

"Kelly, when you see them coming, you are go."

"Roger that."

"B team. I want four men in there to replace him."

"Roger that," a woman replied, apparently next in the chain of command.

Jude glanced around, trying to spot her. She didn't have to try too hard. A gloved index finger pointed her way. She was being ordered into position as one of the four going in.

They flattened out along the rise and waited for the command. Farrell was pulling out the stops. He had a chopper overhead, drawing fire away from the two approaching vehicles, black SUVs with the windows tinted. Gunfire flashed from the house. They were aiming at the chopper. Jude wondered if they knew there were more civilians out back. It didn't look like it.

"Go!" Farrell commanded.

Jude stopped thinking and started running just as the two SUVs screeched to a halt in a cloud of dust, providing a workable screen between the white minivan and the house. As the plygs unloaded into the vehicles, their occupants bailed fast and ran to the back of the house spraying fire along the white stucco.

"We have about twenty seconds to get out of here," Jude said. By now, the plygs had to be on their way to the rear of the dwelling. She tapped two of the guys and pointed into the empty room behind them. "Stay here and pin them down if they come through that door."

The rest of the team picked up a child each, leaving the biggest to run alongside. A young teenage girl had a Downs Syndrome child in her arms. He was the only one not weeping.

The woman with the group clutched the infant she was carrying to one shoulder and seized Jude's arm. "Her baby's coming out the wrong way."

"Don't worry. We have doctors standing by," Jude told her. Addressing Kelly, she asked, "Can you carry her?"

"Sure." He lifted Summer into his arms and called, "Go!"

The first SUV was ten feet away and they made it without incident. The firing had stopped. Even these people were not going to kill innocent women and children. An electronic buzz hurt Jude's eardrums and Nathaniel Epperson's voice boomed out.

"And the Lord sayeth, I shall bring a scourge upon my people to purge the ungodly from among you. And those that are righteous shall suffer with the wicked."

Jude signaled the agents at the front of their group, waving them on. One at a time, they ran to the next SUV. Smoke was rising from the vehicle, creating useful cover. But Jude was uneasy. The thing could go up in flames at any moment. She met Kelly's eyes and knew he was thinking exactly the same thing.

The litany continued. "And those transgressors who seek forgiveness shall beg their brethren to spill their blood in atonement for their sins, as ye would so do now if only the wrath that is kindled against ye were known."

As Epperson poured down hate, they shuffled out from behind the first vehicle, crossing five or six yards to the next. The two agents at the head of their little band were already at the white minivan, about to run the final stretch to safety, when a light flashed from the house.

Jude shouted, "Grenade! Run! Take cover."

She and Kelly didn't get far enough from the SUV targeted by the plygs. The blast threw them off their feet, well clear of the vehicles. Ears ringing, she lifted her head. Kelly and Summer lay inert a few feet away. Next to them, the teenage girl with the Downs Syndrome child was trying to crawl, blood streaming down her face from a head wound. They were completely exposed, too far away from the vehicles to use them as cover. The plygs opened fire at random through the haze of smoke, smashing the boards off the nearest window so they could find better sightlines.

"Engage," Farrell commanded. "Shoot to kill." A swarm of FBI agents cleared the ridge, grouping at the white minivan in an offensive formation.

Jude could hear gunfire but it was as if her ears were under water. She scrambled toward the girl with the head injury and realized that Kelly was hit and unconscious. Yelling for support to bring Summer and the small boy in, she grabbed the girl around the middle, hooked Kelly beneath one arm, and dragged them both toward the minivan. She had barely made six paces when several agents reached them and three more ran by, exchanging heavy fire with the men shooting from the windows.

Handing Kelly and the girl over, Jude turned automatically to go back. But even as she willed her feet to move, her body froze. It was too late. Out in the open, unprotected, the little boy hunkered next to Summer, his hands over his face. The image froze in Jude's mind as bullets rained down on the helpless pair before they could be rescued. Their bodies bounced, blood sprayed, and dust rose in a dense cloud.

Someone yanked her into a run and she hurtled toward the minivan. She could hear Farrell giving orders but could not make out the words, her ears still ringing from the explosion. The gunfire seemed far away and was becoming sporadic. Agents ran toward the rear of the house, joining the two already positioned there. Jude was familiar with the drill. They would capture any subject trying to exit. The fact that they had left Summer and the child unattended could mean only one thing.

As the dust settled, Jude felt tears crawl down her face. All that was left of the lives that might have been were two rag dolls in a crimson pool.

❖

After the shooting stopped, a dark silence descended. In that time, Elias Rockwell arrived under escort. He was not at all what Jude had expected. Early thirties, no sign of the genetic traits that would make walking through a crowd of Colorado City polygamists a déjà vu experience. He wore an expensive three-piece suit, aviator sunglasses, and designer loafers. His hair was blond and fashionably cut to disguise the thinning around his temples. When he wasn't marrying schoolgirls, Jude had the impression he was probably on a yacht or playing golf.

Farrell showed him the scene. They were watched by Rockwell's retinue, six rent-a-goons in cheaper versions of his suit. A few genetic similarities were evident in their ranks.

"This is a shocking tragedy," Rockwell said, as if the unfolding events had nothing to do with him. "These actions are the actions of a few deeply confused individuals, and in no way reflect the philosophy and aims of the new FLDS." He walked a few paces away and got on his cell phone, speaking in an undertone.

Moments later weapons were dropped from windows and a white flag appeared. On closer inspection, it was a pair of long underpants.

"They're ready to surrender," Rockwell informed Farrell and they proceeded to the front of the house.

The plygs emerged, their hands on their heads, and walked quietly down the front steps to assemble in the yard. Jude scanned the faces, seeking Epperson's. She moved to Farrell's side and said, "I have an arrest warrant for Nathaniel Epperson on charges of kidnapping and criminal homicide."

"He's ours," Farrell said. "We can quibble over jurisdictional matters later."

Nauseous, Jude walked around the side of the house once more.

Over the ridge, agents were processing the women and children who had filed from the house, patting them down for weapons and taking their details. The small party rescued under fire were seated under a makeshift canopy, being examined by a doctor. Beyond the white minivan and the smoking wreck of the SUV, the two bodies lay uncovered as yet. Kneeling over them was a slightly built teenage boy in overalls. As Jude approached, he looked up, tears rolling down his face.

"You shouldn't be here," Jude said. "If you go down to the officers, they'll take your information and give you something to eat and drink."

The boy didn't move.

Jude extended a hand. "Come on. I'll walk down with you." This was not a sight for a child.

He shook his head and bent low over Summer. Gently, he lifted her head onto his lap. "She never liked her hair this way," he said, and began unfastening her braids.

Jude watched the tender ritual in silence and understood what she was seeing. After a time, she asked, "Adeline?"

"Mmm-hmm."

"I'm very sorry."

A pair of eyes as dark as Chastity Young's met hers. "Why did they do this to her?"

Jude's throat hurt and she blinked away tears. "In life, some things make no sense at all. This is one of them."

Adeline smoothed her sister's snow blond hair and leaned over, placing a kiss on her cheek. "I wanted her to come with me but she wouldn't."

Jude removed her bulletproof vest and stripped off her shirt, folding it to make a pillow. She handed this to Adeline, who eased her sister's head onto it and stroked her eyes closed. They did not move the little boy, who had his face resting on Summer's nightgown.

"Your aunt is looking for you," Jude said.

"She's here?" Adeline got to her feet.

Jude pointed toward the mountain. "She went over that way on her bike."

Adeline wiped her eyes and picked up a makeshift backpack. Out of this she took the lid of a tin can. "I need to signal her," she explained.

They walked to the edge of the rise and Adeline bounced sunlight off the lid.

"Do you know her cell phone number?" Jude asked after a minute or two.

"Why do I always forget about phones?" Adeline gave a ragged little grin.

Jude handed hers over. "Do you know how it works?"

"Aunt Chastity says I might as well super glue mine to my ear." She dialed and waited. Then her face lit up and she said, "It's me."

Jude took a few steps away and stared out across the merciless plateau as Adeline cried into the phone. She should go get someone to take the bodies, she thought. But she didn't move. Numbly, she watched an eagle soar high above, riding a thermal. She imagined herself up there, floating in the cool tranquility, divorced from the tragedy below, hearing nothing but the wind rushing through feathers and her own mournful cries.

"She's coming." Adeline returned the phone and thanked her. "I told her where Daniel is and she's going to go pick him up first."

"That's great. Would you like me to wait with you?"

"Do you have time?"

"Absolutely."

"Got any water?"

"No, but I can get some. Come on." Jude offered a hand and Adeline took it.

CHAPTER SEVENTEEN

A month later, Jude sat on the front porch of the Epperson house and watched the FBI forensic team load the last of their gear into the backs of a fleet of vans. They'd owned the place since the shootout, and Jude had stayed well clear. Pratt had given permission for her to return for a walk-through once they received the okay from the FBI crime lab. This was supposedly aimed at straightening out a few details missing from her account of the shooting. Jude had a feeling he knew she just needed to come back.

She'd been unsettled since that day, and not just because people had died needlessly. There was so much they would never know; she almost regretted that the Huntsberger case had all but solved itself once Zach walked into the Paradox station. On investigations where clues came slowly and detectives had to create their own luck, there was time to accumulate knowledge and develop theories. The work was methodical, detail oriented, and detached. There was order. And a sense of satisfaction when months of effort led to a good arrest.

By contrast, Jude felt like she'd been swept into a situation that went completely out of her control almost before she could process exactly what was going on. With the benefit of hindsight, she thought she could have made some better decisions. She tried not to feel that she had shortchanged Darlene, and Poppy Dolores—all of Epperson's victims.

Sheriff Pratt was riding high. Shaking hands, kissing babies, appearing in photo opportunities with the Huntsbergers. He'd told the media justice had been done and he truly seemed to believe it, as did most of Cortez. Jude wanted to go after Jeffs and Rockwell, but Pratt said they'd bought themselves enough trouble and her FBI masters said it was someone else's fight. Jude needed to wrap up the final paperwork and get on with her life.

"Done?" she asked a bored-looking technician who emerged from the house.

"Help yourself." The guy strode away like a man who'd been waiting two weeks for a cold beer.

Jude got up and stepped indoors. The place was whitewashed inside and out, consistent with the way the case had been handled in the press. A pack of religious nuts opens fire on women and children trying to flee for their lives. The FBI had everything on video, so there couldn't be sticky questions left unanswered. Jude had seen the footage they released a hundred times over, trying to make certain she was unrecognizable. They'd done a good job of blurring her features and it was comforting to see herself anonymously referred to as a "Denver detective at the scene on an unrelated investigation."

She entered the northeast-facing bedroom that had had the windows knocked out on that day. The bloodstains were still tagged. The splatter on the wall to her right belonged to Nathaniel Epperson, who had died of chest wounds at the scene, robbing them of answers to countless questions, but making his wife Naoma a happy woman, perhaps for the first time.

Jude wanted to spit in his face, but she wouldn't have that satisfaction and spitting on a man's grave was not her style. Feeling cheated, she wandered through the rest of the house. It wasn't like they didn't know what had happened. A fairly clear picture had emerged from the statements given by those of the other wives who were willing to talk, Thankful in particular. Encouraged by a community of former plural wives living in Colorado, she had decided to make the state her home.

After being condemned by Nathaniel Epperson, for reasons unclear to all, Darlene had been taken to her first husband, Hyrum, and told to seek his forgiveness as part of her purification. He had flown into a rage as he sometimes did and mauled her like a dog. Eventually Nathaniel and several of the older sons had managed to drag him off. One of them, Thankful's oldest boy, had told his mother everything, even though they were sworn to secrecy. No one knew exactly what had happened after that, except that Naoma and Nathaniel had been heard shouting at each other, then Fawn Dew and Nathaniel drove off with Darlene and returned without her eight days later.

Jude had been trying to interview Fawn Dew ever since, but she was holed up in Rockwell's compound and it appeared the new prophet had struck a deal with Utah and Arizona. He had agreed to a gradual "modernization" of his flock, including public school education, in exchange for an injection of government funding to tidy up the twin towns and fund community development. His daughter was "unavailable for comment" and Jude had been referred to his attorneys.

Adeline's story had made headlines, and she and Chastity had appeared on a few television talk shows, putting a face to the countless women whose lives were destroyed by the so-called "sacred principle" of plural marriage. Jude had seen them again at Summer's funeral in Salt Lake City. The Flemings had wanted to avoid publicity, so they'd allowed their daughter to be buried with her grandparents. They'd also signed over guardianship. Chastity said she'd paid her brother-in-law twenty thousand dollars for this. Child Protection Services had placed Daniel Epperson in a foster home where another of the "Lost Boys" of Utah was thriving, and it sounded like he was doing fine.

Jude paused opposite a small plaque on the wall of what was once Naoma Epperson's bedroom. *Keep Sweet, No Matter What.* Just reading it made her feel depressed and overwhelmed. Thankful had talked about being brought up in a home where crying was forbidden and children who did were badly beaten.

Something she'd said played again and again in Jude's mind. "I had to learn to be silent. It was the only way I would survive."

She'd been embarrassed talking about her past, as if she should have known better.

Jude returned to the front porch and gazed out at the barns and the scraggly junipers, trying to imagine how the women living here must have felt. It had been too much for Poppy and somehow she had gotten away. Most of the wives admitted she'd been one of them, but seemed afraid to talk about her. Thankful said she was the ninth wife and that her real name was Valerie. She claimed to know nothing about her and Jude could sense that she was uncomfortable. Valerie had been a poofer, she said. There one day, gone the next. Everyone thought she was probably in Canada. Naoma was equally unhelpful. Valerie was one subject she was not willing to discuss and her plea bargain did not require her to do so.

Jude took a plastic bag from her pocket and examined the key and ten-digit code. In their extensive search of the premises and outbuildings, the FBI had found nothing the small key would fit. The number made no sense to anyone. 2329159919. Jude reminded herself to look for the obvious. Living here, staring out at the surroundings, yearning to escape, what must Darlene have been thinking? What secret did the numbers represent? Why had she been singled out by Nathaniel for torture and murder? According to Naoma, God said Darlene had "betrayed" them. Clearly, this was Nathaniel's opinion dressed up as a message from the Almighty.

Jude paced back and forth in the shade, trying to put herself in Darlene's shoes. Pregnant. Helpless. Desperate to contact someone from the outside world and let them know who she was. Had she stolen money and concealed it somewhere, imagining she could get to a town and buy a ticket out? There had to be a reason why Nathaniel lost his temper that day. He must have discovered something. If Darlene had physically hidden money or some other item, it had to be within walking distance of the house. There was nowhere else she could go.

Jude studied the digits again and remembered something she had seen in Darlene's room—a note pinned to her mirror that instructed her younger sister to "leave my lipstick alone." Every *L* in the note had been written *l* and in Darlene's hand, the letter was stunted. To a lab tech in Quantico who thought he was dealing with a phone number, it would be easy to mistake the letter for the number one.

In her mind's eye, she replaced the ones with an L, and for a moment the revised code still didn't make any sense, then she knew exactly what she was looking at. It was dead simple. Jude began counting her paces from the doorstep, walking in as straight a line as she could.

Half an hour and two left turns later, she was staring at a smooth boulder with a small trowel jammed deeply into the earth next to it. Jude dug her way around the boulder until the tip of the trowel struck something metallic. Scraping the dirt away, she eased a small locked metal box from the ground.

The key slid into the lock and turned. Inside the box, a notebook was wedged on top of a pile of papers. Jude lifted it out and opened it at the first page. The owner had drawn a flower. Beneath this was written in a child's hand, "My Story by Valerie Epperson."

Jude flipped the page and found herself staring at a photograph of Naoma as a young woman. On her knee sat a prettily dressed little girl. The caption under the photo read, "Me with my Mom."

Poppy Dolores was Naoma's daughter. Nathaniel Epperson had taken his own child as his ninth wife. But that was not the ugliest secret Darlene had uncovered. Folded in the center of the notebook was a carefully drawn map in the distinctive turquoise ink Nathaniel Epperson used in his fountain pen. It showed the graves of seventeen people buried on the Epperson ranch. Each grave was numbered and a legend appeared on the back of the map. Beside each number was a name and next to that a brief statement of the individual's sin and the method of "elimination." The list was headed up "Atonement."

Nathaniel Epperson was a mass murderer.

❖

"That's fascinating," Mercy said, glancing around the restaurant as she sipped her wine. They were in Denver, but she was still paranoid. "She must have found the box somewhere on the property, seen the value it could have, and hidden it while she tried to figure out how she could use it."

"I think she tried to blackmail him," Jude speculated, mildly distracted by the outline of Mercy's hard little nipples beneath her white shirt. "I think she told him that if he drove her back to Colorado, she would tell him where to find it. That's why she had the note and the key. But then, at some point, she must have realized he was going to kill her, and she swallowed the information. Got the last word, in a sense."

"You think Epperson and Fawn Dew planned it all along? Drove all the way to Colorado intending to kill her?"

"Probably. Then I think they buried the body somewhere, but had second thoughts. They were away for about eight days, according to Thankful."

"They dug her up…yes, that figures with the decomposition rate. But why?"

"My guess is that they came up with a dopey plan to make it look like she'd been in Colorado all along. I think they found the stake when they were looking for a dump site and hammered it into her heart to try and make this look like the work of a psycho killer."

"Which it was," Mercy chipped in.

"They wanted her to be found and identified so we'd focus on locals in the investigation. Hence the social security card. They were just trying to hide the fact that she had been in Utah."

"But she vanished two years earlier. Didn't they realize we'd know she hadn't been dead that long?"

"I doubt forensic science or even basic biology formed part of their education," Jude said.

Mercy smiled. "Basic biology. Now that's a topic we should discuss in private." Her hand drifted across the table and her fingers lightly stroked the inside of Jude's wrist. "Want to get a room?"

Jude did. In the worst way. But she was still bothered about Elspeth. "You already have a girlfriend."

"She's only here every few months. And we just sleep together for old time's sake."

"So the next time she comes, you'll relive those happy memories again?"

Mercy shook her head, half laughing, half serious. "You're being a Neanderthal about this."

"You haven't answered my question."

"I don't owe you an explanation." Impatience seeped into Mercy's voice. "It's my business if I choose to have sex with Elspeth or not."

Jude stared down at the table, wanting to agree and get out of the restaurant and escape to a hotel. "Okay. I'm sorry. You're right. It's none of my business."

"Jude," Mercy said softly, "we can't do this if we're not on the same page. I don't want to hurt you."

"I'm not hurt."

"I don't mind if you see other people."

For some reason, that was no consolation. Jude said, "I know."

That was exactly what she should do, she told herself. See other people. The fact that she only wanted to "see" Mercy was her problem. She signaled the waiter for the check and changed the subject.

"As I was leaving the place I went to the baby graveyard. One of the local women took me. She wants the FBI to investigate the place. There are about two hundred children buried there and in the big cemetery next to it. A lot of the graves are unmarked."

She broke off when Mercy took her hand firmly and stared into her eyes. "Jude, you can't dig up every dead child. It's too late to save them."

They left the restaurant and walked to Mercy's car. In silence, they got in and put on their seat belts. Jude told herself to lighten up. She'd done nothing but talk about the case ever since Mercy picked her up from the airport. She'd had a feeling the whole time that Mercy had something on her mind she wanted to talk about. Not that she'd had the opportunity. They might as well have been sitting in her office talking shop. If Jude wanted Mercy as a girlfriend, she had to do better than this.

Before she could come up with an innocuous conversation starter, Mercy said, "I'm going to drop you at the hotel and go stay with friends in Boulder for a couple of days."

Jude's throat cramped. "Why?"

"Because this is getting too complicated for me."

"No one saw us."

"That's not what I'm talking about." She lifted a caressing hand to Jude's face. "I think you need more than I can give you right now."

Jude covered Mercy's hand with her own, then turned it over so she could kiss the palm. "You can't imagine how much I want you."

Mercy leaned into her, the flimsy silk of her shirt shifting across her breasts with every breath. Her mouth was against Jude's ear. "That's just the problem," she murmured. "I can."

Jude lowered her mouth to the base of Mercy's throat and kissed a path down, unbuttoning Mercy's shirt as she went. She wore a sheer camisole instead of a bra. Her nipples rose against the fine fabric, their dark peach color darker in the shadowed interior of the car.

"We can't do this here," she gasped as Jude bit down softly.

"I don't want your Boulder friends listening while I fuck you," Jude replied.

"You want me to check into a hotel like…this?" Mercy stared down at her camisole. It was glued wetly to her nipples where Jude's mouth had been. She buttoned her shirt.

"I'll check us in. You can sit in the lobby with your legs crossed."

"Gallant to a fault." Mercy slid her arms over Jude's shoulders and cusped her hands behind Jude's neck. "Kiss me."

Jude forgot to be gentle. She kissed Mercy the way she wanted to take her, forcing her lips roughly apart, pushing inside, ignoring her resistance. Pressed to her, Mercy's body felt firm and damp beneath the gossamer barrier of her clothes. Jude drove deeper into her mouth and slid a hand between her thighs. Wet flesh kissed her fingers. Mercy groaned.

Brilliant light flooded the car and someone honked their horn.

Jude lifted her mouth from Mercy's and looked out the back window. "I think they want our space."

"They can wait," Mercy said. But she started the car and bunny-hopped out of the parking spot.

"Want me to drive?" Jude offered.

"No. I have other plans for you."

"I'll save my strength, then."

"Good idea."

They stopped at a set of lights and stared at one another.

"God, you make me hot," Jude said.

Mercy smiled the way she did in Jude's regular fantasies. "Well, we're on the same page with *that*."

"Drive faster," Jude said.

And Mercy did.

CHAPTER EIGHTEEN

Tulley came into work late. He had a black eye.
"It didn't go well?" Jude asked.

"She cussed me out."

"You'll find a nice girl one day." *And so will I*, she thought. Maybe not *nice*. But smart and kind-hearted. Also on the wish list—hot and monogamous in her inclinations.

Smoke'm stuck his head in Tulley's lap, feeling his pain if the subsequent whines were any indication.

"I'm not in any hurry." Tulley massaged the hound's jowls and lifted his ears one at a time, kissing them lavishly.

Jude was curious but decided Tulley's reasons for bachelorhood were his own. It was rare to meet a male who was not hormone driven, quite a relief, especially in the light of the bouquet of flowers flaunting itself on the cherry console where anyone looking in the station window could see it. Agatha wanted the world to know Jude was not the lonely, unwanted old maid people thought.

"Is he still waiting out there?" she asked.

Tulley nodded. She could tell from the quivering line of his mouth that he could barely control his mirth. This made the rhythm of his speech more halting than usual.

"That's one womanizing horndog you got chasing your tail, Detective," he squeezed out before lowering his head to the papers in front of him and howling with laughter.

"Very funny," Jude said and went to the window.

Bobby Lee Parker was leaning up against his Chevy, reading *East of Eden*, a fact he'd impressed her with when he came calling the day before. Today he was wearing faded Levis and a sleeveless white T-shirt that showed off his perfect tan and tasteful tattoos. His truck windows were open and a Garth Brooks love ballad announced the presence of Jude's impassioned suitor to the entire valley yet again. He tipped his hat at her. Jude marveled at his persistence. Didn't the guy have a job to go to?

Tulley brought his laughing fit under control long enough to suggest, "Maybe you should go on one date so it seems like you gave him a chance."

"I don't *want* to give him a chance."

"Because of his past?" As if genuinely mystified, Tulley said, "He's college educated."

"Have you been talking to Agatha?"

"She says it couldn't do any harm."

"Tulley, I don't want a boyfriend. Just like you don't want a girlfriend."

"But you're a lot older than me."

"Take it easy."

Jude willed the phone to ring. Now that Naoma's arraignment was over, things were settling back to normal. Last week they'd arrested a man for putting a goat in his cheating wife's red lace underwear and parading the wretched animal in front of the workplace of the guy she was bonking. The goat was fine, but Jude had to explain the hazards of elastic; the thong had already rubbed some hair off. Colorado had serious animal cruelty legislation, she'd pointed out to the offender, and she would see to it personally that he paid the maximum fine if he took his marital problems out on a four-legged friend again. She let him go after he donated a hundred bucks to the Humane Society.

This debacle was followed by a snake scare, when a local python breeder rolled his SUV en route to a reptile convention in Durango. Youths stole the cage from the crash site and let the pythons loose in the Cortez Safeway, causing mayhem. Smoke'm had sniffed the embarrassed creatures out, ending their reign of terror and earning Tulley a front-page photo in the *Cortez Journal* and a brief appearance on Channel 9 news. The TV reporters had caught him off duty, shirtless, and washing his car. The ensuing footage of him playing fetch with Smoke'm was described by Sheriff Pratt as "more porno than promo." Nonetheless they'd seen a gratifying flood of e-mails from an admiring public, even if most of them were from women who wanted to cook Tulley dinner.

The real excitement of the past month, however, was off the record. Harrison Hawke, apparently inspired by the Gathering for Zion incident, was organizing a series of training sessions on his land and had invited rival white supremacist organizations to attend these "Aryan Defense Days." He'd applied for the requisite permit to shelter two hundred patriots in a tent village, and last week he'd asked Jude if he could meet with her in person to discuss logistics. He wanted to make sure the event was not subjected to harassment because "some liberals can't allow their fellow Americans to exercise their constitutional rights and freedoms."

Jude's handler was wetting himself and wanted her to suck up to Hawke by arranging a police presence to prevent civil rights activists from throwing eggs and waving placards. She could hardly wait. She was supposed to be driving out to Black Dog Gulch for the promised face-to-face in a few hours' time. But first she'd have to get rid of Hawke's competition. She was about to go break the bad news to Parker when the phone signaled a reprieve, and, speak of the devil, it was none other than the would-be architect of a "cleansed America" himself.

Tulley's gag-me-now expression was priceless. His hand over the mouthpiece, he announced, "It's Mr. Hawke from the Christian Republic of Aryan Patriots. He desires to speak to you in person."

Jude picked up the phone and sank down in her chair. Her last conversation with Hawke had claimed an entire afternoon, but he seemed to think they had bonded.

He returned her polite greeting with, "Just checking in. This afternoon still good for you, Detective?"

"Looking forward to it." Jude mustered all the warmth she could. "We have a lot to talk about."

This inspired a sharp intake of breath and Hawke eloquently shared what was on his mind. "There's something I want to say before we meet, to set the tone as it were."

Jude mumbled some encouragement and he launched into one of his monologues.

"Before your time, there was a moment in our nation's history when law enforcement officers stood shoulder to shoulder with patriots like myself in the one great fight white Israel must win. Some present-day activists have forgotten that, and mistakenly believe our former brothers—and sisters—have forsaken us. But I'm here to tell you I know that's not true. Detective, you speak for a silent majority, and I'm here to extend that invitation once again. This will be a moment you look back on, a moment for which your children's children will revere you in the ages to come."

He had prepared that impressive speech in advance, Jude surmised. An excess of solitude, paranoia, and time on one's hands was bound to amplify passions. Or, as in his case, fixations.

Meaning every word, she replied, "Sir, I've always believed that my uniform should stand for something."

"If I had my way, you'd be wearing another uniform," he all but simpered. "A uniform that truly befits a woman of your caliber. You know the one I'm talking about."

Recognizing this as something akin to a marriage proposal, Jude produced a small choked-up sigh. "You've no idea what it means to me to hear you say that, sir."

"Please. Call me Harrison. When we're speaking in private, of course."

"Of course. I'm very excited about the plans…Harrison." This breathless confession earned an incredulous look from Tulley.

"I'm aware that in offering your support, you do so at considerable risk to your reputation in certain quarters. So, I want to thank you." His tone let her know that he was up for much more than thanks.

Courted by two losers on the same day. How did she get so lucky? Falling back on her straight and susceptible routine, Jude said, "One day, I'd like to introduce you to my father. I think you two would have a lot in common." Not least being hair loss and a pathological dislike of Vietnamese people.

"I'm honored you feel that way." Hawke paused, evidently needing to collect himself. "This afternoon, then."

"This afternoon," Jude said softly and hung up.

"Do you know who that maniac *is*?" Tulley demanded.

"I certainly do."

"Then why are you being so nice to him?"

Because my masters think he's Richard Butler's natural successor and I'm supposed to become the object of his unrequited lust. The Bureau was convinced Hawke was trying to rally the fragmented, rudderless neo-Nazi movement—still reeling from Pierce's "freaks and weaklings" speech—by having a get-together along the lines of the legendary Estes Park conclave of 1992.

That gathering had seen the birth of an alliance between neo-Nazis, Klansmen, Posse Comitatus, antiabortion militants, and the Gun Owners of America, all united around a common goal to build "an all-White Christian republic." By 1995, they were urging their loyalists to forge ties with the extreme right at large, in particular Christian fundamentalists. The strategy was notably successful in remaking the gun lobby, adjusting its single-issue focus away from recreation and the right to hunt, to a broader right-wing platform around which every militia in the country could rally.

Lately, despite its spectacular under-the-radar political gains, the movement had seen a rash of in-house fighting and petty power struggles. Various notables had died or been convicted of crimes, including stealing from their own membership. The Aryan Nations had gone bankrupt and since the death of its leader, Richard Butler, the organization had splintered. The National Alliance had just expelled half its leadership cadre, who had regrouped as the National Vanguard. And the KKK had been steadily falling apart for the past decade. All in all, these were worrisome times for rank-and-file neo-Nazis, and humiliating, too. How could Jews and African Americans be blamed for the internal chaos in a movement entirely operated by the "racially superior"?

Tulley was still waiting to find out why she was being a sweetheart to Hawke, and Jude produced a slippery answer. "Because I'm here to protect and defend the rights of all citizens, not just those cut from the same political cloth as me."

"You don't *like* him, do you?"

"My personal feelings about Mr. Hawke are irrelevant. This is work."

Tulley peeled a stick of fresh gum. "If you had to choose between the two of them, who would you pick?"

"I have no idea what you are talking about."

"Hawke or Bobby Lee?"

Jude rolled her eyes. "Like I said, I'm not looking for a boyfriend."

"But if you had to."

Guessing he was uncomfortable with the idea that a creep like Hawke could even be in the running, she conceded, "Bobby Lee.

Okay?"

"Mighty pleased to hear it." From the doorway, Bobby Lee Parker drawled a greeting and strolled into the office like he owned the patent on cool. When he reached Jude's desk, he removed his hat and placed it tenderly on top of the nearest filing cabinet.

She said, "That was a figurative question, Mr. Parker. I wouldn't read anything into the answer."

"All the same, do I need to speak with this Hawke dude, man to man?" He cocked his head in Tulley's direction. "Know where he drinks, Deputy?"

Tulley snickered. "In his bedroom, I reckon."

Bobby Lee flashed his white, perfect teeth. To Jude, he said, "That's not the kind of man who'll put a smile on your face."

"Get out of here," she ordered. "And take your posy."

Strangely undeterred, he said, "Man, you've got it going on Anyone ever tell you, you have the sexist voice since Marlene Dietrich?"

Jude got up. Normally the sight of her—5' 10," built, armed, and annoyed—terminated male overtures without so much as a whimper. Not in Parker's case.

The guy stuck out his arm out and said, "Come on. Make a man happy. Take a walk with me, Detective Dee-Vine."

Why couldn't Mercy show up at her office with flowers and sweet talk? For a few seconds, Jude indulged herself in a pity party, then she laughed at her own lapse into romantic yearning, hooked her arm into Bobby Lee's, and resigned herself to having to be blunter than usual. "Okay," she said. "Let's have a conversation."

Grinning, Bobby Lee picked up his hat and pulled her close. He even smelled good. As they passed Tulley's desk, he paused and offered his condolences.

"The face. That's unacceptable. Was she drunk?"

"Nope." Tulley touched his purple eye. "Just pissed."

"I can tell you're not a man who hits a woman." Bobby Lee tightened his grip on Jude like he knew she was already regretting the impulse to talk with him. "But listen up, my friend. A chick who takes advantage of your fine manners is not worth having. Get some self-respect and dump her."

"I did."

"Good to know." Bobby Lee seemed lost in thought for an instant. Then he asked, "Hey, pal. Want to get a beer later?"

"Sure," Tulley said.

Jude could tell he was pleased. Did Parker think he could win her over by making friends with her associates? He already had Agatha eating out of his hand, after fixing a flat tire for her and carrying her parcels to the door. Jude tried to tug her arm free, but he kept a firm hold and started walking.

As soon as they got outside, he released his grip and she stepped away from him, demanding, "What are you playing at, Mr. Parker?"

"I like it better when you call me Bobby Lee."

"Well, don't get used it. Stop flirting and listen to me. You're wasting your time. I am never going to date you." She offered the excuse she thought would make the most sense to this hormonal cowboy. "The fact is, you're too young for me. None of us can change the way attraction works. I choose lovers in their thirties."

Bobby Lee opened his truck and held the passenger door. "Care to continue in air-conditioned comfort?"

"So long as this doesn't take more than five minutes." Jude got in the truck, thinking: *I need my head examined.*

"You're a hard woman," Bobby Lee mourned.

"So I'm told."

He took the seat next to her and started the motor. The vents threw hot air ahead of cold. Jude was already perspiring, which made her uniform feel like it was hugging way too closely for a situation like this.

She said, "I'm flattered. Really, I am. But there's just no way. Do you understand?"

"That butch, huh?"

Her heart stopped in her chest, then began galloping at double time. Was this what she thought it was? Had the rules just changed in a split second? Coldly, she said, "Call it what you want."

Bobby Lee's brilliant blue eyes wandered lazily over her. "People think they know their own demarcation lines," he said softly, "but I've found there's a lot of slack between no and yes."

Jude knew exactly what he was talking about. She was surprised. Who would have taken Bobby Lee Parker for the philosophical type? In another time or place, she might have allowed herself to be drawn into a conversation beyond the superficial. There was obviously more to him than met the eye. But this was not an anonymous bar somewhere in a big city.

Damply, she said, "That's something we see in my line of work, too."

"Mine changed in prison," he replied, making her willful detachment feel cheap. "A man learns a lot about himself in a situation like that."

"If you don't quit robbing gas stations you'll be having another learning experience soon."

The dark center of each eye dilated, consuming the blue. He said, "I went through a rough patch when I got out. That's in the past now."

"You've found work?" He was probably growing weed for his mother and her pothead pals.

Another surprise. "I'm going back to school."

"Good for you. I really hope it pans out."

"There's one thing I'm gonna miss."

Jude thought gloomily: *here it comes.*

"Love at first sight," he mooned. "Never happened before."

"You'll get over it. College is wall to wall…attractive women."

He wasn't letting up. "I gotta tell you something—that place between no and yes is real familiar to me."

Jude wasn't sure how to translate this statement. Bobby Lee spared her brain cells.

"What I'm saying is I don't limit myself like most folks. So, if you were interested, we could party. But the fact is, it's your deputy that's on my mind."

Jude's first thought was: *no fucking way!* Her voice hit a rare treble. "Tulley?"

"I prefer to call him Adonis." Bobby Lee acknowledged this poeticism with a wry grin. "First moment I saw him, it was exactly like they say. A lightning bolt. Thought I could scope him out if everyone got the idea I was hot for you."

"You sure had me fooled."

"Disappointed? Just say the word and I'll make it up to you."

"I thought you were in love."

"Doesn't affect my competence with others, and for you…I'd go the extra mile."

Jude burst out laughing. "Slut."

"There's no need to be unkind."

Jude wanted to dislike him, but their conversation was refreshingly uncomplicated. Amazed that in a place like this, a young male would come out as bisexual or gay to anyone, she said, "You're taking quite a risk talking to me like this,"

"There's only been two females ever turned me down. The other one was a lesbian. So, I figured..."

"Tulley's straight."

"Poor taste in women, too." Bobby Lee seemed unfazed.

Jude had no idea what to say. She consulted the desolate Uravan landscape and came up with a lame response. "I don't think he shares your feelings."

"That's why I've decided to make friends with him, and hit on you instead."

"Are you trying to make him jealous?"

"No. Just buying myself some access and doing us both a big favor. The Four Corners is not a good place to be gay. Or bi."

Then leave Tulley alone, Jude thought. "There's something I'm not seeing. Who says anyone knows?"

"You're a single female under fifty in a town where guys outnumber chicks three to one. You've been here awhile and you've turned down every guy who's dropped a hint. They're talking about you."

Jude shrugged. "Talk is just talk."

"This works for both of us," he said. "'Specially in your situation."

Jude frowned. Just how closely had the unexpectedly serious-minded Parker been watching her?

"Dr. Westmoreland's a classy lady," he said.

"We're just friends." Anger quickened her limbs. "Are you making some kind of threat?"

"Jesus. Chill. It's not healthy to be wound up like you are. All I'm saying is there's talk. Even my mom's heard."

Jude felt squeamish. This would mean curtains. No more 4:30 a.m. drives back from Grand Junction. No more checking in to separate rooms at the Hotchkiss Inn, miles from anywhere.

She said, "I don't suppose it could do any harm to give them something else to gossip about."

"That was my thinking."

"I seriously doubt you'll get anywhere with Tulley."

"Me too."

Who would buy *her* dating Bobby Lee Parker? Jude shook her head in disbelief that she was even considering this desperate measure. It wasn't like her affair with Mercy was a star-crossed lovers situation. They were strictly about getting laid. All the same, good sex in this neck of the woods was nothing to be sneezed at, and if Mercy got wind that there was talk, their exhausting evenings would be over in a heartbeat.

She said, "What's the big date in Cortez?"

"If you get lucky I'll take you to Blondie's."

Also a popular outing for cops and their wives. Jude could see them now. "Christ," she said.

Bobby Lee moved closer and dropped a tame kiss on her cheek. "No need to thank me, sweetheart."

Jude lifted a handful of Mercy's hair and kissed the smooth curve where neck met shoulder. Several small dark moles nestled in the hollow above her collarbone, as if Mother Nature had flicked some paint on the immaculate almond canvas of Mercy's skin. A scant haze of ultra-fine blond hair was visible on her forearms, picked out by the morning sun. Her hands lay folded over her midriff, their fine-boned perfection thrown into relief, a latticework of pale blue veins visible beneath the pale translucence of her skin.

Jude tried to frame the words she wanted to say. They'd seen each other on and off ever since their evening in Denver. Jude's feeble resistance to sharing Mercy crumbled every time she set eyes on her. Mercy only had to look at her and she was putty. Was she in love? She didn't think so. She was in lust, but love hovered as a possibility. Sometimes she wanted to say that to Mercy, to check in and see if it was still too complicated.

She decided now seemed like a good time to revisit that, but before she could speak, Mercy moved closer and faced her. Playfully, she said, "We should do this again some time. You're a truly accomplished lover."

It seemed like a compliment, only Jude found herself hearing what Mercy didn't say. Feelings were not mentioned. She didn't say she wanted to see more of Jude, that maybe they could start including each other in their lives, not just in their beds. It was always like this.

Sometimes they barely spoke, other than to voice their desires. Their dialogue was almost entirely sexual.

"Thank you. I'm glad I pass muster." Jude could not miss the edge in her own voice. It was not lost on Mercy, either.

"Is something wrong?" She stroked Jude's cheek.

"No." Jude told herself to do better, to take a shot at saying what was really on her mind. "I was thinking. Maybe we could see a bit more of each other. It doesn't always have to be about sex."

"You mean date?"

"Why not? We don't have to be obvious about it. We could meet after you finish work sometimes. Have a drink. Have dinner at each other's houses like a normal couple."

"We're not a couple, and I'm not ready for that."

"I'm not suggesting we get married."

"Aren't you?" Mercy's eyes chilled a little.

"Give me a break." Jude said softly. "We're both grown-ups. I don't suffer from romantic delusions any more than you do. But I think we're being overly paranoid. We like each other's company. All I'm saying is why don't we accept that and make the most of it. You've said you're lonely."

"Yes, but it's not so bad anymore. It makes a big difference knowing that you're there."

Jude rolled onto her back and stared up at the ceiling. Did she really want to be nothing but a convenient port in a storm, a lover who, like a toy, could be picked up and put down at will? Restive, her mind working, she asked, "Mercy, what exactly do you want from me?"

Mercy trailed a hand over Jude's breasts to her stomach and down to the wet parting of her flesh. Slowly, deliberately, she aroused her. "I want this. I want someone I can let go with. I want there to be one place in my life where I don't have to be careful all the time. You give me that."

Jude could barely hold a coherent thought together. Catching Mercy's hand by the wrist, she arrested its distracting pressure and took a risk. "I could give you more than that. I don't want us to be closed to other possibilities."

"This isn't enough for you?" Mercy picked up her strokes with the other hand. With an intent expression, she got to her knees and moved over Jude, lowering her mouth to her throat, biting slightly harder than usual. "The way I see it," she lifted her head, bright blue eyes challenging Jude, "Why mess with a good thing?"

Why indeed? There were people who'd kill for what they had. Jude wanted to discuss this some more, but it could wait. For the moment, her body had another agenda. Ignoring the part of her that craved a deeper connection, she drew Mercy down and kissed the breath from her.

CHAPTER NINETEEN

Eight hundred years ago, the Anasazi abandoned their pueblo villages in the Dolores valley and built a city beneath the massive overhangs of the Mesa Verde 8,000 feet above sea level. They lived in the canyon walls for a century, then vanished without a trace, leaving only abstract designs and a few petroglyphs. Little remained of their cliff dwellings now. The Ute, the Navajo, and the Apache had left them undisturbed in the centuries that followed, but time took its toll.

Jude stood on the rim of the mesa and allowed her eyes to drift slowly along the canyon sandstone ledges. In the harsh sunlight, it was easy to miss the shadow of a doorway or a window tucked into a niche or shrouded by a rocky overhang. But eventually, the eroding remnants of walls and buildings took shape, almost miragelike in the afternoon haze, and she could make out the telltale indentations the Anasazi had gouged into the cliffs as hand and footholds. These, more than anything else, whispered to her of the people who had once clung to them, driven by some unknown fear or yearning.

She wondered what had happened to them. They had cultivated their corn and squash on the mesa top, building dams and irrigations channels; one of their reservoirs, the Mummy Lake, was still visible from the Far View pueblo. They had hunted deer and buried their dead infants wrapped in rabbit skins. They constructed hundreds of miles of roads, but for what purpose? There was no sign that they used wheels or pack animals. Without a written language, they could leave no explanations for the curious latecomers to this land.

The evening before, she had strolled along the Knife Edge trail to watch the sun set over the Montezuma Valley. A few decades earlier, some optimists had built a road along the western face of the mesa, but the gods that ruled this ancient kingdom had rained down boulders and torn at it from below until it was inaccessible. Before long, it would vanish completely, the lost evidence of another civilization. Watching the sun sink behind Sleeping Ute Mountain, drowning the canyons in red, Jude had felt as insignificant as any human was in the greater scheme of things. It was just the feeling she was seeking. Her mom would call it getting things in perspective.

She had made the journey days earlier, through the Dolores rift to the ruins of Chapin Mesa, unable to shake from her mind the image of Summer and the little boy who died with her. She felt responsible, snared by the what ifs she'd been taught to let go of. Hindsight was a rod any detective could use to beat herself up. In the split second when she'd grabbed Kelly and the teenage girl, she'd made a choice to leave the others. Had she chosen differently, they might still be alive. The team would have reached Kelly and the girl first.

Everyone said she'd done the right thing, and that had she gone back alone for the two who died, she would probably have been killed as well. Jude could follow their reasoning but it didn't help. She would always see those two innocents, trapped in that moment before their lives were stolen. She would always feel that terrible powerlessness. The best she could hope for was to reach an accommodation with the events of that day, to forgive herself for not being able to arrest time and entice a different outcome from the Fates.

Jude left the mesa rim and took a circuitous route back to her truck at the Morfield Campground, halting at a cairn one of the guides had pointed out during the walking tour she'd taken soon after she first arrived. It was an ancient shrine near a yellow-leaved cottonwood tree, a mound of gray river cobbles caressed smooth and round by eons of water. The Navajo still prayed and left offerings there—small turquoise beads, feathers, obsidian, and twigs. They only did this on their way to a destination, the guide said; never on the return trip.

Jude broke a twig from a pine tree nearby and placed it with the other offerings, making a wish for luck on her journey. In theory, she was on her return trip, but somehow it didn't feel like that. It felt like she was moving forward, heading into the unknown, trusting in the promise and possibility of tomorrow.

She strolled the rest of the way to her tent and packed up, one of several campers watched warily by a group of deer wandering through the high grass, then drove slowly between the piñon pines and junipers, down the winding, treacherous road toward U.S. 160. Ahead of her lay the Mancos Valley, once Darlene Huntsberger's home. Her parents had raised a small stone monument to her on their farm, just below a tree she liked to climb. They had invited Jude and Tulley out to see it, and Mrs. Huntsberger had made a pie for them. The family seemed to think justice had been done, even if it came without the niceties of a trial. This was the general sentiment about town. Little was known about Jude and Tulley's role beyond the official story—two MCSO officers were dispatched to arrest the prime suspect in the Huntsberger homicide, only to find themselves caught up in a confrontation between the FLDS sect and the FBI. Tulley said he didn't care if their story was not going to end up on TV. He was still getting his promotion.

At Towaoc, Jude took the turnoff to Eddie House's place and pulled into the driveway as the late afternoon light was fading. The air had a chill in it, the first whisper of the coming winter. It would be a relief to see snow, she thought, as she fished around in the back of the Dakota and found her backpack. She slung it over her shoulder and headed for the house, pausing opposite one of Eddie House's bird enclosures. A peregrine falcon studied her from its feeding platform. She whistled and it hopped down and bounced across the ground toward her. One of its wings was extensively taped, but Eddie was hoping it would fly again. The bird remembered her from last time—the visitor with the dead rodent in her coat pocket. It waited expectantly and Jude offered a few pieces of jerky. These the peregrine husbanded in a corner of its cage, apparently planning for lean times ahead.

Waiting at Eddie's door, Jude opened her backpack and removed a plastic binder. "This is for you," she said when he answered her knock. "I'm sorry it's not the original."

Eddie invited her in, asking, "Beer?"

"No, I won't stay, thanks. I just wanted to drop the book by."

Eddie didn't pay this much attention. Waving her indoors, he led her to the living room at the back of the house. Ranch sliders faced onto a small patio with some cedar furniture.

They sat down outdoors and Jude smiled at the sight of Zach and the ghost gray wolf rolling and growling on the small square of lawn Eddie had coaxed from the sullen earth. She'd been visiting a couple of times a week since bringing Zach to him. The kid must have put on ten pounds over the past month, and he was taller. The young man was suddenly emerging from the child.

"Is this the diary?" Eddie asked.

"Yes."

He opened it and read a few pages. "How did she get here?"

Jude took her time answering. She'd learned that replying to Eddie after a normal interval denied him the option to converse at his own pace. Which was why Sheriff Pratt described him as "the strong silent type," she supposed. Their conversations were punctuated by long silences, the kind most people felt the need to fill. Once she'd grown used to this pattern, she found it relaxing.

"I'm not sure," she said, "but it seems as if her mother might have been instructed to kill her, but instead drove her out of the area and told her never to come back."

"Her name was Valerie?"

"Yes."

"Poppy is better."

"I think so, too."

He flipped to the final pages in their plastic envelopes and read the one that had disturbed Jude perhaps more than any. Poppy had drawn a picture of herself with liquid spilling from her mouth, and written, "Mom says I talk too much."

"I think she must have known about the murders for a long time, and her father suddenly decided she was a risk," Jude said.

She pictured a little girl, silently witnessing crimes, knowing there were bodies buried, amassing information until, as a young woman forced to marry her own father, she started questioning what she'd seen and the life she was leading. Perhaps she'd said something to one of the other wives and Nathaniel heard about it. Naoma had remained uncooperative, insisting that her daughter Valerie was in Canada.

"It's good you shot him," Eddie said.

Jude accepted the credit for it. One of her bullets had hit Epperson, one of the eight the M.E. dug out of him. She watched the antics on the lawn as Eddie continued to examine the diary.

"What's your wolf's name?" she asked eventually.

"Hinhan Okuwa. It means Chased By Owls. That's how he came to cross my path. He was a cub. An owl was attacking him."

Jude mused on that, and half a minute later said, "He eluded the harbinger of death."

"The owl gave him to me." More silence. "A Two Kettle Sioux warrior called Hinhan Okuwa fought at Little Big Horn. He did not elude death."

"Ah. So, you decided his name would live on?"

Eddie studied her. As always his expression was hard to read. "Your ancestors…no Native Americans?"

"Not as far as I know. Irish on my father's side and Scottish on my mother's."

He nodded. "Warrior people."

"Yes, very tribal. One of my ancestors, a Cameron, fought the English at the battle of Culloden. I guess you could say that was the Wounded Knee of my people."

"I know of it."

"The circumstances were very different, of course. My people were armed men who died on the battlefield. They had a fighting chance."

The comparison lay in what each event symbolized—the systematic destruction of a people and a way of life. She had visited Inverness the year she turned thirty and had driven out to the site of Culloden, expecting an innocent field like any other, sluiced of its history by the passage of time. But Drumrossie moor was an eerie place, the air heavy, the sound of the wind uncannily like distant weeping. Even at the scenes of unimaginably brutal crimes, Jude had never allowed her imagination to run away with her, yet Culloden seemed haunted.

Standing in silence at the tall stone commemorative cairn, she'd felt the hair on her neck prickle. It was as if the blood that had soaked the earth that day could never be washed away. The dead were present in every blade of grass, in the bark and branches of every tree, in the purple heather that stained the field, as if all that was living had been nourished by the broken, bleeding hearts of the fallen.

The names of the Highland clans were etched on rough-hewn stone slabs marking the spot where their clansmen were buried together in mass graves, along with the few women who had fought beside their husbands. Gazing down at these, Jude had felt a leaden sorrow, a despair so profound she wondered if she had somehow tapped into a chord of grief that echoed through time.

Thinking out loud, she told Eddie, "It was the death of hope, the death of a people more than the death of the individuals."

"Yes. Our voices were silenced."

"I've learned something," Jude said. "Beyond silence, the truth waits. It reaches out."

Eddie's expression softened. "The spirits of the dead seek their honor in the eyes of the living. They must not be denied."

Jude met his gaze and saw compassion mixed with something else. Respect?

"Yes," she said. "Denial...complicity...that's the gravest silence of all."

She looked past Poppy's headstone, across the heartless earth, beyond the mesa to the far horizon. She thought about Ben. Was this why she had never believed him dead—that she could not feel him reaching out to her? That delving into the silence around his disappearance had yielded nothing.

His face glowed in her mind's eye, golden with the setting sun, and she realized that she would never cease her search. She would not go quietly into the night. She would not say good-bye and fall silent.

Her brother deserved more, and so did she.

About the Author

Rose Beecham lives in the shadow of the Rocky Mountains with her partner and animal companions. Her vice of choice is writing; however, she is also devoted to her wonderful daughter, and her hobbies—fly fishing, cinema, and fine cooking. Rose started writing stories almost as soon as she could read them, and never stopped. Under pen names Jennifer Fulton and Rose Beecham, she has published eleven novels and a handful of short stories.

Look for information about her work at www.boldstrokesbooks. com.

Books Available From Bold Strokes Books

Grave Silence by Rose Beecham. Detective Jude Devine's investigation of a series of ritual murders is complicated by her torrid affair with the golden girl of Southwestern forensic pathology, Dr. Mercy Westmoreland. (1-933110-25-2)

Honor Reclaimed by Radclyffe. In the aftermath of 9/11, Secret Service Agent Cameron Roberts and Blair Powell close ranks with a trusted few to find the would-be assassins who nearly claimed Blair's life. (1-933110-18-X)

Honor Bound by Radclyffe. Secret Service Agent Cameron Roberts and Blair Powell face political intrigue, a clandestine threat to Blair's safety, and the seemingly irreconcilable personal differences that force them ever further apart. (1-933110-20-1)

Protector of the Realm: Supreme Constellations Book One by Gun Brooke. A space adventure filled with suspense and a daring intergalactic romance featuring Commodore Rae Jacelon and a stunning, but decidedly lethal Kellen O'Dal. (1-933110-26-0)

Innocent Hearts by Radclyffe. In a wild and unforgiving land, two women learn about love, passion, and the wonders of the heart. (1-933110-21-X)

The Temple at Landfall by Jane Fletcher. An imprinter, one of Celaeno's most revered servants of the Goddess, is also a prisoner to the faith—until a Ranger frees her by claiming her heart. (1-933110-27-9)

Force of Nature by Kim Baldwin. From tornados to forest fires, the forces of nature conspire to bring Gable McCoy and Erin Richards close to danger, and closer to each other. (1-933110-23-6)

In Too Deep by Ronica Black. Undercover homicide cop Erin McKenzie tracks a femme fatale who just might be a real killer...with love and danger hot on her heels. (1-933110-17-1)

Stolen Moments: Erotic Interludes 2 by Stacia Seaman and Radclyffe, eds. Love on the run, in the office, in the shadows...Fast, furious, and almost too hot to handle. (1-933110-16-3)

Course of Action by Gun Brooke. Actress Carolyn Black desperately wants the starring role in an upcoming film produced by Annelie Peterson. Just how far will she go for the dream part of a lifetime? (1-933110-22-8)

Rangers at Roadsend by Jane Fletcher. Sergeant Chip Coppelli has learned to spot trouble coming, and that is exactly what she sees in her new recruit, Katryn Nagata. The Celaeno series. (1-933110-28-7)

Justice Served by Radclyffe. Lieutenant Rebecca Frye and her lover, Dr. Catherine Rawlings, embark on a deadly game of hide-and-seek with an underworld kingpin who traffics in human souls. (1-933110-15-5)

Distant Shores, Silent Thunder by Radclyffe. Dr. Tory King—along with the women who love her—is forced to examine the boundaries of love, friendship, and the ties that transcend time. (1-933110-08-2)

Hunter's Pursuit by Kim Baldwin. A raging blizzard, a mountain hideaway, and a killer-for-hire set a scene for disaster—or desire—when Katarzyna Demetrious rescues a beautiful stranger. (1-933110-09-0)

The Walls of Westernfort by Jane Fletcher. All Temple Guard Natasha Ionadis wants is to serve the Goddess—until she falls in love with one of the rebels she is sworn to destroy. The Celaeno series. (1-933110-24-4)

Change Of Pace: Erotic Interludes by Radclyffe. Twenty-five hot-wired encounters guaranteed to spark more than just your imagination. Erotica as you've always dreamed of it. (1-933110-07-4)

Honor Guards by Radclyffe. In a wild flight for their lives, the president's daughter and those who are sworn to protect her wage a desperate struggle for survival. (1-933110-01-5)

Fated Love by Radclyffe. Amidst the chaos and drama of a busy emergency room, two women must contend not only with the fragile nature of life, but also with the irresistible forces of fate. (1-933110-05-8)

Justice in the Shadows by Radclyffe. In a shadow world of secrets and lies, Detective Sergeant Rebecca Frye and her lover, Dr. Catherine Rawlings, join forces in the elusive search for justice. (1-933110-03-1)

shadowland by Radclyffe. In a world on the far edge of desire, two women are drawn together by power, passion, and dark pleasures. An erotic romance. (1-933110-11-2)

Love's Masquerade by Radclyffe. Plunged into the indistinguishable realms of fiction, fantasy, and hidden desires, Auden Frost is forced to question all she believes about the nature of love. (1-933110-14-7)

Love & Honor by Radclyffe. The president's daughter and her lover are faced with difficult choices as they battle a tangled web of Washington intrigue for...love and honor. (1-933110-10-4)

Beyond the Breakwater by Radclyffe. One Provincetown summer three women learn the true meaning of love, friendship, and family. (1-933110-06-6)

Tomorrow's Promise by Radclyffe. One timeless summer, two very different women discover the power of passion to heal and the promise of hope that only love can bestow. (1-933110-12-0)

Love's Tender Warriors by Radclyffe. Two women who have accepted loneliness as a way of life learn that love is worth fighting for and a battle they cannot afford to lose. (1-933110-02-3)

Love's Melody Lost by Radclyffe. A secretive artist with a haunted past and a young woman escaping a life that has proved to be a lie find their destinies entwined. (1-933110-00-7)

Safe Harbor by Radclyffe. A mysterious newcomer, a reclusive doctor, and a troubled gay teenager learn about love, friendship, and trust during one tumultuous summer in Provincetown. (1-933110-13-9)

Above All, Honor by Radclyffe. Secret Service Agent Cameron Roberts fights her desire for the one woman she can't have—Blair Powell, the daughter of the president of the United States. (1-933110-04-X)